"DREAMS. THAT'S WHAT WE'RE SELL-ING. THE MOST BEAUTIFUL MEN AND WOMEN IN THE WORLD. GODS AND GOD-DESSES. ESCAPE. THAT'S WHAT WE'RE SELLING . . ."

For studio executive Eli Hebron, there was no escape. Not from the bewitching dream web of Hollywood in 1927, on the eve of sound. Not from the irresistible lure of power that sparked the garish circus of studio politics. Not from the seductive Gladys Divine, the hopeful young star-let whose beauty threatened to lead Eli, still stunned from his movie-star wife's suicide, to ultimate disaster.

He was a dreamer, an artist, a poet. But in the glittering world of Hollywood—where deception was a business and the dollar reigned supreme—those who dreamed big . . . fell hard.

THE DREAM LOVER
Lawrence Sanders

Lawrence Sanders

The Dream Lover

BERKLEY BOOKS, NEW YORK

Previously published under the pseudonym of Mark Upton.

THE DREAM LOVER

A Berkley Book / published by arrangement with
the author

PRINTING HISTORY
Coward, McCann and Geoghegan edition / January 1978
Berkley international edition / July 1986
Berkley mass market edition / January 1987

One

THE front door of the Beverly Hills mansion was solid oak. It was painted a glossy white with gilt trim. Eli Hebron came out slowly, testing the day like a swimmer dipping toes. He turned a pale, night-ravaged face to the sky. In the west, over the ocean, there was a stroke of chalk across china-blue. He had lived in California for eight years but still wondered at the high sky, low clouds like rabbits, breasts, bears, thighs, fish, buttocks. And dragons.

And the light pulsated. It didn't move in the east.

Down on the graveled driveway Barney O'Hara lounged against the maroon Hispano-Suiza limousine. He was leafing through *Variety*, sucking a matchstick thirstily. The padded neck brace held his head erect, so he had to hold the paper high. He wore a white linen cap with button, a diamond-patterned cardigan, golf knickers with tassels hanging from the outside garters. Ribbed white stockings. Brown-and-white shoes. His shirt was soft-collared. Wally Reid had started that. The Arrow people had objected, but now they were making soft collars.

Eli Hebron came down the steps, carrying his Spanish leather script case. Taki, the Japanese gardener, trotted around the corner with the flowers: yellow roses and white mums surrounded with maidenhair, all artfully arranged in a trumpet-shaped wicker basket that could be spiked into the grave.

"Thank you, Taki," Eli Hebron said.

Then, a conjuror, Taki produced from his canvas jacket a tiny nosegay of tea roses. Pinkish. Like watery blood.

Hebron took the bouquet, smiling.

"I'll leave it," he promised.

Taki hissed faintly, bowing.

On the way to the Hollywood Cemetery, Hebron tried to read a one-page treatment of *The Bridge of San Luis Rey*. But the words blurred; he stuffed it back into the case. He lighted a Lucky Strike, looked out the window. He leaned forward to watch a file of little kids bouncing down the road on pogo sticks, like a line of sandpipers hopping on the beach. A nice cut.

"Think he'll make it, Mr. Hebron?" Barney O'Hara asked.

The broken neck had done something to his voice. Made it thick and growly. Barney had been one of the four best stunt men in Hollywood. But a year ago, in a saloon brawl for one of Magna Pictures' Westerns, the chair that was supposed to be a balsa breakaway had turned out to be solid pine. After O'Hara had been taken to the hospital, it was determined that one of the propmen had made the switch at the last minute. Barney had been screwing his wife.

So the propman was fired, and when O'Hara got out of traction, Eli Hebron made him his chauffeur and bodyguard.

"Thank you very much, Mr. Hebron," Barney had said gratefully. He had his own wife and six children.

"Think who'll make what?" Hebron asked from the back seat.

"Lindbergh," O'Hara said. "That young aviator. He ain't been seen or heard from since he took off."

"Oh?" Hebron said. "He took off, did he?"

"Sure. The radio said. Yesterday morning. He's still got a chance."

Eli Hebron dreamed of a dauntless young man over the cruel ocean. Alone. Darkness. The engine's roar. Faltering. The plunge. . . .

"If he makes it," he said, "it'll help Paramount's *Wings*."

"It'll tell the cockeyed world," Barney O'Hara agreed.

Her grave was near Valentino's crypt, and almost as new. There was a chill marble angel with upturned eyes and more décolletage than Eli Hebron liked. The stone breasts were veined. The inscription read: "Grace Darling: 1903–1925. In Our Hearts Forever."

He walked from the gate. O'Hara trailed him, carrying the flowers. It was a dazzling day, glittering. They would need sheets on the outdoor sets. Hebron heard the tick of a lawn mower, smelled the green tang of freshly cut grass.

He stopped, startled. Around her grave a score of men and women knelt, wailing.

"What the hell?" O'Hara growled.

"Her fan club, I suppose," Hebron said.

A large woman clad in black bombazine saw them and screeched. She climbed laboriously to her feet, clasped her hands to her bosom.

"Eli Hebron," she screamed. "It's Eli Hebron. Oh, my God, my God."

The others lurched up and swarmed at Hebron, claws reaching. A pirate crew: several chalk-faced flappers, damp matrons, a few frantic young men wearing Oxford bags. Weeping, shrieking.

Some fell on their knees before him, plucking at his trousers, tugging his jacket. Or just putting their hands on him, pulling. He had a terrible desire to surrender, to let himself be hauled down and rent.

Others snatched at the flowers. O'Hara stumbled backward, but they crowded him. The blooms were shredded. Taki's nosegay was crushed. Roses and mums were wrenched away, slyly hidden as souvenirs, scattered on the grass, or kissed and tossed onto Grace Darling's grave.

Until Barney O'Hara, roaring with fury, began to lay about him, using the empty wicker basket as a cudgel.

"Cocksuckers!" he howled.

He drove them back. He grasped Eli Hebron's arm, pulled him free. They dashed for the car, leaving the fans fighting over petals and stems. They heard the cries as they drove away, a shrill cawing.

Too much love, too much longing. He felt soiled by that moist fervor. He told O'Hara to drive back to Beverly Hills rather than to the studio. On Summit Drive they saw Pickfair, a castle in the clouds. Gardeners were at work under straw coolie hats. A woman swathed in chiffon veils dissolved across the terrace.

"Is Pickford working?" he asked Barney O'Hara, who knew everything.

"Doing ballyhoo on *My Best Girl*," the chauffeur said.

"Then it must have been a houseguest."

"Did you catch *Sparrows*, Mr. Hebron?"

"No. Should I?"

"No," O'Hara said, and Eli Hebron frowned. Movie attendance was down. Profits were down.

"It's the radio," O'Hara said, picking up on his reaction. "Everyone's sitting home listening to the A&P Gypsies."

Hebron didn't answer. O'Hara pulled into the curved driveway, up to the portico. When his wife was alive, this home was called Paradiso. Now it was just a number on Benedict Canyon Drive.

"Half an hour," Hebron said. "I want to change."

"Them cocksuckers," Barney growled.

Mrs. Birkin came fluttering, but he waved her away. He walked steadily up the handsome floating staircase. His wife had died in convulsions on the top landing of that staircase, then thumped all the way down. When he reached her, a boneless bundle on the marble floor, she was still wearing the mauve night mask. He had raised it to peer into her eyes. Wet stones.

He had duplicated that scene in *Lost Love:* Sophie commits suicide because she thinks Armand has been killed in the duel. It was artful crosscutting, building terror and suspense as Sophie rolls down the stairs while Armand spurs his horse to the home of his beloved. "As good as anything in Eisenstein," the New York *Times* critic had said. But Marcus Annenberg had never liked that picture.

"It made money," Eli Hebron told him.

The old man smiled his dark smile.

"Not enough," he said.

But Grace Darling had not committed suicide, of course. Not deliberately. An overdose of nux vomica to relieve her depression after *The New Cleopatra* had been such a disaster it was withdrawn from distribution and shelved. She had been Sylvia Janovic of Gary, Indiana. Then DeMille saw the glow, the lucid profile. She starred in *Old Country Girl, Susannah and the Elders, Jes' Plain Folks,* and *On*

the River. That's how her fans remembered her. Eli Hebron remembered lifting the mauve night mask.

In the master bedroom, seeing himself dwindling to
nothing in the facing mirrored walls, he stripped to his
balbriggan drawers and undershirt. He bathed face, neck,
and arms with a cloth dampened with Ed. Pinaud's Lilac
Vegetal. The walk-in closets held fifty suits, a hundred
pairs of shoes, uncounted custom-made shirts, imported
ties, sweaters, hats. Costumes, not clothes.

Because the man from the Boston bank would be at the
studio today, he donned a dove gray shirt with starched
white French cuffs and a stiff, white, detachable Hoover
collar, named for President Coolidge's Secretary of Com-
merce. He put on a Norfolk suit of white linen with bone
buttons. "Beau Hebron" Louella Parsons had once called
him, but he had been told that a month ago, in the men's
room of the Beverly Hills hotel, Charlie Royce had been
overheard calling him a pansy because he wore suede
shoes.

He dawdled a moment before going down to the car. He
looked around that baroque room, wanting to know grief
but feeling only loneliness. He remembered how often she
had played "I'm Always Chasing Rainbows" on the Victrola
and saw her dancing naked around the room in great
swoops and glides, ecstatic. Little Sylvia Janovic of Gary,
Indiana, in her mirrored boudoir. She owned the first bidet
in Hollywood, and the wife of the French consul in San
Francisco had to show her how to use it.

A vulgar woman, his wife. His dead wife. But her
earthiness had anchored him. Now he was floating. Anomie, Dr. Irving Blick called it. He drank a heavy gin
before he went downstairs. He kept a packet of Sen-Sen in
the Hispano-Suiza. They drove to the studio.

*   *   *

Magna Pictures had been organized by Marcus Annenberg and Solomon Getz in 1914. Like most movie pioneers, they had originally been in the cloak-and-suit business in New York. An early investment in nickelodeons led to the formation of a production unit, called Getz & Annenberg Films. A distribution subsidiary, Magna Pictures, was organized in 1917. The company moved to California in 1919.

Sol Getz died in 1921 (he choked to death on a piece of ice). Marcus Annenberg bought out his dead partner's share in 1923, after deliberately allowing the business to become almost bankrupt to depress the value of the widow's inheritance. The company was then consolidated under the name Magna Pictures, Inc., and flourished. Its staple continued to be one- and two-reel comedies and Westerns. But under the supervision of Eli Hebron, Magna began to produce more and more features—dramas, historical romances, sophisticated comedies, and an occasional biblical epic.

By 1927 Magna was producing almost two hundred movies a year, including thirty to forty six-reel features. Hardly on a par with Fox, Paramount, or First National, but a very respectable output. In addition, Magna was enlarging its overseas trade and establishing a chain of company-owned movie theaters in the United States to take advantage of block-booking of its products.

The studios of Magna Pictures, Inc., were at Sunset Boulevard and Vine Street. The main buildings faced Sunset. There were thirty acres of back lots. Magna also owned a ranch in Culver City, where most of its broncos were filmed.

The main compound, surrounded by a wire fence, was a

jumble of wooden buildings: indoor and outdoor stages, labs, writers' bungalows, prop and equipment sheds, permanent sets, and a long, low commissary. The administration building was three stories high, with full balconies and outside stairways.

Mac came out of his hut to open the gate. They heard his Atwater Kent radio playing "Ain't We Got Fun?" It was Jean Goldkette's orchestra.

"Morning, Mr. Hebron," Mac said, ducking his head.

"Hear anything?" Barney asked him.

"About Lindboig? Nah. He's a goner. If God had wanted us to fly, He'd have given us wings."

"Bushwa," O'Hara said.

They had to wait while a rubber-tired tractor passed in front of them. It was pulling a flatbed trailer loaded with bloody French guardsmen. They were heading for a back lot where the Battle of Waterloo was being filmed. It was three days behind schedule and ten thousand dollars over the budget.

Hebron went up to his office, nodding at the people who greeted him. Mildred Eljer, his secretary, took his script case.

"How do you feel today, Mr. Hebron?" she asked anxiously.

"Fine," he told her. "I feel fine."

"Are you hungry, Mr. Hebron? I could have ham-and-eggs sent up. A sandwich?"

"No, thank you." He smiled at her. "How is your mother feeling?"

"Better, Mr. Hebron."

"Good," he said, touching her bony shoulder. "Glad to hear it. Anything. . . . You just ask."

8

His office was all golden oak and leather. The walls were covered with autographed photographs of Magna stars and others. Colman, Vilma Banky, Fairbanks, Horton, Harry Langdon, Ramon Novarro. A photo of Griffith holding tight the jaws of a crocodile and grinning at the camera. Keaton, Valentino, Marion Davies, Swanson, Francis X. Bushman. A still from Georges Méliès' *A Trip to the Moon*, showing a rocket hitting the eye of the man in the moon, making it weep. Emil Jannings, May McAvoy. Bull Montana. More. . . .

On his desk was a list of people who had called. He glanced at it, pushed it aside. He shuffled through a stack of new magazines: *Literary Digest, Liberty, Vanity Fair*. He picked up the *American Mercury* and flipped through to find the "Americana" section. He read a few of the items, smiling, as he sauntered to his windows. They overlooked the yard.

He closed the magazine and looked down. Three cowboys were flirting with a nun, laughing and digging the girl in the ribs. A man led a goat that was dressed in top hat and tails. A troupe of harem dancers filed into the commissary. General Robert E. Lee took off his hat and spit into the dust. Three men hauled a dolly with arc lights. A mechanic fussed over a trick Model T that could break in two, each part powered. Moses chatted with Iroquois Indians, and a French musketeer dueled with a Roman legionnaire. An elephant painted white was prodded toward Outdoor Stage Four. Bea Winks came out of the prop shed, carrying an armload of lace parasols.

Eli Hebron looked at this activity and recalled Chaplin's remembrance of days past when "All you had to do to make a picture was go into a park with a ladder, a bucket of whitewash, and Mabel Normand."

Then he saw Charlie Royce and Franklin Pierce Archer, the man from the Boston bank, striding purposefully toward Outdoor Stage One. Royce was leaning toward the other, talking rapidly, gesturing. Archer, a stretched, stooped man, was listening intently, nodding. The two men were much alike: wearing heavy, dark, vested cheviot suits. Watch chains and high shoes. Costumed, Hebron thought, for a movie about Yankee skinflints.

Depressed, he went back to his desk and buzzed Mildred on the Dictograph.

"Get me Abe Vogel, please," he said.

The agent was waiting when he picked up the phone a moment later.

"Good morning, Mr. Hebron," Vogel said.

"Make me laugh, Abe."

"There's this hotsy-totsy in the business," the agent said promptly. "She works for MGM during the day and Fox at night."

"Not bad," Eli Hebron laughed. "So . . . you called. Who have you got?"

"A new girl. An Esther Ralston type, but dark. Could be a vamp."

"We've got nothing right now for a vamp, Abe."

"Please, Mr. Hebron, take a look. Not beautiful, but something. I think it'll shoot. Have I ever been wrong?"

"Alice Cormack," Hebron said.

"That was last year," the agent protested. "Have I been wrong *this* year?"

Hebron laughed again. "All right, Abe. Bring her around."

"Be there in an hour," Vogel said happily. "Thank you very much, Mr. Hebron."

"Tell the gate to call Mildred; she'll know where I am."

His secretary knocked and came in. "They're waiting in the projection room, Mr. Hebron," she said.

He nodded, and when she closed the door behind her, he took two of the orange pills Dr. Blick had prescribed.

"Something new," Blick had said. "For anxiety. Cheaper than lying on a couch."

Hebron gulped the pills with a swallow of gin from an unlabeled bottle he kept in his desk drawer. Then he went down the outside staircase to the projection room.

It was crowded; assistants sat on the floor. But they had left three vacant seats in the back row, knowing he didn't want to be touched. He sat in the center and lighted a cigarette. Then they lighted cigarettes.

"All set, Mr. Hebron?" Tony Carmichael asked nervously. He was the director.

Hebron nodded. Carmichael called, "Roll it!" to the man in the projection booth. Lights went off. The first slate appeared on the white screen. Cigarette smoke made swirling shadows.

They were rushes: snippets of film that had been shot the preceding afternoon. The Battle of Waterloo. Long and medium views had been taken previously; these were close-ups. French cuirassiers straining against British dragoons. A bayonet duel. Men falling. A horse stumbling on a trip wire, the cavalryman taking a rolling fall. A saber slash. An apoplectic general shouting commands. Field guns firing. Smoke of muskets. Men clutching their chests and crumpling.

Carmichael was competent. He could handle crowds, and he covered himself with front, back, side, and three-quarter views of the same scene. And his cameraman was Harry Wallman who, when he was sober, was as good as Billy Bitzer or Hal Mohr. No heads or feet were cut off. Everything was in focus. Frames were composed.

11

The screen flickered to whiteness. Lights came on again. Everyone looked at Hebron. He lighted a cigarette. Then they lighted cigarettes.

He smoked slowly, tapping a knee with the fingers of one hand. They knew the signs and tensed. He turned his head to stare at Tony Carmichael. It was easier to tell a man that he had no talent at all than to tell him he was competent and nothing more.

In life, and on the stage, a door opens, and a man comes through, walking toward us. But a movie camera could show you that, and the *back* of the man passing through the opened door. That was the essence of cinematography.

Too many directors and cameramen were staggered by that essence and never went beyond it. Or they could not go beyond the marvel of *moving* pictures. When movies were first shown in nickelodeons, audiences stampeded from the theaters, terrified by waves rolling at them or a locomotive rushing into their laps. But that was twenty-five years ago. Movement was no longer enough. The back of a man going through a door was no longer enough. Camera tricks.

"What we have here," Eli Hebron said to Tony Carmichael, to all of them, "is usable footage. Professional footage. But there isn't a meaningful image in the lot. Nothing that hasn't been done a hundred times before. Nothing that anyone will leave the theater and remember until the day he dies. Does anyone here take shorthand?"

A girl with marcelled hair raised her hand.

"I do, Mr. Hebron. I take Gregg."

"What is your name, dear?"

"Doris Bergman. I'm Mr. Carmichael's script clerk."

"Bergman," he said. "Any relation to Sam Bergman?"

"He's my father, Mr. Hebron."

"I know him. A fine cutter. I wish I could afford him."

They laughed with relief.

"Do you have a pencil and pad, Doris?"

"Yes, I do, Mr. Hebron."

"Good. Take this down. This is what I want. One: A dead soldier, face in the mud. Camera at his bloodied head. Slowly pan down to neck, shoulder, along his outstretched arm. Just beyond his reaching fingers is a small, white flower. Catch that in an iris. Harry Wallman?"

"Here, Mr. Hebron."

"You can do that, Harry?"

"Sure, Mr. Hebron. Come in tight on the grabbing fingers and flower, and hold?"

"Correct. Two: A wounded soldier. Bloody. His face covered with dirt. Gritty. Oil his face and sprinkle sand on it. Cut to his legs. He has no legs. We see that clearly. We know he is dying. Cut to his eyes. Above him a white butterfly flutters. Close up to his face. His eyes follow that butterfly."

"How will we get the butterfly, Mr. Hebron?" Tony Carmichael asked despairingly.

"I don't know. Ask Michaldo in Process."

"We could paint it on the negative," Harry Wallman said. "A few frames. It won't cost so much."

"I don't care what it costs," Hebron said, "I want it. Eyes watching that butterfly with longing. Three: An English soldier and a French soldier close together. Both dead. They have killed each other. Almost an embrace. You understand? Four: A dead horse on its back. Legs stiff. Up in the sky."

"We can get that," Stan Haggard said enthusiastically. He was the assistant director. "Four stiff legs outlined against a clear sky. Maybe framed by bare trees stripped by gunfire. Pick up the verticals. We'll get a dead horse from the slaughterhouse.''

"Or kill one," Hebron said. "But the legs have got to be stiff. Five: A dead officer sitting propped against a tree. An old officer. Maybe a general. Papers scattered around him. A painted miniature of his wife and kids. We understand it's his family. But in his lap he's holding—what? In his dead hands he's holding an open locket. Come in tight. A young, beautiful woman with long hair. Who is she? His daughter? His wife when she was young? His mistress? We don't say. We don't know. Let the audience wonder. That is what we want: wonder and images that never fade. That's it. Thank you."

As they were going out, talking excitedly, he took Tony Carmichael aside.

"Finish up today," he smiled, "or you're off, and I'll do the rough cut myself."

"Yes, Mr. Hebron," the director said, his face falling apart.

"Good," Hebron said, patting his shoulder. "You can have your party tomorrow night."

He came through the outer office. Abe Vogel leaped to his feet. Hebron didn't look at the girl.

"In a minute, Abe," he said, waving a hand.

In his office he sipped a small glass of gin. He sat with his eyes closed. He tried to think of a calm sea.

"When these attacks come," Dr. Irving Blick had said, "try to concentrate on images of serenity. A flat sea. Clouds drifting. Quiet things like that. Maybe a bird flying."

But he saw a dead horse's four stiff legs framed by naked trees.

"Send Vogel in now, please," he told Mildred on the Dictograph.

The girl came in ahead of the agent. Small, slender, wearing a red cloche over dark, shingled hair. As Vogel had said, not beautiful. But want in her face, smoldering. A frightening need.

"Mr. Hebron, may I present Gladys Potts. It can be changed, of course."

He got them seated. He pulled the drapes open so bright California sunlight fell cruelly on the face of Gladys Potts. She blinked but lifted her chin.

"How old are you, Miss Potts?"

"Eighteen, Mr. Hebron."

"What experience have you had?"

"Well . . . I—"

"From New Jersey," Abe Vogel said quickly. "Hackensack, Hohokus . . . like that. High school dramatics. A few hours of mob work since she got out here. Don't try to fool Mr. Hebron, sweetie."

"I wasn't—" she started angrily.

"Of course you weren't." Eli Hebron smiled. "I understand. Why do you want to be in pictures?"

"I don't want to be a waitress," the girl said, lifting her chin again. "I want to be rich."

Hebron nodded, staring at her. He opened his top desk drawer. He tore a sheet from a pad of scratch paper.

"The man you love has gone to war," he told Gladys Potts. "This sheet of paper is a telegram saying he has been killed in action. I want you to read the telegram, realize what it says, and react to the news."

"Do you want me to stand, Mr. Hebron?"

"Stand, sit, whatever you like."

She stood, took off her hat, shook her sleek hair free. She was wearing a low-waisted dress of ivory crepe de chine, with sash and side bow. The hem was an inch above her knees.

15

"I'm ready," she said.

He handed her the blank sheet of paper. She took it with a half smile. She "read" it swiftly, then looked up at him, smile fading. Her eyes went back to the "telegram." Now she stared at it a long time. Her face registered blankness, then shock. Her fingers began to tremble. The paper fluttered to the floor. A knuckle rose slowly to her teeth. She stared sightlessly. Then her head went back. Slim throat taut, spine arched. Her body became rigid. She swayed. Fingernails clawed at her cheek.

"All right, Miss Potts," Eli Hebron said. "Thank you, that's enough." He flicked on the Dictograph. "Mildred, will you come in, please? Bring your pad."

The girl sat down again and crossed her good legs. She put on her hat. They waited in silence until the secretary entered.

"Mildred," Eli Hebron said, "this is Miss Gladys Potts. Please set up a test for this afternoon. Stan Haggard is out on the back lots. The Waterloo shooting. I want him to direct. Ask Bea Winks for costume and makeup. I'll set up the scene."

"The cameraman, Mr. Hebron?" Mildred Eljer asked.

"That young kid—what's his name? He did the chase in *My Husband's Wife*."

"Ritchie Ingate," Mildred said.

"Yes, that's the one. Get him if he's available. Abe, have you got an old character? Say, fifty, fifty-five; around there? Foreign-looking. A boulevardier. A man who owns spiffy clothes."

"I know just the man, Mr. Hebron. Calls himself Baron von Stumpf. Wears a monocle."

"Good. Twenty for him for the test. All right?"

"Fine, Mr. Hebron. You want the monocle?"

"Why not? And a morning coat. Or a cutaway. Something formal and wealthy. A top hat if he's got one. If not, we can supply. Have him here as soon as possible. We'll set this up for four or five this afternoon."

"Thank you, Mr. Hebron," Gladys Potts said.

"Keep your fingers crossed." He smiled at her. "Sometimes the camera does funny things."

"The luncheon, Mr. Hebron," Mildred reminded him.

"Yes," he said heavily. "The luncheon. . . ."

The executive dining room was not a room at all. It was one corner of the commissary, surrounded by a waist-high wooden railing. The money people could dine within the enclosure, and supervisors and directors. But not actors, cameramen, or cutters, except by special invitation. Outside, at tables close to the railing, extras and bit players clustered, showing their profiles to the executives, gesturing broadly, laughing loudly. It never helped.

That afternoon, May 21, 1927, the long table was headed by Marcus Annenberg. A frog-faced man. Squat. Hooded eyes. He wore patterned carpet slippers. Liver spots on the backs of his puffy hands. He had survived a severe stroke; sometimes he drooled slightly. He was Eli Hebron's uncle.

(In 1919, something of significance had happened to Marcus Annenberg. He had attended a screening of Griffith's *Broken Blossoms*. He had seen a timorous Lillian Gish cringing before a brutal Donald Crisp. The subtitle read: "Please don't whip me, daddy." This combination of visual image and printed legend had inflamed Marcus Annenberg, a happily married man, father, and grandfather.

(A few days later he went to an expensive parlor house on Wilshire Boulevard. There he hired a prepubescent Chinese girl, the first of many. He beat her with a rod of

17

split bamboo while she, rehearsed, sobbed, "Prease don't whip me, daddy." After his stroke Annenberg resumed his weekly visits, although the parlor house was now in Beverly Hills, and the Chinese girls had to be instructed not to giggle under the feeble blows of the furious old man.)

Today salad plates of fresh fruit and cottage cheese were served. Nehi, Moxie, and Coca-Cola were available, as well as coffee and tea. The waitresses were carefully selected older women, plain, with no movie ambitions.

Eli Hebron sat next to Franklin Pierce Archer.

"Enjoying your visit to California?" he asked the Bostonian.

"I am, Mr. Hebron. Last night at my hotel I met a man who claimed to be a rancher. He looked like a rancher: boots with high heels, leather clothes, sombrero. I asked him how many cattle he had, and he said he didn't raise cattle; he owned a *pear* ranch!"

Hebron smiled politely. Like most Californians, he was inured to the scorn of Easterners. It was easier to accept, knowing how readily actors and writers overcame their contempt to grab the inflated salaries Hollywood offered and how avidly Eastern banks sought to gain control of the enormously profitable movie industry.

"Have you been well taken care of out here, Mr. Archer?"

"Oh, yes, thank you. Charlie Royce has been showing me around."

"Good," Hebron said. "Glad to hear it. Is there anyone special in Hollywood you'd care to meet?"

"Well—uh. . . ." Archer said, his face darkening. He ducked his head. "Not necessarily meet. My wife, she wondered if. . . ." His voice trailed away.

"If what, Mr. Archer?"

"William Powell's autograph," the haughty man said, suffering. "A few words. My wife's name is Betty. Betty Archer. Something personal, to show her friends. Do you think . . . ?"

"Of course," Hebron said gravely. "I'll be happy to arrange it."

The Bostonian turned away almost angrily. He began to talk to Ben Stuttgart, on his other side. Stuttgart supervised the short comedies at Magna, turning them out at an average rate of one a week. He was a graduate of the Keystone Kops, as fat as Arbuckle. Like most movie comedians, he was a morose, embittered man. But no one doubted his talent. He was the first director in Hollywood to see the comic possibilities of process shots: live action photographed in front of a screen showing another film. So his one- and two-reelers were filled with clown-cowboys riding bucking donkeys across the sky and cops in flivvers bouncing over the ocean.

To Ben Stuttgart's right sat Meyer Levine, in charge of foreign distribution. Across the table from Levine was Al Klinger, who managed Magna-owned movie houses in the United States. Next to Klinger was Phil Nolan, a supervisor. He produced nature and travel shorts, with such titles as *Our Friends, the Bees* and *A Visit to the Holy Land*. Julius K. Felder was next to Nolan. Felder was treasurer of Magna Pictures, Inc., and sat in on budget and schedule planning. On Felder's right, directly across from Eli Hebron and sitting to the left of Marcus Annenberg, was supervisor Charlie Royce.

Royce produced Magna's Westerns and a growing number of B pictures. These were low-budget features with second-rank players and limited backgrounds. Royce had been an advance ballyhoo man on the Chautauqua Circuit, with an interest in photography. He started in Hollywood as an assistant cameraman, rose to director and then to supervisor in four years. His movies were marked by extremely brief takes, few subtitles, almost finicky attention to realistic detail. It was said that at a showing of one of Royce's Westerns in a small Texas town, a cowboy rose from the audience and emptied his six-shooter at the screen in an attempt to aid a besieged sheriff.

"We better convert, Mr. Annenberg," Charlie Royce said in his harsh voice, "or within a year you'll have grass growing on Outdoor Stage One."

He was loud enough so the others heard. Men stopped eating, forks poised. They turned to the head of the table. Marcus Annenberg bent far over his salad plate, raising little dabs of cottage cheese slowly to his mouth.

"Why do you say that, Charlie?" he asked mildly. "Sound is nothing new. Twenty years old it is."

"I know, Mr. Annenberg. Edison tried it. But he didn't have the amplifiers. Now the sound can fill the house. The synchronizing to the film is better. Warner's is putting a lot of money in Vitaphone. *The Jazz Singer* is in final cut. For release this year. Not all sound. No dialogue. But Jolson sings, Mr. Annenberg, he *sings!* You think movies will ever be the same?"

"You want songs in your Westerns, Charlie?" The old man leered.

"Gunshots, Mr. Annenberg," Royce shouted. "The pounding of horses' hooves. Indian yells. You'll be able to hear the rapids in a river and the bugles of cavalry. My God!"

Annenberg pushed his plate away, hardly touched. He leaned back slowly. He laced fingers across his paunch.

He sucked his teeth, staring at Charlie Royce. Then basalt eyes shifted to Julius K. Felder.

"Julie," Annenberg said, "what about this sound?"

"Very costly, Mr. Annenberg," the treasurer said nervously. "No one knows how much, but plenty. Right now, with what we got budgeted for new houses and attendance off, I say wait a year. Two years, maybe. Let Warner's take the risk. See what happens. Be conservative. If it goes, we can always get in."

Annenberg nodded. "Phil?" he asked the supervisor.

"For me, it wouldn't make all that difference," Nolan said. "I could use narration, sure, but as for special sounds, what could I do? You travel across a desert or mountain— what sounds? We got footage on wolves running through the snow. What sounds? I mean, it's just not that important. A novelty."

"Al?"

"Mr. Annenberg, what it would cost to equip the houses, I hate to think," Klinger said. "Victrolas and amplifiers, they don't come cheap. Plus teaching my people how to use them. I'm not talking about the production end. But just in the houses—a fortune!"

Annenberg sat nodding, heavy lids almost closed. His face was deeply folded. Ten years previously, at the last Hollywood party he had attended, a costume dansant, he had dressed as Nero, crowned with a laurel wreath. He had won first prize.

Now his jowly head turned slowly to the other side of the table.

"Meyer?" he said.

"It'll kill us overseas, Mr. Annenberg," Levine said angrily. "So we have actors talk. In English! Or sing. In English! So what does that mean in France, Germany,

21

India, China, and so forth? So what good is actors talking? There goes your foreign market right there. That's how I feel."

None of them was eating. Around them was the bustle of the commissary: laughter, loud talk, calls, rattle of plates and cutlery. But they watched only Marcus Annenberg.

"Ben?" he said. "You want sound?"

"Sure," Stuttgart said promptly. "I could use it. Funny sounds. A pie in the face. A guy falling down a well. A balloon bursting. Explosions. A chase. Things like that. Like what the pitman does now on his piano or organ, but better. As for dialogue—nah. Who needs that? It's all action. Comics don't have to talk. But sounds I could use."

Annenberg's head turned.

"Please excuse me from this discussion," Franklin Pierce Archer said. Bleak smile. "I know nothing about it. But I assure you, I find it quite interesting." He turned suddenly to his left. "I'd like to hear your opinion, Mr. Hebron."

"Well," Hebron said softly, looking at Charlie Royce, "I think we may be talking about several different things here. I have no objection to recorded synchronized background music. Mood music, played by good orchestras, great artists. To replace the pitmen. I can understand that. And the special sounds Ben and Charlie were talking about. Gunshots, explosions, bugles, and so forth. It would help, no doubt about it. You're talking about *sounds*. I'll go along with that. But now about dialogue. . . . Players talking. . . ."

He continued to look at Royce. But the supervisor had lowered his head, was busily eating, digging rapidly into his salad.

"Dialogue," Hebron repeated. "Now we're right back in the theater. We've spent twenty years trying to get off the stage, and we're right back on. Movement. Moving pictures. How could the players move? They're tied to that microphone. Lovers strolling across a field of flowers. How would you pick up their voices? Even moving around a set. Going through a door. In a boat, on a train, and so forth. Where's the microphone? So we're back on the stage, frozen. Front view only. Players clustered around a microphone. Is that what audiences want? To see a moving picture of a play on a stage? I don't think so."

Now Hebron looked down at his own plate. His long, pale fingers scrabbled at crumbs on the cloth.

"But even," he said in a low voice, "even if these— these mechanical problems could be solved. . . . Assuming that, would it help movies? Players talking? Would that sell more tickets? I don't think so. Because what are we selling? We're selling dreams. I don't care if it's Ben's comic driving over a cliff, Phil's shots of the Alps, or Charlie's Indian fights. Or my love scenes. We're selling dreams. It's not reality; we know that. Detroit produces Model Ts, and we produce dreams. And adding dialogue brings audiences closer to reality. Diminishes the dreams. Makes them everyday life. You really want to film everyday life, Uncle Marc? That's what our customers pay to forget. And players who talk would be just like everyday life. Who needs it? Who wants it?"

Even Charlie Royce raised his head to look at him with astonishment. No one discussed the philosophy of moving pictures in Hollywood. They were too busy turning out the product. They intellectualized about movies in France, where film societies had been formed. But the French intellectualized about *everything*. In Russia, Eisenstein,

Pudovkin, and others debated theories of cinematography, but that was because they suffered a shortage of raw film stock—not enough to make films, so they talked about them. But in Hollywood the pressures of production were too intense for theories and debate. Make it up, shoot it through, get it out.

"Dreams," Eli Hebron murmured. "That's what we're selling. The most beautiful men and women in the world. Gods and goddesses. Dressed in clothes that no one in the audience can afford. In surroundings of such magnificence that they can only wonder. It's another world. Where beautiful people love and laugh, suffer and triumph. It lifts them. For a couple of hours. Makes them forget their problems and defeats. Escape. That's what we're selling. But the moment the players start talking, the illusion is destroyed. They become the people next door. Who wants to pay fifty cents to see a moving picture of the people next door? The magic is lost. And we—"

"Tell it to the Marines!" Charlie Royce cried, face stuffed with fury. "Why do you think attendance is off? Because people are sitting home listening to radio. *Listening!* Sure, it's only voices, only sounds, but it's *free!* And don't think they don't escape just from listening, just from sounds. So an actor on the stage speaks. He's still Hamlet, isn't he? It's still a dream. I didn't go to college like you, Eli, but I think your ideas are cockeyed. Subtitles don't do anything but interrupt the action. If players could talk, you could explain dull stuff in a few words and concentrate on fast, realistic action to tell the story. Dreams, my ass— please excuse the language, Mr. Annenberg. We're selling entertainment, that's all. We're competing with stage, vaude-ville, and radio. If we fight sound, we're digging our own grave. Last month the Radio Corporation broadcast pictures and sound from Washington to New York. What do we do when that's perfected? Listen, Mr. Annenberg, I say we convert to sound as fast as we can or we're out of business.''

"Charlie," Eli Hebron sighed, "you haven't—"

But suddenly the commissary erupted. Screams and shouts. Laughter and tears. Men and women were on their feet, leaping about, embracing.

"What?" Marcus Annenberg said, stunned. "What's going on here? An earthquake?"

Meyer Levine whirled from the table, leaned across the wooden railing. He grabbed a shrieking Confederate soldier, shook him by the shoulders.

"What?" he yelled. "What is it?"

"He made it!" the actor howled. "Made it, made it, made it! Lindbergh! The radio said! He landed in Paris! Alive! He made it!"

They heard it at the executive table. They settled back in their chairs, smiling.

"Well, well, well," Phil Nolan said. "That's something that is!"

"Let's get him," Charlie Royce said eagerly. "We sign him up. How about it, Mr. Annenberg? He's young, good-looking. Let's put him under contract. The story of his flight. A natural!"

The old man considered a long moment. They all stared at him.

"What will he want?" he asked finally.

"A hundred, two hundred thousand," Royce said roughly. "Who cares? It'll gross fifty million. Call it *The Spirit of St. Louis*. That's the name of his plane."

Annenberg turned to Hebron.

"Eli," he said, "what do you think?"

"You'll never get him for that, Uncle Marc," Hebron said. "MGM or Paramount will go to half a million. At least. Also, maybe RKO."

"Well," Annenberg said thoughtfully, "it wouldn't hurt to ask. Meyer, cable your people in Paris. Start at fifty thousand. What does he know, an aviator? If necessary, go to two fifty. Not a penny higher."

"Yes, Mr. Annenberg," Meyer Levine said. "I'll get it off right away."

"So what if we don't get Lindbergh himself?" Royce demanded. "He don't own the story. I got a young guy who looks exactly like him. How's this? A kid from a small town. He's crazy about flying. Always tinkering with planes—you know? He's in love with this pretty girl next door. She loves him, too, but her parents want her to marry this rich, dull, older guy. Like a lawyer or doctor— something like that. So the kid takes off for Paris alone. To prove himself to the girl's parents—see? She gives him her scarf to wear around his neck. Makes him sandwiches— like that. So we see him struggling through storms, over the ocean. Plenty of cliff-hanger footage. On the edge of their seats! He makes it! He comes home a hero. He gets all kinds of big cash offers. But he turns them down. He goes back to his small town, marries the girl, starts a small, successful airline. Fade-out. How's that?"

"To me it sounds good." Marcus Annenberg nodded. "Clean. American. But fast, Charlie. We've got to get it out fast. Like yesterday."

"You'll have the scenario on your desk this afternoon," Charlie Royce said happily.

The luncheon broke then. They separated, pushed their way through the commissary crowd. People were still laughing, yelling, shaking hands. Pint bottles of bootleg gin had appeared.

Charlie Royce strolled a few steps into the yard, paused to light a cigar. Timmy Ryan, chief of the studio police, came up to him. They grinned at each other. Royce gave the chief a White Owl.

"Good news, Timmy," the supervisor said. "A great day."

"It is that, Mr. Royce," Ryan said. "Thanks for the smoke. I'll save it for dinner—after I take the feathers off! I never thought he'd make it."

"Me neither. Timmy, you think he's a Yid?"

"Lindbergh?" Ryan said. "I wouldn't be knowing."

"Just wondering," Charlie Royce said.

Mildred Eljer was waiting for him in the outer office. She always reminded him of a stork. An earnest stork, with glasses.

"Isn't it wonderful about Lindbergh, Mr. Hebron?" she said.

"Yes," he said. "Wonderful."

She peered at her pad.

"Indoor Stage Two is available at five o'clock for the Gladys Potts test," she reported. "Stan Haggard will come in from the back lots to direct. I finally got hold of Ritchie Ingate at Universal. He'll try to make it but may be a little late. All right, Mr. Hebron?"

He nodded.

"Eddie Durant wants to know what kind of a set you want, and you better talk to Bea Winks about makeup and costume. Most important, Bruno Schmidt called twice and came up once. He's got trouble."

"What kind of trouble?"

"Margaret Gay. She won't cry."

"All right," he said. "I'll go down there in a few minutes. Call and tell him I'm on my way. Tell Eddie Durant I want a store. A Parisian shop of about twenty years ago. That sells women's gloves, hats, perfume. Things like that. A simple set. Sales counter. Maybe a chair or two. Shelves on the walls. Am I going too fast for you, Mildred?"

"No, Mr. Hebron," she said, scribbling busily. "I'm keeping up."

"Tell Eddie not to build anything; just furnish with what we have; it's only a test. Oh, yes—a mirror. A full-length mirror on a swivel. What do they call them?"

"A pier glass, Mr. Hebron?"

"Is that it? Well, anyway, we've got one in storage. Oval. Bought it for *The Last Kiss*. It's around somewhere. Then call Bea Winks and tell her I want Gladys Potts like a Parisian shopgirl of about twenty years ago. Long skirt. Fluffy blouse. Do something with her hair. And her eyes are too small. Tell Bea to make them bigger. Anything else, Mildred?"

"Just phone calls, Mr. Hebron. Agents mostly. And that Santa Monica real estate company. About your beach lot."

"They'll call back."

"Did you eat, Mr. Hebron?" she asked anxiously.

"Sure," he smiled. "A cottage cheese salad. Delicious."

"Good," she said approvingly.

He went into his office. He closed and locked the door, drew the drapes. He poured a small glass of gin. He lay on his leather couch, put an arm across his eyes. Occasionally he raised up to take a sip of gin.

It was the physical energy of Charlie Royce that daunted

him. He had been in California for eight years, Royce for four. It made a difference. The California scene—heat, sky, sea, the whitewashed openness—caused a scurvy of the will. Big money contributed. And the flood of golden lads and lasses from all over the country to become stars. But essentially it was the hot sun, high sky, murmuring sea. A lotus-land that eroded resolve and left nothing but dreams. It had not yet softened Charlie Royce.

He finished his gin. He rinsed the glass in his small lavatory, not glancing at himself in the mirror. He went down into the yard again, not going through the outer office but using the French door that led directly to the balcony.

They were shooting the third movie version of *Madame Bovary* on Indoor Stage One. It had a six-week schedule and a budget of four hundred and fifty thousand dollars. It was being directed by Bruno Schmidt. He was one of many lured to Hollywood from the German UFA studios. All of them were addicted to low-key lighting, thinking to create another *The Cabinet of Dr. Caligari*.

Schmidt was a short man, not much taller than his megaphone. He wore cavalry breeches and high leather boots. On outdoor sets he wore a white pith helmet and carried a riding crop, looking about nervously for snakes. But his one completed picture for Magna, *Roses Are Red*, a sophisticated comedy, had been a surprising success. One scene was still being talked about in Hollywood: The negligee-clad heroine, to escape a would-be seducer, jumps from her hotel balcony and slowly, almost lovingly, slides down a thick flagpole. The scene was Eli Hebron's idea, but he was willing to let Bruno Schmidt take the credit.

The director grabbed Hebron's arm the moment he stepped inside Stage One.

"She vill not veep," the German wailed. *"She vill not veep!"*

"All right, Bruno," Hebron said. "I'll handle it. You go outside, have a smoke, calm down."

He pushed the director toward the door. When he was gone, Hebron beckoned the assistant director.

"What's the scene, Max?"

"It's a little thing, Mr. Hebron. Emma is giving up her baby, and she looks down into the cradle. That's all. Schmidt wants a close-up. He wants Gay to cry, and she can't do it. Or won't do it. Seven takes, and we haven't got it yet. It's all lighted, Mr. Hebron. I made sure of plenty of light like you told me."

"All right, Max. Kill the arcs and let everyone cool off a minute. Where's Gay?"

"Over there in the corner, Mr. Hebron."

Margaret Gay was Magna's ranking female star. She was under personal contract to Eli Hebron. She was a striking brunet, with a close resemblance to Norma Talmadge. But she had a fey, wistful quality that filmed beautifully. She received fifty proposals of marriage a month, by mail, from Oklahoma oilmen, Arabian sheiks, and Hungarian noblemen. *Photoplay Magazine* had paid tribute to her "Unspoiled, innocent, insouciant allure, fresh as a dewy morn, that makes even the most torrid love scene devoid of all that might offend."

She was sitting in a canvas chair, back to the camera. Eli Hebron walked over quietly, bent to kiss her cheek lightly. She looked up.

"Eli," she said, with a sad, sweet smile, "that fucking Kraut bastard is killing me."

"There," he said, patting her shoulder, "it's going to be all right, darling. We'll do whatever you say."

"You're fucking right," she said. "Eli, he wants me to cry, and I just *can't*."

"Could we use a few drops of glycerin, dear?"

"*Pretend?*" she said. "Eli, I've got millions of fucking fans out there. They love Margaret Gay because they know she never pretends. They know she gives them everything in her heart, honest and sincere. She can't fake an emotion, Eli. Margaret Gay can't disappoint the little people."

Hebron motioned. Another canvas chair was brought and slid under him. He sat on the edge, leaned forward. He clasped her hands in his and looked at her earnestly. She was twenty-three years old and was making ten thousand dollars a week. Last year her movies had grossed almost fifteen million.

"Darling," he said, "you have cried. You know it and I know it. A woman who feels as deeply as you do—a sensitive woman, a delicate woman—must have cried many times."

She put head back, closed her eyes. He stared at that cameo profile, the porcelain skin.

"Oh, yes," she said dreamily. "I have wept, Eli. Many, many times."

"For what reason, dear?"

She opened her eyes. She looked at him with that otherworldly smile that drove men mad.

"I cry every time I hear 'Fascination,' " she said. "I was playing that fucking tune on the Victrola the first time I got screwed, and every time I hear it I cry."

Hebron nodded. He stood up, beckoned to the assistant director again.

"Max," he said in a low voice, "they're shooting the ballroom scene of *Jazz Mothers* on Stage Three. They've got a dummy orchestra. Send someone over to see if one of those extras can actually play a musical instrument.

31

Piano, fiddle, piccolo—I don't care what. But he's got to be able to play 'Fascination.' Find someone; get him over here."

"Right away, Mr. Hebron."

Twenty minutes later Bruno Schmidt was sitting in his director's chair alongside the camera. Margaret Gay was bending over a wooden cradle, reaching toward a hidden rag doll baby. Eli Hebron stood behind the lights.

"Take eight," the script clerk called.

"Action!" Bruno Schmidt shouted hoarsely through his megaphone.

The script clerk showed his slate in front of the lens, identifying the number of the scene. Then he stepped aside.

Off in the dimness, a lachrymose, mustachioed man, wearing a nipped-waist tuxedo, began to play "Fascination" on his violin.

Margaret Gay leaned over the cradle, weeping.

Writers' Row was a street of ten bungalows set behind the commissary. "Between the garbage dump and the toilets," newly arrived writers invariably remarked.

Originally, each bungalow had been equipped with two desks, two swivel chairs, two typewriters, two file cabinets. Over the years, writers had attempted to relieve the austerity of their cells. Those hired would bring in pictures, lamps, an armchair, perhaps a sofa, Victrola, books, magazines, a small Crosley radio, etc. Fired writers invariably left these personal belongings behind, determined to forget all about Magna Pictures, Inc., and move on to more comfortable surroundings at United Artists, MGM, or Universal.

Bungalow Five was occupied by Edwin K. Jenkins and Tina Rambaugh. Both writers were assigned to Eli Hebron.

Jenkins was an ex-newspaperman from Wichita, Kansas. He had come to Hebron's attention when he had a short story published in *The American* magazine. It was Jenkins' first and last published story. He had almost been fired when Marcus Annenberg had asked for a very brief screen treatment of the Bible and Jenkins had submitted: "Jesus wept."

Tina Rambaugh was seventeen years old, a plain, chubby girl. She had won her job by regularly submitting plots for moving pictures to Eli Hebron. None of her one-page outlines was purchased or even stolen, but the supervisor was impressed by the girl's persistence. She was hired to write subtitles and proved to have a flair for sophisticated dialogue and double entendre. Her work had, more than once, come to the attention of the Hays Office.

All the woodwork in Bungalow Five—desks, chairs, file cabinets, walls—had a dingy, whittled look. There was one broken armchair, the springs exposed. A large cardboard cutout of Theda Bara leaned against a wall. Alongside Edwin K. Jenkins' desk was a brass spittoon, used as a wastebasket. Over Tina Rambaugh's desk, framed on the wall, was a blowup of a subtitle from Erich von Stroheim's *Greed*. It was considered by many the funniest subtitle ever written: "Let us go over and sit on the sewer."

"Ed," Tina Rambaugh said, staring at her typewriter, "you know all about speech and proper grammar, don't you?"

"Ain't I been tellin' you?" he said lazily.

"Do you prefer 'The next day . . .' or 'The following day . . .'? Or do they mean the same thing?"

"Depends."

"What does *that* mean—depends?"

"If action takes place on Monday, and the next scene is

on Tuesday, it could be either 'next day' or 'following day.' But suppose you have a big daytime scene where the hero and heroine make love. Maybe they don't meet again for another month. Then you could use 'The next day . . .' but not 'The following day. . . .' "

"I don't get it," she said.

"Neither do I," he said. "Does it make any difference?"

"I suppose not. I'll use 'The following day. . . .' "

She typed it out on her subtitle sheet, then consulted the scenario she was working on. Jenkins flipped slowly through the current issue of the *Saturday Evening Post*, looking for a plot to steal.

"Find anything?" she asked him.

"A good one by Clarence Budington Kelland," he reported. "Nice twist at the end. But it takes place in a swamp."

"Switch it to the studios of Magna pictures," she advised. "Ed, why don't you write an original?"

"They don't pay me enough. Want a drink?"

"No. You drink too much."

"And you talk too much."

"How long have you been out here, Ed? Six years?"

"That's right. The best years of my life."

"You're another," she said.

She pounded at her typewriter. He poured a water glass of straight gin from a pint bottle he kept in the bottom drawer of his file cabinet. He added a few chips of ice from a burlap-wrapped bundle in a small pail beneath his desk.

He was a tall, lanky man, farmerish, wearing a rumpled suit of shiny alpaca. A bad case of smallpox in his youth had left his cheeks raw and pitted. Sandy hair was parted in the middle and brushed back. "Like Bix Beiderbecke," he often said. "My hero."

"How's the novel coming?" Tina asked.

"You go to hell," he said.

She paused, fingers on the keys, looking at him thoughtfully.

"Ever think you can't write a novel in California?" she said. "Ever think it's impossible, that *no one* can write a novel in California?"

"I'll bite," he said. "Why not?"

"It's just not novel country. No tradition. This is short-story country."

"I'll drink to that," he said, and did. "I would now like to propose a toast to Charles Augustus Lindbergh."

" 'Augustus'?" she said. "Is that his middle name?"

"Sure."

"How do you know?"

"I was a newspaperman once. And a good one."

"So you've told me," she said. "Several times."

"Snot," he said. "Well, you're a virgin. I'd rather be *anything* than a virgin."

"It's not so bad," she said, not looking at him. "I have plenty of time."

"Forget it," he said. "What gink would give you a tumble?" Then, when he saw her face, he said, "Jesus, Tina, I'm sorry. What a rotten thing to say. Forget I said it. Please."

"That's all right," she said, sniffing a little. "You just say things like that because you're frustrated and miserable and want to take out your hostilities on someone else."

"Thank you, Dr. Freud," he said.

She laughed, got up from her swivel chair, came over, and kissed his pitted cheek. Then she went back behind her typewriter again.

"You're the bees' knees," he said. "The cat's pajamas."

"Your slang is dated," she told him.

"You keep rolling your stockings, and you're going to get into trouble, fatso."

She thrust one plump shoulder at him, puckered rouged lips, ran fingers through her marcelled hair.

"Think I could be a sheba?" she asked him.

"Sure," he said. "Like I could do a tango with Dagmar Godowsky. Hello, boss. Come to see if the slaves are still chained?"

Eli Hebron let the screen door slam behind him. He stood, hands on hips, looking around the office.

"We're trying to reproduce the atmosphere of the starving artist in the garret," he said. He felt at home with writers.

"You're succeeding," Jenkins assured him. "Pull up a chair."

Hebron looked at the exposed springs of the armchair, then perched on the edge of Tina Rambaugh's desk.

"What are you working on, honey?" he asked her.

"Subtitles for *Down on the Farm,* Mr. Hebron."

"When can you finish up?"

"This afternoon."

"Good. Ed, what are you doing?"

"Swiping," Jenkins said. "Where would Hollywood be without the *Saturday Evening Post?*"

Hebron looked at the glass on his desk.

"What's that?" he asked.

"Ice water," Jenkins said.

Hebron leaned over, picked up the glass, took a sip.

"Good," he said. "Better than what the studio buys. Who's your legger?"

"That guy they call Sammy," Jenkins said. "You've seen him around. Short and fat. Wears a raincoat on the hottest days. Inside the coat he's got these fifty pockets sewed on. For pint bottles. He sells to all us peons."

"Where's the stuff from?" the supervisor asked.

"Imported," Jenkins said. "Long Beach."

"Well, it's got a nice flavor," Hebron said. He didn't return the writer's glass, but continued to sip it as he talked. "I want the two of you to do a synopsis for me."

Tina Rambaugh looked up with interest. Then she stood and walked around in back of Jenkins, so they were both facing the supervisor. She put her hands lightly on Jenkins' shoulders.

"There's this young fellow," Hebron said. "A Keaton type—but more warmth. He's married or he's got a girlfriend—it's up to you. The girl is nice, solid, sensible. The fellow has a job, like milkman or something like that. Steady, but not a lot of money. And dull."

"Children?" Tina Rambaugh asked. "If they're married?"

Hebron thought a moment.

"No," he said finally. "No kids. They steal everything. Now this fellow is a romantic. He's always dreaming. We'll call this *The Dream Lover*. That's just a working title. And we *show* his dreams. He's a pirate, a tycoon, a great lover, a Lindbergh—all kinds of things. You understand? He can't endure the monotony and quiet despair of his existence, so he has these fantasies. He's Fairbanks, he's Valentino. Beautiful women throw themselves at his feet. He loves them and leaves them."

"Trouble with the Hays Office," Jenkins said.

"No," Hebron said, "I don't think so. Because it's going to be obvious these are just dreams, not reality. The dream sequences we'll shoot with a diffusion lens. It'll give the image a dreamlike quality. The audience will understand it's all in his mind."

"I get it," Tina Rambaugh said. "His dreams interfere with his career. Have I got it right? He makes crazy mistakes like delivering milk orders to the wrong door because he's always dreaming. Forgets to collect bills, forgets where he left his horse, and so forth."

"Sure," Jenkins said. "I see it. Always in trouble because he's always dreaming. In his dreams he's strong and determined. He shoots Indians, a real Tom Mix. But in life he's Harry Langdon."

"You've got it." Hebron smiled. "The real-life scenes we shoot on drab sets. You know—three walls and a table. But the dream scenes are gorgeous—palaces and harems and luxury liners and expensive Manhattan apartments. Like that."

"Is this a comedy?" Jenkins asked.

"Well, it is and it isn't," Hebron said. "In a way, it's a defeat expressed in comic terms. Because, you see, in the end he gives up his dreams and knuckles down."

"Why does he do that?" Tina Rambaugh asked.

"I don't know," the supervisor said. "That's your problem. But how's this? He decides to make one of his dreams come true. He meets a vamp and tries to play the sheik, like his dreams. She leads him on, and then she drops him. Takes all his money and laughs at him. So then he goes back to his nice, solid, sensible wife or girlfriend. Fade-out. How's that?"

"I like it, boss," Jenkins said. "Could be funny as hell and also touching. Everyone dreams. I think it'll play. Where did you steal it?"

"I don't know," Hebron said, frowning. "I've been thinking about it a long while. I don't believe I read it anywhere; it just came to me. This Lindbergh thing. . . ."

"How about this?" Tina Rambaugh said, looking at

Hebron. "In the final scene, when he realizes he's got to put his dreams away and get back to reality, and he goes off into the sunset with his nice, sensible wife—why, you also shoot that scene with a diffusion lens. So the customers are left wondering if that solution is a dream, too."

"Jesus Christ," Ed Jenkins said, tilting his head far back to look at her. "How old did you say you were, kiddo? Sixty? Seventy?"

"It's a possibility." Hebron nodded. "A very ironic ending, Tina. Well, give me that as a possibility and also an alternative ending."

"How long do we have?" the girl asked.

"Tomorrow?" Hebron said. "Late tomorrow. Enough time?"

"We'll have it," she told him.

"Good," Hebron said. He slid off the desk, drained the gin, handed the glass to Jenkins. "If you have any ideas for casting, I'll be happy to hear them. Keaton and Langdon are out. Too expensive. See you tomorrow."

He waved a hand and was gone. The screen door slammed. Edwin Jenkins looked at the door. He looked down at the empty glass in his hand.

"Why don't you play the lead yourself, boss?" he said in a low voice.

Tina Rambaugh bent to kiss his pitted cheek again. His free hand slid up her fat leg, over the rolled stocking. Fingers clamped on the bare thigh below her bloomers.

"One of these days . . ." he said thickly.

Edison had provided the vocabulary, Griffith the grammar. But the style was the responsibility of the individual supervisor or director. And, frequently, of the cutter.

A talented cutter (film editor) could make a ham-handed

director look like Thomas Ince. Similarly, a malevolent cutter, for whatever personal reason, could splice together an atrocity from ten reels of the same rushes. Eli Hebron made certain Magna's film editors got prominent credit lines. He knew their worth.

More important, he enjoyed cutting. He worked as closely as his time allowed with his editors, both of them bending over a hand-cranked twin viewer, inspecting rushes, going over the frames again and again to add, delete, change the sequence of scenes or, if necessary, to order scenes reshot. Only when both agreed on the final cutting copy (sometimes with the director's approval, sometimes without) was the negative cut to match it, and prints made for distribution.

The cutting room at Magna Pictures, Inc., occupied one corner of the lab building. There was nothing elegant about it: a small, jumbled enclosure with long wooden tables, stools, overhead racks festooned with strips, loops, miles of film. Cans of film stacked on the floor. NO SMOKING signs and buckets of sand everywhere.

Three cutters were permanently employed at Magna. Freelancers were hired for single pictures when the schedule backed up.

The head cutter, Myron Mattfield, was young (twenty-four), pale, and almost as short as Hebron. He had a hacking cough that everyone suspected was TB. Mattfield worked all of Hebron's pictures; they had the same sense of timing. A close-up of a mother's face, for instance, as her son marches off to war, would be wasted if cut too short. If allowed to run too long, it would lose its impact. The gift was in knowing how many frames of that wrenched, tearstained face should appear on screen. It could not be done by formula or stopwatch.

Eli Hebron had once tried explaining this creative process to Marcus Annenberg, who never could understand how his products were made.

"It's like writing a poem, Uncle Marc," he said. "Or a song. You have long lines and short lines. And you vary mood and tempo. There's a rhythm to it. When it's right, you feel it."

"But how do you know it will sell?" the old man had asked.

This afternoon Myron Mattfield and Eli Hebron were viewing a cutting copy of *Mrs. Robinson Crusoe*. In the movie, Friday was a girl who eventually married Crusoe after an Episcopalian minister was providentially washed ashore. Neither supervisor nor editor was satisfied with the final cut.

"It's the beach scenes, Mr. Hebron," Mattfield said. "Where they're walking hand in hand. Once, fine. Two is all right. The third time they go walking down that damned beach, you begin to yawn. And the fourth . . . !"

Hebron nodded. The wooden roof of the lab was low; it radiated heat. He had loosened his tie, opened his collar button. The base had left a light green disk on his neck. He paced up and down, hands on his hips.

"Where's Dupont?" he demanded.

Gregory Dupont had directed *Mrs. Robinson Crusoe*. Halfway through filming Abe Vogel had told Hebron that Dupont was marking time at Magna while he argued contract terms with Columbia.

The rushes had been satisfactory; Hebron had no complaints. Still, he expected the director to be on hand for the final cut of his first Magna release.

Myron Mattfield had a severe coughing attack before he could answer the supervisor. He bent far over, holding a handkerchief to his mouth. Hebron turned away, waiting.

The coughing sickened him: hoarse, deep, phlegmy. Finally it eased; Hebron turned back to see Mattfield jam a sodden handkerchief into his pocket.

"He worked with me on the rough cut, Mr. Hebron," Mattfield said, still gasping. "Then he told me to finish up. I haven't seen him since."

Hebron nodded.

"Dupont is a fool," he said. "There are ways. . . . All right, Myron, we don't need him. I think you're right about those beach walks. If we cut the last two, what do we lose?"

The cutter looked at his counter. "We'll run about four minutes short, Mr. Hebron. We could pad the chimp footage. Chimps are always good for a laugh."

Hebron shook his head.

"Those scenes are right the way they are," he said. "This is a picture about people, not animals. We need something else."

He continued his pacing. Mattfield waited patiently. He couldn't do his job until other men did theirs.

"How's this?" Eli Hebron said. "We go back to camera. We shoot more footage. Another beach scene. Friday goes for an early-morning swim. Bathing suit made out of leaves. The surf washes her footprints away. When she comes out of the water, to play a trick on Crusoe, she walks *backwards* from the ocean onto the sand. Cut to her footprints. She hides behind a rock, giggling. He comes along, sees her footprints in the wet sand. Apparently going *into* the ocean but not coming out. He gets frantic. He dashes up and down the beach. He's out of his mind—she's drowned! Then he sees her laughing behind the rock. He rushes to her, relieved but angry. Then they both laugh. They wrestle on the sand."

"Sounds good to me, Mr. Hebron."

"Maybe I'll shoot it myself," the supervisor said. "I know exactly what I want."

"And Greg Dupont gets the credit," the cutter said cynically.

"Credit?" Eli Hebron said. "What credit? Dupont should learn to read his contracts more carefully. It said nothing about credits."

In the garage Barney O'Hara was lounging with the other chauffeurs. They were arguing about the second Dempsey-Tunney fight, scheduled for Chicago in the fall.

"The Mauler will take him," O'Hara said authoritatively. "He's learned how to handle the cute stuff. Hello, Mr. Hebron. Want me?"

He drew Barney aside, and they talked cars. Hebron owned three: the Hispano-Suiza limousine, a black LaSalle four-door sedan, and a yellow Packard straight-eight roadster. The LaSalle was generally kept at the studio. Barney O'Hara drove to work in his own Hupmobile Eight and left it parked in Hebron's garage during the day.

"Barney, I won't need you anymore today. You can drive the limo back. I'm going to be working late."

"How will you get home, Mr. Hebron?"

"I'll take the LaSalle or call a taxi. See you in the morning."

"Thanks, Mr. Hebron. If you need me tonight—unexpected like—be sure and give me a call."

"I'll do that, Barney. Thank you."

He walked purposefully toward the indoor stages, paused to light a Lucky Strike. He waited until he saw the maroon Hispano-Suiza pull through the gate. Then he went back to the parking lot and got into the LaSalle. It was stifling. He rolled down the front windows and waited a few minutes. Then he started up, waved at Mac at the gate, and drove to a two-story building on La Brea. He parked in front of a shop that sold Mexican jewelry, castanets, and jumping beans. Hebron walked around to the back. He climbed the outside staircase, walked down the balcony to a door with a tacked sign: MADAME ORTIZ, ADVISER. He knocked and entered. The opening door hit a bell, and it jangled.

The room smelled of incense and frijoles. There was a beaded curtain hanging from an archway leading to an inner room. On the walls were paintings on black velvet of bleeding saints. There was a worn couch with a leather pillow branded "Souvenir of San Diego." In the center of the room was a card table and two folding chairs.

A fat Mexican woman came from the inner room, pushing through the curtain. She was carrying a pack of greasy playing cards. She had a large wen on her chin with black hairs sprouting from it. Strings and strings of beads encircled her bulging neck, some hanging to her knees. She wore a ring on every finger.

"Meester," she said.

"I don't have much time," Eli Hebron said.

They sat down at the table. She laid out the cards, setting each down with a little snap. She stared at them.

"Well?" Hebron asked.

"Like last time," she said. "This mans, he don' like you."

"The dark man? The big one?"

"Yes. He do you dirt."

"How?" Hebron asked.

"I don' know. Moaney maybe. He cost you moaney. I see a woman. A girl. Young girl. She will bring you 'appiness."

"You sure?"

"The cards they never lie," she said severely. "The future is written. It is all here. You will make moaney. Plenty moaney. The bad mans will try to take away."

"But I'll find happiness with the young girl?"

"The cards say."

"Is she fair? A blond girl? Or dark?"

Madame Ortiz peered at the stained cards.

"Dark," she said. "Beware of her."

"Beware?" Hebron said. "But you said she will bring me happiness?"

"Is so." The woman nodded. "But beware. That is all I see."

He gave her five dollars and left.

Eddie Durant, a gum-chewing guy, was more carpenter than set designer. He was good on the breakaway stuff for the slapsticks. He could be trusted on Western saloons and ranch houses. But free-lancers were hired to design more complex and luxurious sets for Hebron's features. That didn't make Eddie sore. He was the only man at Magna who knew where to find a specific item in the big prop warehouse. He figured that made his job safe.

When Eli Hebron strode into Indoor Stage Two, Eddie Durant and his helpers were putting the finishing touches on the Parisian shop for the Gladys Potts test.

"Look okay, Mr. Hebron?"

"Looks fine, Eddie. Move the mirror closer to the counter."

"Sure. How tall is this dog?"

"She's not a dog, Eddie."

"Sorry, Mr. Hebron. How tall is the lady?"

"It makes a difference?"

"Sure it does, Mr. Hebron. She'll be standing by the sales counter—correct?"

"Yes."

"So we don't want it too high. Make her look like a midget. Or we can cut it down and make her look taller."

"Eddie, you're a genius."

"I keep telling you, Mr. Hebron."

"She's about my height."

"Tall," Durant said diplomatically.

"Cut it down, Eddie," Hebron told him, sighing.

Stan Haggard, who would direct the test, was already onstage. He was showing two electricians where he wanted the lights. The cameraman, Ritchie Ingate, hadn't shown up yet.

Hebron went over to a corner where Abe Vogel was standing with a stalwart, imposing older man wearing a top hat, swallowtail coat, striped trousers, short boots with pearl gray spats. He had a spade beard that looked dyed. A monocle was screwed into his right eye.

"Mr. Hebron," the agent said nervously, "this is Baron von Stumpf."

"A bleasure," the man said, holding out a gloved hand.

"Glad to meet you, Baron," Hebron said, shaking the glove. "Is the beard yours?"

"Pull," the man said, thrusting his chin at Hebron.

"I believe you." Hebron smiled. "You look fine. Just what I wanted. Where's the girl, Abe?"

"Makeup and costuming, Mr. Hebron," Vogel said. "We were right on time."

"I'm sure you were," the supervisor said. "Relax. We're waiting for the cameraman. Then I'll sketch the scene."

Bea Winks came through the door. She was leading

Gladys Potts by the hand. The girl had been fitted with a wig of tight blond curls, a shiny mobcap. Her short-sleeved blouse was a cascade of braid-trimmed ruffles. She was wearing a laced corselet and a full skirt of crimson brocade, billowed by pink petticoats. Cupid's-bow lips had been painted on her mouth, a star-shaped mouche pasted on her cheek. Her face was vapid enough to be on a *College Humor* cover. She looked close to tears.

Eli Hebron exploded.

"You fucking idiot," he screamed at Bea Winks. "You call this a Parisian shopgirl? Where are your brains—in your *tuchas?* What the hell's wrong with you, you stupid cunt? She looks like a Gypsy whore."

They had all frozen. No sound, no movement. Staring at the supervisor.

"Have I got to do everything around here myself?" he yelled. "Get all that shit off her face. Just make her eyes bigger, that's all. The blouse should be long-sleeved, simple. Like a man's shirt. Deep neckline to show cleavage. All right, a single ruffle at the neckline. A wide black leather belt. A straight black skirt, a hobble skirt, to her ankles. White blouse, black skirt. Can you understand English?"

"Yes, Mr. Hebron," Bea Winks said in a low, trembling voice.

"I'll be in my office," he shouted at all of them. "Call me when you're ready. And this time get it right, for Christ's sake."

He left them shaking, white-faced.

He stormed past a startled Mildred Eljer, slammed the door of his inner office. He gulped two of the orange pills. He filled a glass with warm gin and sipped, swinging back and forth in his swivel chair. After a while he buzzed

47

Mildred on the Dictograph and told her she could go home. She started to say, "Mr. Hebron, are you—" but he disconnected.

He swung about, staring out the high windows.

All of them—executives, supervisors, directors, actors, cameramen, technicians—worked long hours. Actors arrived at the studio at six A.M. for makeup and costuming. Shooting began on the outdoor sets when the sun was up, didn't end until dusk. Indoor stages were sometimes in use till midnight. The floods illuminating the yard frequently burned all night. The assembly line never stopped. The demand never stopped. New York slum dwellers, African natives, Chinese coolies sat on cushioned seats, wooden benches, and packed earth, watching the flickering magic, dreaming.

After a while, the gin finished, Eli Hebron lay down on his leather couch. He put one arm across his eyes. He may have dozed.

He roused when the phone rang. He stumbled across the dim office to his desk.

"Mr. Hebron? This is Stan Haggard. We're ready for you, sir."

"Ritchie Ingate there?"

"He's here, Mr. Hebron. We're all set."

"Be down in a few minutes."

In the lavatory he ran cold water over the veins in his wrists. He combed his fine dark hair straight back from the brow. Reginald Denny. He adjusted collar, tie, shirt, trousers, jacket. He staggered a moment and had to grab the sink to steady himself. He wasn't drunk, and it wasn't a physical illness. Dr. Irving Blick had told him that. "A vertigo, Mr. Hebron. A disordered state. A kind of disorientation."

"Can it be cured, Doctor?"

"Well. . . ." Blick had shrugged.

They were waiting for him, nervously, on Stage Two. The arcs were on. He walked over to Gladys Potts. The heavy makeup had been removed. There was a light dusting of white powder, a touch of rouge to accentuate her lips. Dark outlines had been used to magnify her eyes. They seemed enormous, luminous. She had been fitted with a heavy black wig, the false hair up in a swirled braid piled atop her head. It gave her a regal look.

She was wearing a long-sleeved blouse of white voile with a white camisole underneath. The collar was a deeply cut ruffle, hinting at small, round breasts. The black belt, cinched hard, gave her a waist no larger than a fat man's neck. A long, tight skirt fell to her ankles. Buttoned boots.

The tight belt forced her torso into a constrained posture. There was a sweet S curve from shoulders and bosom through the tiny waist to flare of hips and bottom. Hebron raised his eyes. The girl was smiling now.

He turned to Bea Winks.

"I'm sorry I blew up, Bea. Please forgive me."

"That's all right, Mr. Hebron," she said stiffly. "Is this what you wanted?"

"Beautiful," he said. "Just what I saw. Everyone, please, come in closer."

They clustered around him.

"Here's what I want. . . . This young lady, Miss Gladys Potts, is a shopgirl in Paris. About twenty years ago. She's poor, very, very poor. But she works in this expensive shop, and naturally she dreams of the day when she can own these beautiful gloves and scarves, and this perfume and jewelry, and so forth. She wants these things, but she is a good girl, an innocent girl. You understand?"

They all nodded solemnly. They understood: the girl hadn't been fucked yet.

"Now the scene is this. . . . In comes a wealthy nobleman, Baron von Stumpf here. He has come to pick out a gift for his wife, his current mistress, someone. But his eye is caught by the shopgirl, a delicious morsel. He can't take his eyes off her. She is aware of his interest, but she is incapable of flirting. Then he selects several things. He can't make up his mind. He has her try on these things so he can see how they'll look. A hat, gloves, a scarf, necklace, so forth. She models for him. He admires. Finally, he selects a necklace he likes. Or a scarf, hat—it can be anything. He asks her, does she like it? She likes it. He has it wrapped. He pays for it. And with the money, he hands her his card. Close-up of card. Any piece of cardboard will do, Stan; this is only a test. Then the man gives the gift to her! Presses it into her hands. Then he leaves, smiling. The cat that ate the canary. She's stunned. She's never had such a magnificent gift. Should she accept it or shouldn't she? She tries it on again, whatever it is—scarf, hat, necklace—and turns this way and that, examining herself in the mirror. It looks beautiful. Finally, she takes his card and is reading it at the fade-out. We know, from the expression on her face, that she's made up her mind: She's not going to be a poor shopgirl anymore. That's it. Anybody got any questions?"

"I am a rake?" Baron von Stumpf rumbled. "A parlor snake?"

"That's correct."

"Good," the baron said.

"Anything, Stan?" Hebron said.

"I think I've got it, Mr. Hebron. Five minutes?"

"At the most. Preferably shorter. A chance meeting. An

incident with significance. A life changes in a moment. Pack it in. As much as you can in as little time as possible. Miss Potts?''

"I know what you want, Mr. Hebron," she said.

"Anything you object to? Anything that doesn't ring true?''

"It rings true," she said.

"Good," he said. "Relax. Try not to be nervous. We're all your friends. We want as much as you do for this to be a success.''

He turned and started out. If he stayed, they'd freeze with anxiety, fearing another explosion. Outside, in the yard, he was conscious of someone behind him and turned.

"She likes you, Mr. Hebron," Abe Vogel murmured.

The supervisor stared at him. The activity of the studio went on about them: tractors hauling lights, a troop of marching Union soldiers, a man carrying an enormous balsa cross, a herd of sheep being driven to a back-lots pen.

"How do you know, Abe?"

"She told me.''

Hebron nodded slowly. "I have to work late. When she's finished, send her up to my office.''

"You want her to change first, Mr. Hebron?"

"No. In costume.''

"Should I wait for her?"

"Don't do that, Abe. I'll see she gets home.''

"I want to thank you, Mr. Hebron, for giving the girl a chance. I think she's got *It*. You'll see.''

He told her to leave on the blouse, camisole, and bandeau beneath. He helped her unhook the hobble skirt and steadied her as she stepped out of it. She was wearing rayon dance pants. She took those off. He told her she could keep on the boots and stockings. When she lay back on the leather couch, he found the garters were tight. He drew them and the black cotton stockings down to the tops of her boots. He rubbed gently at the wales the garters had left on her thighs.

Her eyes were open. She stared at the dim illumination of the yard coming through the closed drapes.

He touched her legs. At the same time his fingers stroked her skin, the edge of his hand brushed the cushions of the leather couch. It was the same: cool, smooth, almost glassy. He wiggled his hands beneath her. She had a back like a weasel's.

When it became evident, to both of them, that he wasn't going to do it, couldn't do it, she sat up, bent over him, took him in her mouth.

"That's it, girlie," he said.

He closed his eyes. She was very good. Slow. Almost thoughtful. He made a sound. She did not go away but stayed with him. Finally, finally, she pressed him back, rose, and went into the lavatory, her hand on her mouth. She came back and lay down again. She put her knees up, spread her thighs. He pried gently with his forefinger, found something that brought her hips thrusting from the couch. He continued, looking at her curiously. Her head whipped, side to side.

"Oh!" she cried.

Later, she said, "Thank you, Mr. Hebron."

While she was dressing, he said, "Would you like a drink? I have gin and scotch. Good scotch. The real stuff."

"I'll have some scotch, please. With water."

"We have a new Frigidaire in the outer office. Would you like ice?"

"Yes, please, Mr. Hebron."

She was finishing hooking up the skirt when he came back with the drinks. Scotch for her, gin for him. He handed the drink to her, then sat on the couch and pulled her gently onto his lap. They touched glasses and sipped.

"This won't make any difference, will it, Mr. Hebron?" she asked. "I mean about the test?"

"Oh, no," he said. "No. I hope it's good. How do you think it went?"

"I was nervous," she said.

"Of course. We understand that. But I gave you a good director and cameraman. The costume and makeup were right."

"When will you know, Mr. Hebron?"

"We screen test for all the supervisors and directors on Saturday morning," he said. "I'll call Abe on Monday. One way or another."

"Could you let me know before that?" she said. "Could you call me on Saturday, Mr. Hebron?"

"All right," he laughed. "Leave your number. I'll call you Saturday."

She kissed his hair. "You're a sweetie," she said.

"Am I?" he said, surprised.

"You really are." She nodded. "And you're very handsome."

"Thank you," he said. "I'll call a taxi for you."

Timmy Ryan parked his Nash Special 6 coupe on Ventura. He turned off the engine and killed the lights. He had changed to mufti at home, but he had brought the White Owl cigar Charlie Royce had given him. Now he lighted up and puffed contentedly. He had smoked almost half of it when a '22 Hudson coach pulled up behind his car and parked, bumper to bumper.

Ryan, still smoking placidly, watched in his rearview mirror. He saw a man get out, lock the door carefully, walk up to the Nash. The door on the passenger's side opened. Bernie Kaplan climbed in.

"Bernie," Ryan said genially, *"vos makst du?"*

"That's a lousy accent you got," Kaplan said. "And a lousy cigar."

"Oh, yeah?" Timmy Ryan said lazily. "There's no accounting for tastes. Got anything?"

"It's a yawn," Kaplan said. "Dull, dull, dull. Timmy, how long is this going on?"

"Till I tell you to stop. The money's right, ain't it, Bernie?"

"Oh, there's nothing wrong with the money," Kaplan said hastily. "The money's good."

"That's what I thought," Ryan said. "So?"

Kaplan drew a small notebook from his inside pocket.

"I can't read it," he said. "Can you put on your dash?"

"No," Ryan said.

"Well, there's not much anyway," Kaplan reported. "The usual shit. Except this afternoon he left the studio. Drove to La Brea. A Mexican place."

"When did this happen?"

"About four o'clock. Went around the back, up the stairs, into a place. It's a Madame Ortiz. A Mex. An old dame. She tells fortunes with cards. Is that anything?"

"Could be," Ryan said. "How long was he there?"

"Ten minutes, tops."

"You got the address?"

"Timmy, Timmy." Kaplan sighed. "You think I'm a mutt? Certainly I got the address."

"Anything else?"

"Nothing. I told you, it's a yawn."

"Where is he now?"

"Beddy-bye. All tucked in."

"All right, Bernie. Thanks."

"Timmy," Kaplan said, "who's paying for this?"

Ryan turned his head slowly to stare at the other man in the dimness.

"Bernie," he said, "you know what happened to the cat, don't you?"

He parked the LaSalle on the driveway. He walked up the steps, carrying his script case. The door opened, and Robert came hustling out, tugging down his striped waistcoat.

"Good evening, Mr. Hebron," he said, taking the case. "A lovely night."

"Yes," Hebron said. "How was your day off?"

"Very enjoyable," Robert said. He spent his free time serving as usher at Aimee Semple's Angelus Temple. "A big crowd, and collections were good. A very successful meeting."

"Glad to hear it. Put the case in the study, will you, Robert? I'm going up and bathe. I'll be in all night."

"Shall I run the tub, Mr. Hebron?"

"No, I can manage, thank you."

"Have you dined, Mr. Hebron?"

He had to think a moment.

"Not since lunch," he said. "A salad. But I'm not hungry."

"Mrs. Birkin has a nice roast of beef, Mr. Hebron. A cold plate? A sandwich?"

"I don't think so, Robert. Maybe some fresh fruit. What do we have?"

"A fresh pineapple, Mr. Hebron. It looks quite good. Pears? Oranges?"

"The pineapple sounds nice. Is it cold?"

"Oh, yes. It's been in the box all day."

"Fine. I'll have a bowl of pineapple chunks. You can leave it in the study. I'll be working there. And would you garage the LaSalle, please? Then you might as well turn in; I won't need you anymore tonight."

"Thank you, Mr. Hebron."

"Thank you, Robert."

He stood at the foot of the stairway, looking about vaguely. A stranger in his own home.

It had been decorated in Art Moderne style by a student of Saarinen, recommended to Eli Hebron by Cedric Gibbons. It had cost a great deal of money, more than a hundred thousand. Photos of the interior had appeared in art and architecture magazines. Once a month, for charity, Hebron allowed a guided tour.

There was furniture by Jallot and Ruhlmann, a clock by Tony Selmersheim, Lalique glass, a signed bronze figure by Marcel Bouraine, a commode by Pierre Chareau. Everything was Egyptian, with prancing nymphs, globes of frosted glass, inlaid wood, female deer, fountains, drapes in foliage prints, doves everywhere. The house was a glittering museum. The Victrola-Radiola combination was in an amboyna wood cabinet designed by Louis Sognot.

He went up the stairs wearily, his hand on the banister. He ran his bath while he undressed. His body seemed to him pale and flaccid. The failure with Gladys Potts dismayed him. With his wife, with Grace Darling, he had been potent. "My Jewish sheik," she called him fondly, raking his back with her nails. "No, not like that. Yes, like that. Like that! Do it! Do it!"

He reclined in the hot tub and closed his eyes. Images. Her back had been like a weasel's. The hair, the triangle, was black, without curl, lying softly. A little pelt. She smelled faintly of something growing. Did she shave her legs? One night, a month after his wife died, Hebron had called Bea Winks for a girl. The one she sent—very dark, somber, vaguely foreign—had been shaved completely. No body hair at all. Her nipples had been pierced. She showed Hebron; she could wear rings in her nipples. She gripped him inside, like a fist of hot muscle. She started, stopped, started, stopped. She had him crying. He never asked for her again.

He went down to the study, barefoot, wearing a white robe of rough wool. Grace had given him that. It was styled like a monk's robe, with a cowl and a rope belt.

He turned on the Radiola, fiddled with the dial. He got a San Francisco station playing a medley of tunes from *Show Boat*. It was Ted Weems' orchestra.

Robert had placed the script case alongside the desk of cherry wood and verdigrised metal from the Primavera atelier at Au Printemps. A frosted glass bowl of pineapple chunks, with cubes of ice, was on a linen napkin on the desk blotter. Hebron tried a piece. It was cold and sweet.

He poured himself a glass of gin from a bottle in the Chareau commode. The bottle bore a label that read "Olde London Gin," but Hebron supposed it was a fake. He added a few drops of bitters to kill the strong juniper flavor. Rather than make a long trip to the kitchen, he fished cubes from his bowl of pineapple and slid them into his drink.

He read scenarios and treatments steadily. Even after the San Francisco station went off the air at midnight, he continued reading. He liked the synopsis of *The Bridge of San Luis Rey* but doubted if Magna could outbid the larger studios on rights to the novel. There was also an original scenario submitted by a New York agent that he thought might work, with some rewriting. It was about a man in love with his brother's wife. All three of them lived in the same small farmhouse.

Eli Hebron could see the key scene. The husband and wife in bed. The brother lying on the other side of a thin wall. Hearing their giggles and sobs and moans. The bed creaking. Lying there and hurting. Moonlight through the window to show his sweated face. A good scene.

The story ended with the single man killing not his married brother but the wife. Eli Hebron wasn't sure that rang true, if brotherly love would prevail over passion. Would audiences accept that? Would they believe it? The murderer would have to suffer for his crime, of course. Would have to hang. Was that what the man wanted from the start—to be together in death with the woman he loved? Eli Hebron put the script aside. An interesting idea. A disturbing idea.

It was almost three in the morning before he finished. He put scenarios and treatments back in the case. The pineapple was finished, ice melted. He poured his third glass of gin—this one warm. He went out the French door of the study onto the wide terrace. Carrying his drink, sipping occasionally, he wandered down the pebbled steps to the swimming pool. He sat on a marble bench, still warm from the sun's heat.

A soft night, a balmy night. Quarter moon in a cloudless sky. As he stared at the pool, he saw the gleaming surface of the water moving gently. Not ruffled by a breeze—there was no breeze—but stirred in the center by something deep and mysterious. The pool was not constantly fed; the water should have been still. But it moved, radiating from some obscure disturbance at the center. He could not understand it.

He stared until his eyes glazed. He felt corroded by loneliness.

After a while, drink finished, he went up to bed. He took two pills—white ones this time—and slid between silk sheets. When he fell asleep, he was thinking of the man who killed his brother's wife. Yes, he thought, a man might do that. For love.

Bea Winks rented a home in West Hollywood. It was a three-story, barny structure on Crescent Heights: fifty years old, Victorian in design, with a screened porch, dormer windows, minarets, gables, balconies, scrollwork, and a fake widow's walk on top, surrounded by a cast-iron railing.

The inside was Victorian, too. Lamps of stained glass with beaded fringe. Dark oak furniture upholstered in velvet. Drapes of green felt. Worn Persian carpets on the parquet floors. Dried bouquets under glass bells. French dolls and Dresden figurines. A moose head and a suit of Japanese armor. The house belonged to a wealthy widower who, following the death of his wife, had moved to Paris and went to see Josephine Baker at the Folies four nights a week.

The only room in the house Bea Winks had rescued from Victorian clutter was her bedroom on the second floor. The original fringed lamps and four-poster bed remained, but the room had been lightened with chintz, ruffles, bright cushions, a mirrored cocktail table (with hammered silver shaker), and a couch of tobacco-tan satin.

Charlie Royce slumped on the couch, his brown congress gaiters parked on the cocktail table. He had unbuttoned his vest, loosened his tie, opened his collar. He was drinking a Pink Lady.

Bea Winks, wearing a brocade mandarin robe, sleeveless, closed to the neck with heavy frogs, also sat on the couch. Her bare feet were tucked under her. She was sipping a Pink Lady, too. The silver shaker was still half full and dripping moisture.

Beyond them, on the four-poster bed, a young girl lay on her stomach, propped on her elbows. She wore a pink shimmy. There was a tiny Siamese kitten scampering over the coverlet. The girl was teasing it with her long, honey-colored hair, laughing delightedly when the kitten clawed at it or fell on its back, legs waving wildly.

"I told them to call me here," Charlie Royce said. "Are you sure you'd mind if I smoked a cigar?"

"I'd mind," Bea Winks told him.

"All right," he said equably. "I can wait. Then what happened after the test?"

"I don't know," she said moodily. "The girl just disappeared. In costume. I don't know what happened to her. I left."

He looked at her a moment, amused.

"What's the matter, Bea?" he jeered. "He cut off your water?"

"Not my type," Bea Winks said shortly.

"But she's right for the job," Royce said.

"You hope."

Bea Winks was a thin, nervy woman with bobbed hair, hennaed. Her bare arms were muscled. Her toenails were painted red, something Charlie Royce had never seen until he got to Hollywood. Her face was pulled, bony, with pressed lips and a longish nose. Royce guessed her age at thirty but never asked.

He was refilling their glasses from the shaker when the wall phone rang. It was in a wooden case attached to a wood wall plaque: the cookie-cutter type. Bea Winks uncoiled from the couch, went over to answer it.

"Yes," she said, "he's here."

She held the earpiece out to Royce. When he took it, she went back to the couch, curled up again. She stared at him over the rim of her glass. The honey-haired girl began kissing the kitten's nose.

"Yes, Timmy," Royce said. "Uh-huh. . . . Yes. . . . It might be. Did you get the address? . . . Fine. . . . Yes. . . . Let me think about it, Timmy. I'll let you know. . . . You, too. . . . Good night."

He hung up and came back to the couch.

"He went to a fortune-teller," he reported. "This afternoon."

"A fortune-teller?"

"That's right. An old Mexican woman. She tells fortunes with cards."

Bea was silent a moment, then said, "Do you believe that stuff, Charlie? Fortune-telling?"

"Of course not," Royce said.

"I don't know," she said softly. "I had my fortune told a long time ago, and this woman said I'd never get married."

Royce guffawed.

"And I know why," he said.

The phone rang again.

"This is the big one," Charlie Royce said. "Keep your fingers crossed."

He rose and lumbered over to the phone, a heavy, looming man.

"Yes?" he said cautiously. "Yes, Abe, it's me. What happened? . . . Uh-huh. . . . Uh-huh. . . . You spoke to her? . . . Good. . . . Abe, I keep telling you, there's nothing to worry about. You'll be protected. . . . Sure. . . . Of course. . . . You can depend on me, you know that. . . . Yes, Abe, I understand. You're absolutely right. . . . Good night, Abe."

He turned from the phone, scowling.

"Lousy hebe," he said. "He's having second thoughts."

"How did it go?" Bea Winks asked.

Royce brightened. He smiled at her. "Fine," he said. "Just like I figured."

"I hope you know what you're doing," she said.

"I know," he assured her. "Believe me, I know."

Bea Winks put her drink on the cocktail table. She stood up and yawned, stretching her bare arms wide. He watched her pad over to the bed. She sat alongside the young girl and began stroking her hair.

Charlie Royce filled his glass again and went over to the bed, too. He pulled up a cretonne-covered armchair. He slumped down, stretched out his long legs, ankles crossed.

"Go right ahead, girls." He grinned at them. "Don't mind me."

Two

FOLLOWING the success of Rudolph Valentino, Magna Pictures, Inc.—obeying the dictum of Marcus Annenberg: "Always be first with the second"—rushed to discover and develop their own Latin Lover. After a search enlisting the efforts of agents on both coasts, they found their star on their ranch in Culver City. He was playing Apache chiefs in Westerns.

His name was Giuseppe Cavelli. He had come to Hollywood because all his friends in Altoona, Pennsylvania, told him he did a marvelous imitation of Enrico Caruso singing "Over There." He was slender, dark, handsome. He had bedroom eyes. Eli Hebron put him under personal contract. His name was changed to Nino Cavello, he was ordered to let his sideburns grow, and he was hustled into *Desert Love*. The movie proved to be Magna's biggest moneymaker in 1923. All Cavello pictures since then had been wildly profitable; not a turkey in the lot.

Nino Cavello's reputation as a Great Lover was carefully created and nurtured by Magna's publicity department. He was seen at the best restaurants in Los Angeles and New York, dining with beautiful women. Press photos were released showing him standing on the windswept deck of a white yacht, bathing beauties lounging in the background. Nino stood with feet spread, fists on hips, chin lifted, eyes brooding, his shirt unbuttoned to reveal a shaved chest. Stories and interviews were peddled to newspapers and magazines in which he told of the one great tragedy in his life: He had not yet found a woman he could love, truly love, with all the passion he felt surging within him.

As a result of this campaign Nino Cavello received the largest volume of fan mail of any Magna star, larger even than Margaret Gay's. Many of the letters addressed to him, opened and answered by the publicity department, contained tufts of pubic hair from his delirious admirers.

Despite his success, the money he earned, the public acclaim, Nino Cavello was a shy, quiet, religious boy. He had brought his mother, father, brothers, sisters, grandparents, and several cousins west to live with him in his Beverly Hills mansion. He blushed easily, was embarrassed during his love scenes, and invariably became seasick on the yacht Magna rented for his publicity stills, even though it was moored at a Santa Monica pier. He had twice been assaulted in public by jealous husbands claiming he had broken up their marriages. It was quite possibly true, although Cavello had never met the ladies involved.

Now Nino Cavello himself wished to get married. The bad news was brought to Eli Hebron on Saturday morning by Henry Cushing, head of Magna's press and publicity department. Cushing was a portly man with a congested complexion. He always wore navy blazers with gold buttons, gray flannel bags, and white buckskin shoes with long, fringed tongues. He had started as ballyhoo man for a Balaban & Katz theater in Chicago. He was widely known and respected as the man who had chained a moth-eaten and lethargic lion in the lobby of the theater during the screening of Elmo Lincoln's *Tarzan of the Apes*.

"Who's the girl, Hank?" Eli Hebron asked.

Cushing groaned, wiping the sweat from his face with a sodden handkerchief.

"Her name's Rosa Sinigalli, Mr. Hebron. Her old man owns a vineyard up in Napa. She's eighteen, stands about five one, and she's gotta weigh two-fifty. Also, she's got a mustache."

"How did Nino meet her?"

"His old man knew Rosa's old man back in Naples. Boyhood pals. So when Cavello moved out here, he looked up his old friend, and the families got together. Mr. Hebron, if it goes through, Nino's dead."

"We could dress her up," Hebron said slowly. "Let Bea Winks do a job on her. Then give the wedding a big splash. 'Marriage of the century!' That kind of thing."

Cushing shook his head, still sweating.

"Not with Rod La Rocque and Vilma Banky getting hitched. Who's going to give any space to Nino Cavello marrying some fat pasta fazool with a mustache? You've got to talk him out of it, Mr. Hebron. He's got one in the can and one shooting. If he does this to his fans, you might as well make mandolin picks out of those films. He's outside, Mr. Hebron, with his priest. Will you talk to him?"

"His priest?"

"Father DiGioia. He's from Nino's church. They're real

close. And why not? Nino gave them a new altar last year. Twenty grand, at least.''

"All right, Hank," Hebron sighed. "Bring them in."

Father DiGioia was a small, slight, sorrowful man wearing steel-rimmed spectacles with glass so thick his eyes looked like minié balls. He sat primly on the sofa, knees together, hands clasped prayerfully in his lap.

"Well, Nino"—Hebron smiled at the star—"Hank's told me the news. Congratulations."

"Thank you, Eli," Cavello said faintly, ducking his head. "She's a good girl."

"And attractive," Hebron said. "Hank says she's very attractive."

"A good cook," Cavello mumbled. "A marvelous cook."

"You've met the girl, Father?" Hebron asked the priest.

"Oh, yes, Mr. Hebron. A fine girl. Excellent family. She will make a good wife for Nino. Everyone is pleased."

"Glad to hear it," Hebron said. "The only thing that concerns me is Nino's welfare and happiness. I hope you all understand that."

"Of course," Henry Cushing said, nodding violently.

"And the only question I have is about the age of the girl. She's seventeen?"

"Eighteen, Eli," Cavello said, blushing.

"Well, that's still—what, Nino? Ten years younger than you?"

"Yes, Eli. Well . . . almost eleven."

"I'm thinking about how the American people will feel about one of their favorite actors, really a national hero—that's what you are, Nino: a national hero—marrying someone so much younger. You know, Nino, millions of Americans look up to you and respect you. They trust you. I want to make certain we do nothing to destroy that respect, to betray that trust.''

''Father?'' Cavello said, looking toward the priest. ''I'll do what you say.''

''I do not feel the difference in ages is an obstacle,'' DiGioia said slowly. ''Italians feel differently from Americans about these things, Mr. Hebron.''

''Of course you do,'' the supervisor said heartily. ''I understand that. But still, Father, you must realize that Nino's fans *are* Americans, and we must take into very careful consideration their beliefs and convictions and traditions.''

''I still say she is not too young,'' Father DiGioia said stubbornly. ''Her father gives his consent. He is eager to see the two families joined.''

''And the girl?'' Hebron asked.

''She is eager, too,'' the father said tonelessly.

Hebron nodded. He rose, walked to the windows, stared down at the activities in the yard. It was Saturday, but the studio would be going full blast until one o'clock and probably later. Then the Saturday-night partying would begin in Hollywood. Hebron himself had received three invitations, including a Charleston contest at Pickfair.

''Father DiGioia,'' he said, without turning around, ''could I have a few words with you? In private, please.''

The little priest stood up immediately and came over. He stepped close to Hebron, eyes blinking behind those thick glasses.

''First of all,'' Hebron said in a low voice, ''I want you to know I have the highest respect for a man of the cloth.''

''Thank you.''

''I've met Monsignor Mulcahy several times. A fine man. Do you know him?''

"Yes," DiGioia said.

"He blessed our movie *In the Beginning Was the Word* before it was released. That deeply religious movie has been shown in twenty-one foreign countries, including Africa and godless Russia, and has grossed more than forty million dollars."

"I am happy to hear it," the priest said.

"About this marriage . . ." Hebron said, lowering his voice even more. He was still staring down into the yard, his hawkish face half in bright sunlight, half in shadow. "I'm sure Nino has chosen a good girl, a fine girl."

"He has," DiGioia nodded.

"But I am concerned by her youth—the ten years' difference in their ages. I know you feel this is of no importance. But honest and sincere men may disagree."

"Of course," the father said. "I understand your concern. But I assure you—"

"What I fear," Hebron went on, "—and I fear this as a Jew, a member of a race that has been reviled and abused since time immemorial—I fear that if Nino Cavello marries this very young girl, it will not only affect his career adversely, but will also reflect unfavorably on all Italians in America. Let's face it, Father: Your people have not had an easy time overcoming the prejudice against Italians in this country. 'Wops' and that kind of thing. . . ."

"That is true, Mr. Hebron." The priest nodded sadly. "It has not been easy."

"But if the greatest Italian star in motion pictures was to marry this very young girl, don't you see how that would reinforce the prejudice? You know and I know that Nino and Rosa are both good, decent human beings who deserve whatever happiness they can find with each other. But we also know the American public would not be so tolerant and broad-minded. They would see only a wealthy movie star grabbing a girl ten years younger than he, and they would say, 'Those Italians. Those foreigners. Those animals!' And their unreasoning hatred would become all the stronger."

The priest blinked furiously.

"I had not considered that, Mr. Hebron," he faltered. "It is something to think about."

"Oh, yes." Hebron nodded. "It is a problem. If it was just Nino's future, then I'd say go ahead with the marriage as soon as possible. God bless Rosa and Nino! But I would not care to see this wedding result in increased prejudice and stupid contempt of the great Italian people."

"Then you are against this marriage, Mr. Hebron?"

"Oh, no," the supervisor said hastily. "No, no, no. These two young people are obviously in love, and should be allowed to seek a lifetime of happiness together. All I suggest is that the marriage be postponed. A year perhaps. Two years. In two years the girl will be twenty, and I assure you a ten-year difference in their ages at that time will have a much smaller effect on the American public. A female of twenty is considered a young woman. At eighteen she's still a girl."

DiGioia nodded slowly.

"Father, Nino will do what you tell him; I can see that. Will you consider carefully what I have said and then advise him?"

"I will do that," the priest agreed. "I will consider it and pray that I decide wisely."

"Good. Now there is one other thing I'd like to mention that has nothing to do with this matter. For some time Magna Pictures has felt that we should play a bigger role in the affairs of the Los Angeles community. After all, the motion-picture industry is the largest in the city, and we should be making a stronger effort to further the city's welfare.''

''I agree, Mr. Hebron.''

''We have decided that the best way we can do this is to make direct contributions to the city's churches and temples, whatever the denomination, creed, or sect, to encourage religious education and foster those qualities of reverence and faith in a Supreme Being that have made this country great.''

''A splendid idea, Mr. Hebron.''

''I have been appointed to administer these direct cash grants, and I hope I may prevail upon you to accept a five-thousand-dollar contribution to your church from Magna Pictures. To be used in whatever way you see fit to encourage clean living and morality in our great city.''

The priest grasped his hand fervently. ''Thank you, Mr. Hebron,'' he said, his eyes moist. ''Thank you, thank you, thank you.''

After Nino Cavello and Father DiGioia had departed, Eli Hebron said to Henry Cushing, ''I figure we've got a year, maybe two. What I want you to do, Hank, is find some tootsie for Nino. A fresh-looking smack with hot pants. She should talk Italian.''

''I got it, Mr. Hebron. To take his mind off Rosa.''

''Right. Someone with sex appeal—you know?''

''I'll find her, Mr. Hebron.''

''Good,'' the supervisor said. ''And if she can cook, so much the better.''

Timmy Ryan parked his Nash in front of the Mexican curio shop on La Brea. He got out of the car, cheerfully humming ''Danny Boy.'' He was wearing his uniform, the peaked cap bearing a brass insigne: Magna Pictures. He tossed the cap onto the front seat before he locked the car. Now the only identification showing on his blue cop's uniform was the ornate gold badge on his chest: Chief.

Still humming, he strolled around to the back, a florid, doughty man. He climbed the stairs to the doorway of Madame Ortiz. He walked in and unhooked his choker collar, waiting.

She came waddling through the bead curtain. Her eyes, bright and hard as immies, looked first at his uniform. Then her stare moved up to his face.

"Private cop," he smiled at her. "See here? It says Chief. If I was chief of city police, would I be here now?"

"What you want?" she asked suspiciously.

"My fortune told," he said pleasantly. "Nothing else. My love life. I want to know all about my love life, dearie."

"Sit down," she said.

They sat opposite each other at the rickety table. She slapped down the cards.

"You will meet a new woman," she told him.

"Think of that?" Timmy Ryan marveled. "A new woman!"

"A beautiful woman," Madame Ortiz said, peering at the greasy cards. "She will breeng you much 'appiness."

"Glad to hear it," he said.

"But beware of a dark, foreign mans," she said.

"I will," he assured her. "Her husband?"

"Yes." Madame Ortiz nodded. "Her hosbon. Beware of heem."

"I surely will," Ryan said. "What else?"

"Nothing," she said. "Five dolair. You pay."

"Five simoleons for that?" Ryan said. "You got a nice thing going here, mama."

He took a wallet from his back pocket. He carefully counted out fifty dollars in ten-dollar bills, licking thumb and forefinger. He pushed the bills to her side of the table. While Madame Ortiz was staring at the money, Timmy Ryan slid a Colt's .38 Police Positive from a hip holster and placed it gently on the table before him. He turned it slowly so the muzzle pointed at Madame Ortiz. She looked back and forth, money to revolver.

"What?" she said.

"Now, Madame Greaseball," Timmy Ryan said softly, "I'm going to tell *your* fortune."

The screen door of Bungalow Five was propped open.

"What're you doing?" Eli Hebron asked. "Letting the flies in or out?"

"Ain't no flies on us, boss," Edwin K. Jenkins said. "What can we do you for?"

Hebron tossed the two-page treatment of *The Dream Lover* onto Tina Rambaugh's desk. He plucked the glass of iced gin from Jenkins' desk, took a deep swallow. He put the glass back. He jerked his chin toward the treatment.

"I can't tell you how bad it is," he said. "I can't *tell* you."

"Sure you can," Jenkins said. "And will."

"Too broad," the girl said. "I told you, Ed."

"Too broad," the supervisor nodded. "Correct, Tina. You're not writing for Mack Sennett, you're writing for me. Now look . . . the hero can do funny things in real life. That part's fine. It fits. But his dreams have got to be serious. Absolutely serious."

"I thought you said this was a comedy, boss?"

"I said it was and it wasn't. It's also a touching tragedy about a man who tries to make his dreams come true and fails. If you make the dreams comic, you lose the point. The whole thing becomes a farce. Ever hear of a comic dream? I mean it." He looked at them, back and forth. "Either of you ever have a funny dream? I don't mean a *strange* dream, I mean a *funny* dream, a comic dream. Either when you're sleeping or a daydream, a fantasy? I've never had a comic dream, a comic fantasy, and I don't think anyone else has either. Dreaming is serious. You've got to give those dream sequences dignity. They give a kind of intellectual spine to the story. Am I getting through to you?"

"Yes, Mr. Hebron," Tina Rambaugh said. "You want the hero's dream life to be as important as his real life."

"*More* important," he said. "Those dreams, in the picture, are going to be everyone's dreams. They'll see them, and they'll say, 'Yes, that's so. I've dreamed that.' Or they'll understand how our hero could dream that. In his real life, he can be a stupe, but the dreams have got to be meaningful and true."

"You want another treatment, boss?" Jenkins asked.

"Do you understand what I just said?"

"Sure, I understand," Jenkins nodded.

"Do you, Tina?"

The girl nodded.

"Then I don't want another treatment," Hebron said. "Get going on the scenario. Meaningful images. Remember that: meaningful images."

On the way out, he closed the screen door.

"He's a genius," Tina Rambaugh said.

"He's a simp," Ed Jenkins said. "All right, in some ways he's a genius, and in some ways he's a simp."

73

"Aren't we all?" she said.

"You're so fucking profound I can't stand it," he said, picking up his glass of gin. "Oh, to be young and virginal again."

"So we're back to that, are we?" she said.

"Back to what?"

"My virginity."

"Don't be so goddamned touchy," he said. "You got any clean paper? All right, let's get started. First rough. *The Dream Lover.* Page one. Following credits, the camera comes in on—"

"Does it bother you?" she asked him.

"Does what bother me?"

"My virginity?"

He looked at her. She was staring at him steadily across their desks. He saw a plump, girlish face, unlined. Behind it, underneath, actor in a mask, was another face he dimly glimpsed. Hard. Intent. And solemn.

"You're something, you are," he breathed.

"Oh, yes," she said. "I'm something."

Charlie Royce had many ambitions. One of them, private, was to be President of the United States. Another, public, was to film a better fight scene than the one in the 1922 version of *The Spoilers,* with Milton Sills and Noah Beery.

Most supervisors kept away from the stages and lots during shooting, unless asked by a director to solve an intractable problem. But Royce drove his directors crazy by constantly breathing down their necks, changing camera angles, demanding bits of business, bullying the actors, and occasionally canning the director on the spot, finishing the picture himself.

On that Saturday morning the supervisor, his director, cameramen, and crew were on Indoor Stage Four. They were preparing to film the big saloon fight between ranchers and rustlers in *Drive to Abilene*. Eddie Durant and his carpenters had put together a realistic set, with bar, back mirror, tables and chairs, upright piano, swinging doors, a stairway to a balcony, etc. Most of this stuff was balsa, half sawn through, ready for easy breakage. Some of the tables and chairs were precariously balanced on unglued legs.

The actors included the leading rancher and rustler, featured players, and their gangs. There was also a piano player in derby and striped shirt with sleeve garters. He would continue playing and drinking during the melee, for comic relief. A few dance hall girls would cower against the far wall, registering fear.

The ranchers wore clean white or cream-colored Stetsons, shirts, and chaps. The rustlers wore black, dirty Stetsons, shirts, and chaps. The rustlers were unshaved and chewed tobacco. The ranchers were washed, neat, and smoked thin, elegant cigarillos. The leading good guy was fair, the bad guy dark. The bad guy also had a thick black mustache. American audiences knew what that meant: He was probably a foreigner, maybe even an anarchist. He certainly didn't go to church.

Ordinarily, in a mob scene like this, three cameras would film it all in one take, and that would be that. No rehearsals because props would be smashed. But in this case, driven by his ambition to capture a scene of unparalleled and convincing mayhem, Charlie Royce had insisted on an early run-through. Everyone had waded in enthusiastically. Chairs and tables had been crushed convincingly. Whiskey bottles of tea had been splintered, and the balcony railing had broken realistically as a stunt man hit it and plunged down onto a big bag of sawdust off camera.

But Charlie Royce wasn't satisfied. He told his director where to reposition the three cameras. He moved lights around. He had Eddie Durant rebuild the set with more breakaway props. And he thought of a nice piece of business: One of the dance hall tootsies would stand at the piano, arm about the player's shoulders, and she would continue caressing his cheek as furniture flew.

They were set up again, ready for the take, by ten o'clock. Charlie Royce left them waiting and went out into the yard. He found Sammy the Bootlegger selling a pint to Mac at the gate.

"What have you got?" Royce demanded.

Sammy opened his long raincoat, displaying the tiers of full pockets.

"Gin, scotch, and rye," he said. "The real stuff."

"Sure," Royce said. "How much?"

"A deuce for a full, guaranteed pint."

"Six for ten," Royce said. "I'm a supervisor."

"I know who you are, Mr. Royce," Sammy said. "All right, for you, six for ten. What?"

"Two of each," Royce said.

He brought Sammy back to Indoor Stage Four. The unlabeled bottles were uncorked and passed around.

"Everyone drinks up," Royce ordered. "Not the crew, piano player, or girls. Just the fighters."

He passed among ranchers and rustlers, watching them carefully.

"Drink up," he kept telling them. "It's free; drink up. It's paid for. What's wrong with you?" he asked one young rancher.

"I don't drink, Mr. Royce," the boy said, blushing.

"Sure you do, sonny," the supervisor said coldly. "You want to be in a Charlie Royce picture, don't you?"

Obediently, the lad took a mouthful of rye, choking and spluttering.

They all laughed, loosening up. Royce waited about ten minutes, then told the director to set up. The actors moved into position. Some of them were grinning vacuously.

"Now let's see some real action," Charlie Royce yelled at them. "This is a grudge fight. No holds barred. You can hit, kick, gouge, bite, for God's sake. I want to see blood. Five dollars to the first man who bleeds! This is the take. This is for real. Show me something if you want another day's work at Magna. All right, let's shoot."

The fight started, cameras grinding.

A man was hit and went plunging through the swinging doors. The back mirror shattered. Tables collapsed. A chair was thrown through the front window. The stunt man plunged from the balcony. Someone tumbled down the stairs and was out cold. Broken bottles were brandished. Curtains were ripped. A man was brained with a brass gaboon. The drunken actors swung wildly, fell down, staggered up, lurched about, struck furiously at anyone. Hair was yanked. Shirts were ripped. Men wrestled frantically. Men collapsed, wincing with pain. Chair legs were used as clubs. Pictures crashed from walls. Ten-gallon hats went sailing. An infuriated roar came from the soused actors. The piano player pounded on his keys as the dance hall girl caressed his cheek.

Sound, Charlie Royce thought. If I only had sound!

Near the bar, two actors, rancher and rustler, stood toe to toe and slugged. A nose was mashed. Blood spurted, gouted, dripped.

"Get the blood!" Charlie Royce screamed at his cameramen. "Get the blood!"

Magna Pictures dealt with thousands of theater owners, managers, and booking agents all over the country. And there were others—bank executives, politicians, reporters, and critics—to whom Magna was beholden. Many of these men seduced young girls with the aid of their vaunted relationship with Magna Pictures, Inc. The girl inevitably ended up at the studio gate in Hollywood, handing Mac a letter addressed to Marcus Annenberg or Eli Hebron, requesting a screen test for "this adorable, lovely, and talented young miss."

Usually one look was enough to see the girl possessed no physical attractions not already in oversupply in Hollywood. But she could not be summarily dismissed, her sponsor ignored. So a system of "blind tests" was devised. These were very brief tryouts in which set, costume, and makeup were eliminated and the camera was not loaded with film. A dozen could be run off in an hour.

The girl was then given a polite rejection and urged to return home. She rarely did. An earnest letter was sent to her sponsor. It thanked him for his interest in Magna Pictures, informed him that a screen test had been made of his protégée, but regretfully, the girl had exhibited no potential for a motion-picture career. And so everyone was satisfied. Except the girl, of course.

Actual tests were treated seriously and given professional production. The industry was expanding at an incredible rate. Movie attendance might be down temporarily, but annual output continued to increase; new faces, new talents were always in demand. It was said that

MGM's budget just for tests already exceeded a million dollars a year.

Magna filmed about a dozen tests a month and hoped two or three might be successful. Tests were absolutely necessary. A player could be attractive, graceful, and expressive on the Broadway stage. Then, by the camera's peculiar magic, he came across on the screen as a flat-footed lout with buckteeth and a Pinocchio nose.

Each Saturday at noon, executives, supervisors, and directors and cameramen under contract gathered in the projection room to view the most recent tests. Occasionally tests borrowed from other studios were also screened. Anyone was allowed to express an opinion. The final decision was normally the responsibility of the supervisors.

As usual, the projection room was filled to capacity on this Saturday morning. Junior executives and cameramen sat in the carpeted aisles. The atmosphere was informal; smoking was permitted, and it was the custom to comment on the players' appearance and talent while the film was running.

The first test screened was a love scene, unusual in that both boy and girl were newcomers to movie work. Usually, in a test, a neophyte would be paired with an experienced player to help ease the tyro's anxiety. But in this case the young couple, married, had come to Hollywood after success on the London stage, playing leads opposite each other.

The love scene was shot out-of-doors. She comes running across a meadow, laughing. He follows in pursuit, trying to catch her. They circle a tree, she evading his grasp. Finally, he catches her hand. He tries to pull her close. There is a comic bit as the tree is between them, foiling their embrace. Finally, he drops her hand, takes a jackknife from his pocket, mimes a question: Shall he carve their initials on the tree trunk? She drops her eyes in girlish embarrassment, nods yes. He cuts their initials within a heart. They run their fingers over the carving, come close to each other. Clinch. Kiss. Fade-out.

The first time the girl appeared on screen, running across the meadow, someone in the darkened projection room said, "*Hello* there!" The comments came thick and fast during the test.

"He's a stick."

"A stick? He's a board!"

"The girl moves."

"Too bad he can't."

"That's nice—catch her eyes!"

"His ears are too long."

"Good bit with the tree. Who directed?"

"I did."

"Nice bit, Maxie."

"Thanks. She could take direction."

"But he couldn't?"

"Or wouldn't. Very haughty. I could see up his nose."

"Veddy British."

"Maybe he was nervous."

"Nervous? He played Hamlet for nine months in London."

"Let him try that in Sheboygan."

"I like her looks."

"Good profile."

"All the way down. Did you catch it when she turned. She's got the goods."

"And you'd like to share them."

"Don't be vulgar. But the answer is yes."

"Oh, my God, is he carving that tree or chopping it down?"

"That kiss—I can resist it."

"Maybe they're Eskimos, rubbing noses."

"He kisses like a mackerel feeding."

Fade-out. The screen flickered white. Houselights came on. They looked at one another, blinking.

"Charlie?" Eli Hebron asked courteously.

"She'll do. She's no Nazimova, but she's something. He's nothing."

"Anyone else?" Hebron asked.

Everyone seemed to agree the girl would do, but not the boy.

"But they're married," someone said. "Maybe she won't sign without him."

"She'll sign," Eli Hebron said. "What God hath joined together, let no one put asunder except a Hollywood contract."

There was general laughter. They settled back for the second test. It was a routine by a comic acrobat, an act he had played in vaudeville for nine years. He comes up to the side of a barn with a folding ladder, bucket of paint, big brush. He tries to put up the ladder, gets entangled in it, falls down, puts up the ladder, climbs it, finds he has forgotten the paint, starts down, falls off the ladder, starts up again with the paint bucket, discovers he has forgotten the brush, slides down the ladder, paint sloshing, picks up the brush and forgets the paint, knocks over the ladder, falls down, spills more paint on himself . . . and so forth.

"Rubbery-looking guy."

"The costume isn't so funny."

"Good timing."

"Frozen face. Another Keaton imitator."

"Keaton would do it funnier."

"Keaton could do *anything* funnier."

"Hey, look! Nice pratfall."

"That's a good bit—bumping down the steps on his *tuchas*."

"My God, he hasn't got a bone in his body."

"Timing is good."

"Too slow. Get on with it, pal!"

"It's his vaudeville act."

"Now you know why vaudeville is dying."

"He just hasn't got it."

"He's got it but doesn't know what to do with it."

The test ended. The lights came on.

"Ben?" Hebron asked Stuttgart, the supervisor of Magna's one- and two-reel comedies.

"Nah," Stuttgart said. "What he does is funny, but *he* ain't funny."

"There's a difference?" someone asked.

Stuttgart snorted. "You bet your sweet patootie there's a difference. I didn't hear any belly laughs while it was running. Maybe a few snickers. But you don't *feel* for the guy. If you felt for him, like Chaplin, you'd be holding your ribs. Forget him. He's just a trained acrobat. He hasn't got it."

"All right, Ben," Eli Hebron said, "we'll forget him. But if he goes to Columbia and makes a mint for them, *then* we'll remember!"

More laughter.

"Roll the Gladys Potts test," Hebron called up to the projection booth.

"Gladys Potts?" someone said. "She must be from Pennsylvania. Pottsville, Pottstown, and Chambersburg."

Still more laughter. But when she appeared on the screen, the laughter ended abruptly.

"Jesus," someone said.

"Holy Christ," someone said.

Hebron saw at once that Stan Haggard, the director, had understood what he had wanted. Haggard had moved the girl mostly in profile to catch that soft, erotic S curve from coiled hair, balanced head, stalk neck, wide shoulders and bosom, through cinched waist, to flare of hips and bottom, fading away to the hobbled skirt. The girl moved a little stiffly at first, but that may have been nervousness or the tight skirt. She loosened up as the test progressed; her movements began to flow. She walked well. When she picked something up, she *held* it.

Hebron couldn't take his eyes from her image. The cameraman, Ritchie Ingate, must have used thin gauze over his lens or a light coating of Vaseline. There was a soft, luminous quality to the scene. The girl's piled hair seemed to have a halo about it. Her skin glowed. When she turned full face to the camera, Hebron saw the short upper lip, gleam of teeth, expression of young anticipation and desire.

She moved confidently through the mime, modeling for her bearded customer: a scarf, a hat, a necklace. She dabbed a drop of perfume on her bared wrist, held it out. The monocled nobleman bent low to sniff appreciatively, holding her fingertips.

"Beautiful," someone breathed.

At the end, when the old roué has departed, she is left holding the gift and his card. She opens the package. She puts on the necklace. She admires herself in the full-length mirror, turning this way and that, preening. Her unlined face shows wonder and delight. She moves toward the camera. Her cleavage fills the screen, gems glittering against creamy skin. Then the camera tilts slowly, slowly upward. The necklace, slender throat, girlish chin, then her eloquent eyes burning with avarice and resolve. Fade-out.

The lights came on. They all sat in silence, stunned. Finally. . . .

"Who directed?" someone asked hoarsely.

"Stan Haggard," Hebron said. "Ritchie Ingate was behind the camera. Well? Anyone?"

"I'll take the old geezer with the beaver," Ben Stuttgart said. "He's a natural for a banker or chief of police."

"Charlie?" Hebron said. "What do you think?"

"The girl's a sensation," Royce said immediately. "Just great. If you can't use her, I can start her next week as a schoolmarm. Not the lead, but a meaty part."

Hebron was pleased but revealed nothing.

"Anyone else?" he asked.

Then they all were talking at once. He had never heard such unanimous enthusiasm for the test of an inexperienced girl. He sat back, glowing, and listened, knowing he had been right. She had the talent, the presence, the drive. And beauty that wasn't much off camera but filmed like money in the bank.

"All right," he said finally. "I guess we're all agreed. Abe Vogel brought her over. I'll sign her on Monday. Charlie, you start her out."

"Fine," Royce said heartily. "The kid's a winner, Eli."

Hebron was grateful for his approval.

"We'll have to change that name," he said. "Anyone got any suggestions?"

"Gladys is all right," someone said. "The Potts has got to go. How about Gladys Galore?"

"Gladys Joy?"

"Gladys Love?"

"Gladys Sweet?"

"How about Gladys Divine?" someone suggested.

"Gladys Divine," Hebron repeated. "I like that. Charlie?"

"All right with me," Royce said. "Short enough to fit on a marquee with no trouble."

"Gladys Divine it is," Hebron said. "Thank you, everyone. Have a good weekend. See you on Monday morning. Sober."

There was laughter and loud talk as the projection room emptied. Eli Hebron was left alone, sitting in the center of the back row. The houselights were turned off. Still he sat, brooding in the empty little theater. Gladys Divine. Her initials would be G.D. His dead wife's name was Grace Darling. He remembered the stacks of satin teddies still piled in a chiffonier in the mirrored boudoir. The monogrammed teddies. . . .

He had no attack of anomie. But he swallowed an orange pill anyway. Preparing, he supposed, for another lonely weekend. He made a large iced gin and sipped it as he worked at his desk. He reviewed budgets and schedules. He initialed contracts. He approved or rejected expense vouchers. He signed checks and discarded charity appeals. Most of the day-to-day business of Magna Pictures, Inc., passed across his desk. He was the heir apparent. Marcus Annenberg had sons-in-law who were all doctors, in Cleveland, Minneapolis, Atlanta. They thought the movie business disreputable.

(A lot of Americans thought that way—reformers, Fundamentalists, Billy Sunday, the Christian Endeavor Society, the churchmen who weekly cried out in anguish against the jazz babies and gin-soaked orgies of Babylon on the Pacific.)

Mildred Eljer had departed for the weekend. So had the rest of the secretarial staff. Executives left. The administration building stilled. Activity in the yard slowed and stopped. Eli Hebron, working, heard a few shouted farewells. Laughter. Model Ts and Oaklands starting up and grinding away through the gate. Quiet came; the absolute quiet of late Saturday afternoon. He worked on. He had nothing better to do.

It was almost five P.M. when he finished up. His gin bottle was empty, his out basket filled. He rose, stretched, wandered to the windows to look down on the yard. A few sweepers and maintenance men, but no players. The players had vanished, to their homes, games, parties. To their loves. . . .

He went down into the yard. The radio was sounding softly from the gate hut; Gene Austin singing "My Blue Heaven." Hebron strolled about, hands in pockets, whistling the tune idly. He walked slowly through deserted stages, through a dusty saloon, empty ballroom, abandoned emperor's palace. His footsteps sounded.

He plodded down a street of sleazy false fronts: a section of 1890 New York followed by a Western town followed by a Southern plantation followed by Victorian London. The dream street stretched to the back lots and ended in a pasture where he saw a gaunt dog dashing about crazily, chasing a swooping finch.

He went back to the yard, wondering. A short, fat man passed him, said, "Good night, Mr. Hebron," and trotted on. He saw that long raincoat and called, "Sammy?" The man stopped and turned.

"Yes, Mr. Hebron?"

"You're the legger?"

"Yes, Mr. Hebron."

"Anything left?"

"One pint of gin. The real stuff."

"I'll take it."

He gave Sammy a five. When the bootlegger fumbled for change, Hebron said, "That's all right."

Unexpectedly, the man said, "God bless you."

"Thank you," Hebron said faintly, pleased.

He went into darkened Indoor Stage Two to uncork his bottle and have a sip. There was a man working in the far corner, a sweeper. Hebron knew him: Andy Something. He was an old-timer in the business, dating from the early Biograph days. He had never played anything but bits. Now he was a sweeper. Everyone thought it was easy. It wasn't easy. Hebron took a deeper swallow, went back to his office.

He poured gin into a glass and added ice. He turned on his desk lamp but sat back in the gloom. He drank almost half the gin before he leaned forward into the light. He opened his desk drawer, found her number, called. . . .

A harsh, woman's voice: "Yeah?"

"Could I speak to Miss Gladys Potts, please."

"Jus' a minute. I'll see she's in."

He waited more than a minute. But then he heard her light, breathless "Yes? This is Gladys Potts."

"This is Eli Hebron," he said.

"Oh! I'm sorry you had to wait, Mr. Hebron, but this is a rooming house, and the phone is downstairs in the hall, and I don't have my own phone."

"You will," he said.

Silence.

"You'll have your own phone," he said, "because your test was a success. I'll call Abe Vogel on Monday, and we'll get together on terms. I want you under personal contract to me."

She began to cry.

"Oh, Mr. Hebron," she sobbed. "You're not joking?"

"No, I'm not joking."

"I was really good?"

"You were really good," he assured her. "Everyone loved you."

"Everyone loved me," she repeated in a tone of such dreamy contentment that his breath caught.

"Miss Potts," he said, "I was wondering, if you have no plans for this evening, if you'd care to have a bite to eat with me. We could go somewhere."

"I have no plans," she said instantly. "None at all. I'd love to see you, Mr. Hebron. To thank you for all you've done for me."

Gratefulness was not what he wanted. But it was, he reflected sourly, all he had a right to expect.

That afternoon, while Eli Hebron worked alone in his office at Magna Studios, Charlie Royce and Timmy Ryan were on their way out to the Valley. Royce was driving his big Chrysler Imperial 80, a four-door tourer with a folding windscreen for the back seat. The car had wire wheels, with spares mounted in front fender wells. Royce had added a heavy pedestal searchlight on the left running board. The car was all black. Like Henry Ford, the supervisor believed only fancy men drove light-colored cars.

The road out to the country was unpaved, graveled in stretches, rutted dirt in others. It had been a dry spring; a plume of dust followed them. Royce had the car up to forty, and once he almost lost it in a skid on a tight curve. But Timmy Ryan, wearing civilian clothes, smoked his Dutch Masters placidly, looking around benignly at orange groves and truck farms.

"She went for it, did she?" Royce asked him.

"Grabbed it," Ryan said, talking around his cigar. "The lady will behave."

"You gave her the whole hundred?" Royce asked suspiciously.

"As we agreed," the cop said blandly. "In matters of this sort, it's best not to skimp, Mr. Royce."

"Much farther?" the supervisor asked impatiently.

"Next turnoff to the left," Timmy Ryan said, looking about. "Nice country around here. Good growing land, they say. Might pick up a walnut grove for myself. If all goes well."

"It will," Royce vowed. "It's going good so far, isn't it?"

"It is that, Mr. Royce."

"Any complaints on the money?"

"None whatsoever," Ryan said. "Jim-dandy, the money. And it goes out just as fast as it comes in."

Royce grunted.

"Here's the turnoff, Mr. Royce. That's it. Just a mile or two now. It's at the bottom of the hill. Take my youngest son, for example. Just twenty, he is, and after me day and night for a new car. These kids!"

"What do you drive, Timmy?"

"A Nash six. Two years old. Good condition; I take care of it. You've heard about Mr. Ford's Model A? Be out late this year, they say. Might take a look at that, if it's cheap enough. For the boy. He's a good lad. Here we are, Mr. Royce. Just pull around in back so this beauty can't be seen from the road. No sense in taking chances, now is there?''

It was a sad, beaten, tar-shingled shack, raised on brick piles on a small patch of hardscrabble land. There was one stunted, dusty orange tree in the front yard. In the back, a dented Model T coupe with wood-spoked wheels was parked alongside a tin washtub set on sawhorses. A few scrawny chickens pecked about. A goat wandered around the corner of the house as they got out of the car.

''Jesus,'' Royce said disgustedly, ''it's a shithole.''

''It is that,'' Timmy Ryan said, beaming. ''We found the crown jewels in a pigsty.''

They all sat in the kitchen, around a table covered with peeling oilcloth. The room itself wasn't much. A zinc sink with hand pump. A stained icebox. The stove was a wood burner. There was a 1926 Montgomery Ward calendar tacked to the unfinished wall. It showed a plump baby playing with a puppy. There was grease on the table oilcloth, shiny on the sink, thick on the stove. The smell was something.

At the table, across from Charlie Royce and Timmy Ryan, were Bertha Potts and Leo Potts, mother and older brother of Gladys. The father, Walter Potts, had ''taken off for parts unknown,'' according to Bertha.

She was a stumpy, embittered woman, wearing a stained cotton shift. During the week, she worked as cook at a White Castle in Burbank. Her hair was stringy gray, not bobbed but jammed into a torn hair net. Small eyes glittered in a dumpy face. Her voice was high, querulous. Charlie Royce found it hard to believe that the girl he had seen on the Magna projection room screen a few hours previously had been popped by this toad.

Brother Leo was more obviously his mother's child, in

manner, if not appearance. He was a lank, pale youth with strands of dirty blond hair falling across a forehead as shiny as the greased sink. He dressed like a Hollywood lounge lizard, with flannel plus fours, argyle hose, a cardigan over a soft-collared shirt with a clumsily tied ascot that revealed his soiled neck. He fancied he resembled Conrad Nagel and often, in front of a mirror, practiced quirking one eyebrow.

Leo, giggling, uncapped four bottles of home brew. He poured the greenish beer into jelly jars. Timmy Ryan seemed to find it palatable enough. Royce took one sip, then pushed the jar aside distastefully.

"All right," he said, "let's get down to business. You got the certificate?"

Bertha Potts rose heavily, moved across the room to the open cupboard over the sink. She was wearing heelless slippers. They flap-flapped on the worn linoleum. She took down a brown bag of ground coffee, opened it, took out a folded paper.

"So that's where you were hiding it, Maw!" Leo Potts said, showing pointy teeth. "Ain't you the sly one!"

"You're damned right," his mother growled. "With you sneaking around. . . ."

She scaled the paper onto the table in front of Charlie Royce. He unfolded it to read the birth certificate of Gladys Alice Potts, born in Zanesville, Ohio, on January 21, 1912.

"Told you she was fifteen," Bertha Potts said.

"Ah, the sweet, innocent babe," Timmy Ryan said happily.

"Innocent?" Leo said. "So's your old man!"

Charlie Royce glared.

"What do you mean by that?" he demanded.

"I don't chew my cabbage twice," muttered Leo.

"Well, we'll need this," Royce said curtly. He folded the certificate, slid it into his inside jacket pocket.

"Just to copy it," Ryan said quickly to the mother. "You'll get it back."

"See that I do," she said, staring at him. "It's all I got."

"Is there any other evidence of the girl's date of birth?" Royce asked. "Like a family Bible, for instance?"

"A Bible?" Leo Potts hooted, trying to raise one eyebrow. "That's a laugh."

"Now, now," Ryan said sternly. "No blasphemy here. We'll get you a Bible, Mrs. Potts, and you can write in the date of your marriage and the births of your dear children. All right, Mr. Royce?"

"Good idea, Timmy. Take care of it." He turned to the others. "The girl will be put under contract at the studio next week. You keep away from her—is that understood? You don't visit her, and she doesn't come out here without my say-so. Got that?"

"Under contract?" Leo Potts whined, face twisting. "You mean she got hired for the movies? Well, cheese-'n'-crackers, when do I get my test?"

"I told you," Royce said stonily, "as soon as I can arrange it. You're getting paid, aren't you?"

"I know, but after all—the movies!" He lighted a Sweet Caporal ineptly, fingers trembling.

"One thing at a time, lad," Ryan soothed. "One thing at a time. Don't worry; you'll have your chance at the silver screen. You just trust Mr. Royce here, and he'll see you through. Isn't that the truth, Mr. Royce?"

"Sure," the supervisor said. He stared at the sulky

youth. "Don't rock the boat, Leo. I got too much riding on this. I wouldn't like it if you made trouble."

"He'll behave," Bertha Potts said coldly. "Or I'll whup his ass. He ain't too big for that."

"Aw, Maw," the boy said.

"Timmy," Royce said, jerking his chin toward the Potts woman.

Ryan took a thin packet of ten-dollar bills from inside his jacket. A paper clip held them together. He handed them across the table. Leo grabbed, but his mother was there first. She folded the bills, stuffed them down the front of her cotton wrapper. She grinned derisively at her son.

"If you want them," she said, "you know where to find them."

On the way back, both Royce and Ryan lighted cigars to kill the taste of squalor.

"The girl should be paying me," the supervisor said, "for getting her out of that place."

"She'll find a way to show her gratitude, I have no doubt," Ryan said dryly. "And a sweet little twist she is. Hardly as big as your hand. But a lot more fun—hey, Mr. Royce?"

She asked him not to call for her.

"I don't want you to see where I live," she had said on the phone. "It's such an awful house."

"All right," he said. "Shall I meet you somewhere then?"

He hoped she would not select a popular hotel or restaurant. If he were seen with her in public, it would be in Louella's column on Monday. "What well-known and handsome pooh-bah of the flicks has apparently made a full recovery from the sorrow of his beautiful wife's tragic death a year ago? At least he was seen Saturday night squiring a lovely unknown in one of our town's classiest bistros. Welcome back to the land of the living, E.H.!''

She suggested they meet in front of Grauman's Egyptian. He readily agreed and told her to watch for a yellow Packard roadster with a white top. He asked if she'd enjoy a night picnic on the beach. She said she'd like that very much. He told her to bring a sweater or jacket; it might be chilly.

He drove home in the LaSalle. He asked Mrs. Birkin to pack a picnic dinner for two in the small hamper. He filled his long flask with gin, the short with scotch. He had Mrs. Birkin include those in the hamper, too. Then he went up to bathe. While he was dressing—blue blazer, white flannels, a silk scarf at his throat—he realized how much he was enjoying these plans and preparations. He tried not to dream a scenario for the evening, to avoid disappointment. He swallowed an orange pill and started out.

The sidewalk in front of the theater was crowded, but he saw her almost immediately. She was standing near the curb, watching passing cars anxiously. Two sailors in summer whites had stopped a few yards behind her and were giving her the eye.

She was wearing a short, accordion-pleated skirt of white silk. Round-toed black shoes with a buttoned strap, called Mary Janes. A blue middy belted low on her hips. The shawl collar closed loosely with a darker blue scarf. Hebron could understand the sailors' interest.

He pulled up in front of her, leaned over to open the door.

''Hop in,'' he smiled.

She came scrambling into the car, with a flash of white skin over rolled stockings. One of the sailors whistled.

She slammed the door, bent to him immediately, kissed his cheek.

"Am I ever happy to see you!" she said. "The fleet's in. What a snazzy car!"

"Not half as snazzy as you," he said. "You look lovely."

"Really? I didn't know what to wear. Is it really all right?"

"Perfect," he assured her. "Very nautical. Got room for your sweater and purse? You can put your feet up on the hamper; you can't hurt it."

"Okeydokey," she said.

She put her feet up, then rolled her stockings below her knees.

"I've got Herbert Hoover knees," she laughed. "I don't care."

"I don't either," Hebron said. "We'll head for the beach. All right?"

"Whatever you say, Mr. Hebron."

He pulled out cautiously into traffic. It looked as if everyone in Hollywood were heading for the beach.

"I think you might call me Eli, don't you?"

"I'd like that." She nodded. "But when other people are around, I'll call you Mr. Hebron."

"You're very wise," he said. "And what do your friends call you—Glad?"

"Sometimes," she said.

"Well, I'll call you Glad. Glad and Eli. It seems to fit."

"Mmm." She sighed contentedly. She snuggled a little closer to him, took his right arm lightly in both her hands.

"Are you really eighteen, Glad?" he asked her.

"I really am. Eighteen going on eighty."

"You'd better be," he smiled. "You know, we investigate everyone before we sign contracts. You look so young in your short skirt and sailor blouse. But maybe that's because I'm so old."

She pulled away, a little, and looked at him.

"How old are you, Eli?"

"I'm forty. Does that seem ancient to you?"

"Of course not." She snuggled back again. "Besides, I like older men. The boys my age I go out with are just interested in one thing. You know?"

"The older men you go out with are, too, I'm afraid."

"Silly," she said softly, pressing his arm.

They drove on awhile in silence. Windows were down, but he became conscious of her scent. A sweet, young, soapy perfume. She wasn't wearing a hat; her dark shingled hair flipped in the breeze.

"Why did you ask if I was eighteen, Eli?"

"I told you—what you're wearing tonight. It's lovely, but it's not the way I see you. I see you as more mature, more sophisticated. Worldly. That's why I asked for that costume for the test."

"I hated that first thing she put on me. Oh, it was such a beautiful costume you made her use, Eli."

"You made it beautiful," he told her.

"Thank you," she said faintly. After a while she said, "Eli, that thing you had me do—the shopgirl who decides she's not going to be poor anymore, and she accepts a gift from a strange man—did you make that up?"

"I sure did," he said. "An original Hebron production."

"Was there any reason you wanted me to do that particular scene? Any special reason?"

"I thought you'd do it well," he said. "I thought you'd understand a girl like that. Maybe it was because of what you said when I asked you why you wanted to be in pictures. You said you didn't want to be a waitress; you wanted to be rich. That's the first time anyone has been that honest with me."

"It was honest," she said.

"I know it was," he said. "Would you like to smoke? There's a tin of Luckies in my jacket pocket on your side."

"Thanks," she said, "but I have my own. Fatimas. Would you like one?"

"No, thanks. But you go ahead. And light me a Lucky, will you? I'd better not take my hands off the wheel. I'm not a very good driver."

"You're a marvelous driver," she protested. "I can't drive at all."

"I'll teach you," he said. "Would you like that?"

"Oh, Eli," she said, "you're so *good* to me."

She got their cigarettes going. She held both of them. Occasionally she put the Lucky Strike to his lips so he could take a puff. She did this naturally, without fuss, and it seemed very dear to him.

He took Wilshire Boulevard out to the beach. Then he turned north into the darkness beyond the Promenade.

"I ordered a moon for tonight," he said, "but God must be on strike."

"It's perfect the way it is. The ocean is beautiful. Can you hear it, Eli?"

"Yes," he said, "I can hear it. My wife and I were thinking of building a beach house along here. But then she died. Maybe I'll build in Malibu. It's opening up now."

"She was very lovely," Gladys Potts said in a small voice.

"Yes. She was. You remind me of her in many ways. Different coloring, of course. No physical resemblance, although you're the same size. But both of you free and easy and open. Do you have a boyfriend?"

"Oh, no," she laughed. "I'm nobody's baby."

"Would you like to be my baby?" He laughed in return. "I could be your sugar daddy."

"I'd like that," she said, putting her head on his shoulder.

"We should be looking for a place to pull off and have our picnic. I don't know what my cook put in the hamper. I hope it's good; I'm hungry. Are you hungry?"

"Uh-huh."

"I know there's a flask of gin in there and a flask of scotch for you. If you'd like a drink now. . . ."

"No," she said, sighing. "Not now. I really don't drink, Eli. That scotch I had in your office was the first drink I've ever had in my whole life."

He turned his head a moment, to look at her in amazement.

"You're joking?"

"No, really. I've had home brew. But never whiskey."

"Did you like it?"

"It was all right. Sort of medicinal."

"Try the gin tonight, Glad. Maybe you'll like that better."

"All right. I'll do whatever you say, Eli."

"I think we've gone far enough. Let's try the beach."

There was no traffic. He made a slow, careful U-turn, headed southward again. Then he pulled off the road, onto the hard-packed verge. He turned off the lights. It was a dark night. The moon was muddled behind a skim of sliding clouds. A sea breeze rustled the palms, and the aloe stalks and eucalyptus in the hills above the road. The air smelled of salt, kelp, the heavier musk of the deep sea.

"Too cool for you?" he asked.

"No," she said. "Eli, can we neck awhile?"

"All right."

She came eagerly into his arms. One hand rose to the back of his neck. Her lips were sweet, soft. He kissed her gently, at first. Kissed the corners of her mouth. Brushed his lips back and forth. Then his tongue pried. Her mouth opened instantly. Their wet tongues touched, pressed. She drew away.

"That was a French kiss, wasn't it?" she asked breathlessly.

"Yes."

"I knew it was."

She strained to him again, mouth open, tongue searching. He felt her body suddenly swollen and hot. He pulled away from her.

"Glad," he said thickly, "let's slow down."

"Don't you like it?"

"I love it."

"Well then? All right," she said, catching his mood. "Then let's just cuddle."

"Let's cuddle," he agreed.

He held her tightly. She made a deep sound, a purr of contentment. He touched her hair timorously. It was damp; it smelled of the sea. He drew wispy fingers lovingly down her temple, chin, soft throat. Then he moved her gently away. They sat a moment in darkness, twisted, peering at each other. He put up the windows.

"What are you doing?" she whispered.

"Don't be frightened. I'm going to strike matches. I want to look at you."

He took a wooden match from a little Diamond box and scraped it. A small flame flared up. He saw it reflected, flickering, in her eyes. She looked at him, unafraid. The match burned down; darkness closed in. He lighted another and held it close to her face, staring. She did not flinch. He lighted two more, moving the flames slowly about. Then they sat in darkness again.

"I don't understand," he said. "Now you look so young, so girlish. Untouched. But I saw someone deeper, more mature. Someone mocking and mysterious. And that's how you appeared in the test. That's how the camera saw you."

"They say the camera never lies, Eli."

"I'm not so sure of that. I'm confused by your appearance now, your actuality, and my image of you. The camera caught the image—everyone agreed on that—but not the actuality. That's odd, isn't it?"

"Eli, maybe it was the makeup and costume and lighting."

"Of course," he said. "That's what it was."

"Are you disappointed in me?"

She bent forward quickly, put her head in his lap, face pressing.

"I will, Eli," she murmured, "if you want me to."

"No, no," he said, caressing her hair. "No, don't do that. You're so sweet, so sweet. Just be still a moment."

He stroked her hair slowly. With a fingertip he touched the inner path of her ear, the lobe, curve of cheek, closed eye, warm lips, yielding neck. In the darkness, he could not see what the matches had revealed. He saw only the filmed and screened image. The dream. . . .

"A drink," he said suddenly. "I need a drink. And something to eat. Shall we try the beach? I have a blanket in the rumble."

They found a place on the sand shielded from the wind by a low dune. But they could see the dully glittering sea. It was a pool of mercury, gently heaving. They sat cross-legged on the blanket, facing each other. They unpacked the hamper excitedly, tearing wrappings away. Mrs. Birkin had packed cold fried chicken, a jar of potato salad, tomatoes, radishes, cucumbers, fresh fruit, slices of peach pie, a thermos of coffee that was still warm. Gladys began eating immediately.

"May I try the gin, Eli?"

He unscrewed the top, handed her the long flask. She took a cautious sip, then a deeper swallow.

"Ooh," she said, "I like that. It has a funny flavor. Like bitter fruit. Now you drink some. . . ."

So he did. They dug a little hole in the sand for the flask, so it wouldn't tip. They gnawed the chicken legs and passed each other salad, tomatoes, radishes, the pie.

"Talk about yourself, Glad. Abe Vogel said you were from New Jersey, but that's all I know."

"Abe got it all mixed up," she told him, eating busily. "He said Hackensack, Hohokus—like that. Montclair, New Jersey—that's where I'm from. It's in the northern part of the state."

"I know where it is."

She said her father taught mathematics at a private school nearby. He was close to retirement. Her mother had also been a teacher, of literature, but she had retired five years ago. Gladys was an only child.

"Were you happy?" Hebron asked.

She assured him she had an idyllic childhood. She was

born late in her parents' lives; they doted on her. She could have anything she wanted, they loved her so. She spoke of her handsome father, her beautiful mother. The wide, tree-lined street they lived on. The tall home with white pilasters. Garden. Flowers everywhere. . . .

He caught the dreaminess in her voice, the choked longing. His febrile imagination filled in the gaps: a long-haired child in a white pinafore skipping merrily across a velvety lawn. Ambling dog. Laughing friends. Cars chugging on a quiet street. Petting the nose of the old horse that pulled the ice wagon. A sunlit schoolroom. Fragrant odors in a gleaming kitchen. Knelt prayers at bedtime. All warm, shining, and brave.

"Let's take a walk," he said. "Down the beach. Just dump everything in the hamper. I'll take the flask."

They strolled hand in hand: young lovers. They kicked at shells, stomped on kelp, and laughed to hear it pop. They paused, occasionally, to kiss: brief salt kisses, her tongue thrusting.

"Ooh," she breathed, "I do like that."

There was enough illumination for him to see her wide eyes, parted lips. Her flesh seemed so limpid to him that a touch might leave a bruise. Once, almost thoughtfully, she stroked him lightly between his legs. More in wonder than in lust. He could not fathom her.

She stopped suddenly, faced the sea.

"Hello, ocean!" she shouted. She tilted her head back. "Hello, sky! Hello, clouds! This is Gladys Potts!"

He took her by the shoulders, turned her to face him. He was laughing.

"No," he said, "not Gladys Potts. I forgot to tell you. We're changing your name. Now you're Gladys Divine."

She was silent.

"Don't you like it?" he asked anxiously.

"It's beautiful." She sobbed, burying her face against his chest. "Beautiful, I love it!"

She wrenched away, turning her face upward again. Her eyes were wet and shining.

"Hello, moon!" she yelled. "This is Gladys Divine! You'll be hearing from me!"

He slid an arm about her shoulders, hugging her close. They wandered on in silence, made a wide circle, started back.

She looked at the small waves splashing.

"I'm going swimming," she said.

"No," he said. "Don't do that."

"Wading?"

"All right. To your knees. No deeper."

She waited until they were at their blanket again. Then she unbuttoned her Mary Janes, kicked them off. She rolled her silk stockings down, peeled them away. She ran into the water. He followed, anxious.

"Oooh," she said, holding her skirt up on her white thighs. "Cold, cold, cold!"

"Not too far," he cautioned.

But she waded in until the sea was lapping at the lace trim on her rayon bloomers. She strode back and forth, kicking the water to froth, roaring with merriment. He stood on dry sand, sipping gin from a silver flask, watching her happiness. An indulgent father.

She came running out, yelping with cold. The pleated white skirt was plastered to her thighs. She was shivering exaggeratedly, hugging herself. He rushed her back to the blanket. She stood, holding up her skirt. He knelt before her. He took off his silk scarf, wiped her wet legs dry. She looked down at him gravely as he worked gently and assiduously. She touched the top of his head.

"I'm going gaga for you," she said.

They lay on one side of the blanket. He threw the loose side across their legs. She was trembling. He held her close. She put her knees and feet between his thighs. She stopped shaking.

"Better?" he asked.

"Gladys Divine," she said dreamily. Then: "What about *you*, Eli?"

He told her a few things. How his parents had died of influenza, and an older brother of infantile paralysis. How his uncle, Marcus Annenberg, had paid for his education at NYU, then brought him west into the business. First, as a reader, then a script clerk, assistant director, director, supervisor. . . .

"You like the movies?" she asked innocently.

"Oh, yes," he smiled. "It's a world. A new world. . . ."

He tried to tell her other things, personal things, but she snuggled closer, her warm tongue laving his neck. He could not go on.

"Pet me," she said. "Please, Eli."

"All right."

The skin of her legs was cool, sea-chilled. But pressing, he could feel warmth stirring, blood coursing. Her belly, beneath the middy, between bloomers and brassiere, was flat and fluttering. Boned rib cage. She was so slender, so twiny. The muscled weasel's back turned in his grasp. She committed herself to him. Not by throwing arms and legs wide, but by surrendering her flesh gladly to his curious touch. Springy; she was springy. Young and yearning. All he wanted was to stroke and wonder.

He thought suddenly that sex could become addictive. A

drug. Like nicotine or alcohol. Or the orange pills. To blunt the anguish. . . . He saw a movie there: a man addicted to sex. He saw images and scenes: a man in thrall. . . . But an impossible picture to shoot, unless you used surreal images.

And Marcus Annenberg would be right: It wouldn't sell.

The office of Marcus Annenberg looked like a Bronx apartment. It was clumped with overstuffed furniture in a brown floral pattern. Tinted photographs of dead relatives in gilt frames. Heavy brown velvet drapes perpetually closed. A bowl of wax apples. Illumination came from a wooden floor lamp with a pyramid shade of brown silk with beaded fringe.

Annenberg was at his enormous rolltop desk, with fifty pigeonholes and, to Eli Hebron's knowledge, at least five secret compartments. The president of Magna Pictures, Inc., sat in a brown leather wing chair. He was covered to the waist with an afghan knitted by his wife. It fell to his ankles. His carpet slippers peeked out.

He sat with spotted hands clasped limply across his paunch. His hooded eyes seemed heavier than usual. As he talked, white spittle gathered in the corners of his mouth.

"They're stalling," he told Hebron in a grumpy voice. "What are we asking for—the moon? Two years ago the loan went through hunky-dory, no questions asked. Now they send a buttinsky out here to poke around. I don't like it."

"They'll come through, Uncle Marc," Hebron soothed him. "They know we're good for the money."

"They'll come through—but when? Business is bad, I admit it. So a lot of houses are up for peanuts. Now is the time to buy. You agree, Eli?"

"Not only to buy theaters, but to improve production. Better pictures. It's no time to cut back, Uncle Marc."

"I agree two hundred percent. My throat," the old man said, touching his Adam's apple. "Something in there I don't like. This morning I woke up, I felt it."

"What is it? What does it feel like?"

"Like something caught in my throat. Like maybe a crumb. When I swallow, it hurts."

"Should I call Dr. Blick?"

"That quack? No. Maybe tomorrow *he'll* have it, and I'll be fine. Eli, you saw the gross on *Red Robin?*"

"Yes, Uncle Marc. Disappointing."

"Disappointing? Hah!"

"Margaret Gay always does better in the small towns. Those figures aren't in yet. Just the big cities."

"You think she takes dope?" the old man said, peering at Hebron.

"Gay? Take dope? Of course not!"

"I heard." Annenberg nodded gloomily. "That stuff you put up your nose—what is it?"

"Cocaine? Where did you hear that about Gay?"

"Around," the old man said vaguely. "No scandal, Eli. We can't have a scandal. If you think it might be true, get rid of her. Those Boston goyim shouldn't have an excuse not to give us the money."

"There won't be any scandal."

"You're a good boy, Eli. A good boy. . . ." He drowsed.

"I want to read you a synopsis, Uncle Marc."

"So read. I'm listening."

Hebron slowly read aloud the treatment of *The Dream Lover,* by Edwin K. Jenkins and Tina Rambaugh. He hurried through the dream sequences, to be filmed with a diffusion lens. But he carefully enunciated the parts he

106

knew Marcus Annenberg would enjoy—the slapstick mis-
adventures of the hero in real life. He ended by telling how
the milkman would give up his fantasies and return to a
happy existence with his wife. But this final scene would
be shot with a diffusion lens to leave the audience wondering if the hero's future happiness was also a doomed
dream.

Hebron finished reading and looked up. Annenberg's
chin was down on his chest. He was breathing deeply,
regularly, with a heavy rumble. The supervisor stood quietly, began to tiptoe to the door.

"Eli," the old man called hoarsely.

Hebron turned.

"Yes, Uncle Marc?"

"Change the ending. It's not American."

It was not necessary to go through the Beverly Hills
hotel lobby to reach the bungalows. Each had its private
entrance, from a path that wandered through a thick tropical garden surrounding a swimming pool. The bungalows
rented for a hundred dollars a day. Or, more commonly, a
night.

Charlie Royce lived in Bungalow Six, called Maui. (All
the bungalows were named for Hawaiian islands.) He
rented by the month and paid twenty-five hundred dollars
for a comfortable efficiency apartment: living room, bedroom, bathroom, a kitchenette with a new Kelvinator. The
bungalow also had a Brunswick Paratrope and an Atwater
Kent in a Pooley cabinet. Both phonograph and radio
operated directly from the electrical supply, without B
batteries. The radio had an attached antenna.

Royce, from his years as advance man on the Chautauqua Circuit, was comfortable in hotel rooms. He liked the

convenience of maid service and room service. He owned few possessions. He had no intention of renting or buying a home until he married. Or was making enough money to afford a Beverly Hills mansion larger and more luxurious than Eli Hebron's.

He entertained infrequently, and when he did, it was usually a catered affair in the hotel proper. So he was able to convert his bungalow living room into a kind of private office. He had the hotel move in a desk, swivel chair, filing cabinet, small safe, and a dictating machine that recorded on wax cylinders. He had recently purchased one of the new Remington electric typewriters and was becoming proficient in its use.

Charlie Royce had never been seen in public twice with the same woman. His name never appeared in the gossip columns or fan magazines, although he was mentioned frequently in the trade papers. In Hollywood society he was considered a dull loner, with his vested cheviot suits and leaden sense of humor. A male dinner companion once said of him, "I spent a week with Charlie Royce last night." That was Hollywood's judgment, too: a talented man, an ambitious man. Maybe, someday, an important man. But with all the verve and élan of Calvin Coolidge. Charlie Royce had never been invited to Pickfair.

As a Magna supervisor Royce could have had a different starlet every night. But he didn't want to endanger his position by getting a reputation as a couch caster. So, occasionally, he called Bea Winks to send over a professional, even though he was the kind of man who found it humiliating to pay a woman. But a close relationship with a loving partner had no place in his present plans. He enjoyed crossword puzzles, which he worked with a Waterman fountain pen.

Royce was a big, bluff man with a threatening posture: hunched, aggressive. His ruddy features colored even deeper under stress or excitement. He was excessively clean, sometimes bathing three times a day. He would have been surprised to know that two of Bea Winks' whores had compared notes on his performance, and both had commented on the odor of his pale body. It was sharp, acrid, but not unpleasant. The professionals also agreed he had brutish tendencies. But nothing they couldn't handle. . . .

But in recent weeks Charlie Royce had little time for social activities. In addition to his job at Magna—which frequently demanded twelve to sixteen hours a day—he had been busily engaged in a number of other endeavors. To all these efforts he brought singleness of purpose, solemnity, and granite resolve. He was as aware as Eli Hebron of what happened to will and purpose under the hot California sky. He had given himself five years. It now appeared he could do it in less. . . .

Franklin Pierce Archer had instructed him not to use proper names in his reports, and initials only when necessary. Royce sat down before his new typewriter, threaded in paper, with a carbon and copy, and started typing without hesitation.

You will find inclosed herewith the latest information I have been able to assemble on the plans of the major studios to convert to sound. As you will note, Warner's— probably because of its current financial condition—is far ahead of the others. The details of the Vitaphone deal are attached. The figure most often mentioned is $800,000. Fox is also moving rapidly into sound with their German system. It will be used first in Fox-Movietone news-reels. Most of the others have adopted a wait-and-see attitude, although exploratory work is going on.

Warner's is using synchronized phonograph discs. I

have attached details of two additional systems now under development. One: A separate film carrying the sound track, synchronized to the visual film. Two: The sound signal carried on the same film (along the margin) producing the screened image. Both these systems, particularly the latter, show great promise.

As you requested, I am also inclosing a proposed budget, should Magna convert to sound. Figures are based on the Warner's-Vitaphone disc system. I must emphasize that the dollar totals stated are hypothetical. This is such a new development, there are no definite prices available for such things as microphones, recording equipment, theater phonographs, amplifiers, and so forth.

I am also inclosing, per your instructions, a list of expenses incurred to date in assembling this material. The total is larger than I anticipated but not, I believe, unduly so. It was necessary to pay technicians and others at several studios, as well as payments to trade reporters, patent attorneys, and so forth. In matters of this sort, it is best not to skimp.

Finally, I believe you and your associates should be aware of two recent developments. First, the physical (and mental) condition of M.A. continues to deteriorate, and I feel he is no longer capable of exercising firm and prudent executive control. Second, I have heard disquieting rumors concerning the private life of E.H. It is said he has formed an illicit relationship with an underage girl. If true, this can only result in damaging publicity for Magna Studios when it becomes a matter of public knowledge, as it inevitably must. I shall try to uncover the truth of this unfortunate matter and report to you more fully in my next letter.

I wish to close by expressing to you once again my gratitude for your confidence in me. I urge you and your associates to give the greatest consideration possible to the inclosed documents. As I said to you during your recent visit, I feel strongly that conversion to sound will enable Magna to take its rightful place among the leaders of the industry. *Not* to convert, as quickly as possible, will have a serious effect on the financial strength of the company.

I consider the objections of E.H. to sound films to be without merit. He speaks of "art" and "dreams." Our only concern should be with the competition of stage, vaudeville, and radio. Our only purpose should be producing a profitable entertainment product.

Charlie Royce did not sign this letter. He addressed the envelope to Franklin Pierce Archer. And, as instructed, he used Archer's home address, rather than that of the Boston bank which employed him. Royce put the letter aside to mail the following morning. Then he went in to bathe. He soaked in the tub, smoking an El Producto. He did not reflect on his activities and plans; he wondered why he derived so much enjoyment from dropping by Bea Winks' place and watching her and her current tootsie perform.

It was Hollywood, he decided. It was alien to him, with the fascination of the foreign. It was a free, easy, open existence, totally different from his own life, from everything he had been taught. It was a life of sunshine and laughter, of short, intense loves, imaginative sex, of drinking and drugs. It was a way of life that seemed to deny the past and ignore the future.

In comparison, his own life, full of dark complicities and lumpy desires, occasionally seemed to him as dated and faintly ridiculous as the pretensions of a dauphin. He longed sometimes, as at Bea's, to become a part of that white-flannel world, the silver-flask world, the loud-jazz and quick-fuck world. What it amounted to, he admitted morosely, was an inability to feel joy. How did you have fun?

Bathed, he rose from the tub and extinguished his cigar

butt in the draining water. He dried his thick, hard body, put on his pajamas. Before going to bed, he laid out his clothes for the following day: B.V.D. underwear, Interwoven socks with Paris garters, high-top Florsheim shoes, Hickok belt, Society Brand tweed suit, Van Heusen shirt with detachable Windsor collar, Botany tie, wide-brimmed Knapp-Felt fedora.

He looked down at this costume draped on his couch. He saw Charlie Royce sitting there. But of course, the clothes were empty.

When he sent Barney O'Hara to pick her up in the Hispano-Suiza, he knew he had made a fateful decision. Now people would know.

He waited in the entrance hall, pacing nervously. Occasionally he drew aside the drapes at the front window to peer out. When he saw the car turn into the graveled driveway, he went outside. He didn't know whether to wait for her under the portico or go down to the car. He didn't know what to do. Finally, he went down to the car in a rush. She was lolling in the back seat like a princess. Barney O'Hara had hopped out and was holding the door for her.

"We have arrived, m'lady," O'Hara said solemnly, and Gladys giggled. Hebron was happy they were friends.

She came out of the car legs first, sliding, her short skirt riding up above the rolled stockings. He kissed her cheek. But she paid no attention. She was staring at the house, eyes widening.

"Welcome to Paradiso, Glad," Hebron said.

She looked at him.

"You *live* here?" she breathed.

"I live here," he smiled.

"It's grand," she said. "Just grand."

"Go up to the porch, Glad. I'll be with you in a minute."

She paused to pat the fender of the Hispano-Suiza. "What a flivver!" she said.

Barney O'Hara laughed. They both watched her walk up to the door, short skirt swinging. Her white cloche was tilted perkily.

"Sorry to bring you out on a Sunday, Barney," Hebron said.

"Anytime, Mr. Hebron."

"I'll make it up to you. I thought she'd enjoy riding in a limousine."

"She sure did," O'Hara grinned. "Kept feeling the leather."

"What do you think of her, Barney?"

"I ask you very confidentially," O'Hara sang, "ain't she sweet?"

Eli Hebron smiled. "See you tomorrow morning."

He took her inside. Robert came forward. Hebron introduced them. The butler bowed gravely.

"Lunch in two hours or so, Robert."

"Yes, Mr. Hebron. In the dining room?"

"Oh, no. It's such a lovely day, could we have it on the terrace, please?"

"Of course, Mr. Hebron."

"Let me show you around," he said to her. "We'll start with the grounds."

He led her to the back French doors out to the terrace, lawn, garage, swimming pool. He pointed out how Taki was trying to create a Japanese garden with plants, trees, and rocks artfully placed on the sloping grass. She didn't say much, but he noted how she touched: feeling a rhododendron leaf, running fingertips along a marble bench, bending suddenly to dabble in the swimming pool. She inspected a bronze sundial that bore the inscription "Time waits for no man." She peered into a tiled birdbath, tweaked the nose of a cement cherub, looked up to watch jays flashing overhead.

"Do you have a dog?" she asked.

"No. We had one, but he died."

"What from?"

"The vet said it was just old age. Bosco was really my wife's dog. I think it was loneliness."

She nodded. "Yes," she said, "that's what it was."

When she wandered beneath the trees, he saw how sunlight dappled her. Shadows were violet. Light was a rosy glow. She floated across the lawn. He looked back and saw grass springing up slowly in her footprints. He wondered if he could catch that on film.

Then he took her back into the house. He showed her through the ground floor: living room, den, projection room, dining room, kitchen. She met Mrs. Birkin and lifted the lid of a pot to sniff the steam.

"Yum," she said.

"For tomato curry, miss," Mrs. Birkin said.

"Yum-yum," Gladys said.

Mrs. Birkin beamed.

She went up the stairway ahead of him. He admired her legs in white silk stockings: slender ankles swelling to muscled calves. The clever backs of her knees. She paused once, smiled at him over her shoulder.

"It's a swell house, Eli," she said. "I'd love to live here."

"Would you?" he said.

He showed her through all the bedrooms, an empty

room that might have been a nursery, and the bathrooms with their marble walls, tubs, sinks, and gold fixtures.

"Really and truly gold?" she asked.

"Really and truly," he nodded. "Not solid," he added hastily. "Plated."

Finally, he led her into the master bedroom. The mirrored boudoir.

"Oh," she said softly, looking about. "Oh, oh, oh."

"It's very feminine, I know," he said, trying to laugh and not succeeding. "My wife decorated it. Or had it decorated. And I didn't want to change it."

"Of course not," she said. "Why should you?"

He sat on the bed. He lighted a cigarette with shaking fingers. He watched her stroll about. She peeked out the windows overlooking the pool. She inspected the dressing room. She poked her head into the bathroom. She came back to stare at a silver-framed photograph of Grace Darling by Eugene Robert Richee, standing on a chromium table. Then she went close to one of the mirrored walls. She took off her cloche, shook her shingled hair free, stared at herself.

"I'm ugly," she said.

"Don't say that," he said. "You're beautiful."

"Not as beautiful as she was."

"Yes," he said. "As beautiful. In a different way."

"I saw all her pictures."

"Did you? She was very good."

"She certainly was. Did you ever direct her, Eli?"

"No. She worked for Universal and MGM. We decided it was better that way."

"Did you give her advice?"

"Sometimes," he said. "Only if she asked for it."

She came over to sit on the bed alongside him. She

fished in her purse, pulled out a crumpled pack of Fatimas. He held a match for her.

"Was she happy, Eli?"

"I think so. Until the last picture. It was very bad, and she couldn't stand it. I read the scenario. She asked me, and I told her not to do it. It wasn't right for her. But she went ahead and did it. I think I could have saved it. The cutting was bad. It needed more footage. At least two more scenes. But it wasn't my picture; I couldn't interfere. I knew it would be a disaster. These things happen. I've had flops. They hurt. But you learn to take them and go on to something else. She couldn't go on."

She turned to stare at him.

"You loved her very much, Eli." More statement than question.

"Oh, yes," he said. "Very much. She had a spirit. Not just her beauty, but a spirit. The camera caught it. I wanted her to do light comedies and sophisticated love stories. Wistful things. Like Pickford and Gish. She did that wonderfully. But she wanted to do heavy drama, and it finished her. It's a mean, brutal business."

"Yes," she said sadly, "it is. You grow up fast."

They leaned forward together, stubbed out their cigarettes together in an ashtray, shaped like an open poppy, on the bedside table.

"Well!" he said brightly. "Shall we go downstairs and—"

Five minutes later, the bedroom door locked, they were standing naked, side by side, close to one of the mirrored walls. He had pulled the drapes; the sunlight was muted. Diffusion lens, he thought idly, and wondered if there was a hum in the air.

They gazed at their reflected image, eyes locked in

glass. They were almost of a height, both slender, both showing bone and muscle. Tendons and tight skin. He darker than she. Their hips touched. His fingertips traced her spine. She shivered; her mouth opened. They moved closer to the mirror, straining to see.

She reached across herself. She took him in her hand. They watched, fascinated. He stood trembling, not hearing their deep sounds or a roaring. Her soft hand, her soft fingers. They observed the image, caught. Until he came: white spurts against the silver screen. They stared as it slid slowly down.

He wondered if you could pray to a God you didn't believe in for the happiness of someone you loved.

He couldn't get her out of the glassed shower stall. He had bathed, in minutes, and was out. But she insisted on staying, shouting with pleasure as water plastered her short hair flat, splayed from her shoulders, sheened belly and thighs.

The frosted glass was etched with cranes, African Negroes, jungle foliage. Behind, dimly, he saw wet flesh flow, features hazy, the dark of hair. He backed away a step. He held his two hands at arms' length, thumb tips touching, fingers together and pointing upward. In this three-sided frame he saw the scene he wanted to film. But that was another take.

When she came into the bedroom, laughing, he was already dressed, and had wiped the mirrored wall clean. She came scampering, naked, toweling her hair. She whirled about the room, giggling as her image leaped from glass to glass. He was tempted to play his wife's phonograph records, to keep her dancing, and then to dress her in his wife's monogrammed lingerie. He did none of these things.

They went downstairs hand in hand, smiling for no

reason. She had perched her hat atop his head. He wore the cloche jauntily, cocked over one eye. They ran onto the terrace. Robert, with great solemnity, was moving a silver cocktail shaker up and down in short, sharp strokes.

"I took the liberty, sir," he said. "Daiquiris. Would the lady care for a cherry? For sweetening?"

"I think the lady probably would," Hebron laughed. "Better make it two cherries. Or three."

They lunched at a table of white cast iron with a glass top. From the center rose a large open umbrella that shielded them from the sun. The umbrella was designed as a giant canvas daisy. The cushions on the white cast-iron chairs were also decorated with daisies, as were the woven place mats.

Robert served the tomato curry with freshly boiled shrimp. The chilled salad, in a glass bowl, was all greens: romaine, endive, water cress, chickory, escarole. And there seemed to be no bottom to the shaker of daiquiris.

They sat at adjoining sides of the square table. They ate slowly, almost lazily. They paused frequently to look at shimmering reflections on the surface of the swimming pool or to watch the antics of a woodpecker attacking a palm bole furiously. Then they heard the grind of an airplane. They stopped eating to stand quickly, dash out from under the umbrella, search upward. A biplane, red as blood, came over Beverly Hills, quite low, wings waggling. They were delighted when a helmeted and goggled pilot leaned from the front cockpit and waved down at them. They waved frantically back.

"Have you ever been up?" Hebron asked her after they were seated again.

"No, and how I'd love to!"

"We'll do it," he said. "We'll go up together. Would you like that?"

"Oh yes!" she cried. "Up, up, up!"

"That's not what worries me," he laughed. "It's how we'll come down, down, down!"

She leaned forward with a little shrimp held in her fingers. She moved it to his mouth. He took it obediently, and kissed her fingertips. When he did that, she raised her fingertips to her lips and kissed where he had kissed, looking at him with a stare he could not fully comprehend.

"Why do you look at me like that?" he asked.

"Like what?"

"Sad and puzzled and determined—all at once."

"Oh, that! I'm just nearsighted."

"You're not!" He paused. "Are you?"

"No," she said. "I was just thinking about the bedroom. The mirror. And how happy I am. Are you happy, Eli?"

"Oh, yes. Happier than I've been in a long time. I've been laughing all day. You must think I'm an idiot."

"A very *nice* idiot," she said. She slipped off one of her shoes, caressed his ankles with her stockinged toes.

"What a lot of tricks you know," he smiled.

"I know another one," she said. "Give me your hand."

He held his hand out to her. She took it softly, turned it palm upward. She bent over it, touched the center of his palm with the tip of her tongue. Then licked avidly. Her eyes turned upward, watching him.

"Does that get you hot?" she whispered.

"It gets *you* hot," he said. "I can tell."

"Everything about you gets me hot," she said. "Can we go up to the bedroom again?"

"No," he said, frightened.

"All right," she said equably. "What's for dessert?"

Robert took their empty dishes away. He brought them slices of fresh peach floating in port.

"Oh, Robert," she said, "you'll make a souse of me."

"I trust not, miss," he said seriously.

After he left, she spooned up great portions of peach and port and said, lips dribbling, "If I get cockeyed, you'll have to put me to bed, won't you?" Then, when she saw his expression, she said, "I was just joking, Eli. I'm not getting drunk. Really I'm not. I just feel good."

"I feel good, too. Being with you makes me feel good."

He saw that look again, the look he could not fathom and gave up trying.

Robert cleared the table, leaving only the shaker and their glasses. They sat indolently, sipping their drinks slowly. After a while, at the same moment, their hands floated up, together. They sat contentedly, holding hands.

"Tell me a story, Eli," she murmured.

"All right. There was this beautiful little girl from New Jersey who came to Hollywood because she wanted to get in the movies and get rich. And she met this man who put her in the movies, and she became rich and famous. All the world loved her, and she was very busy, and handsome men kept trying to meet her and take her out and make love to her."

"And what happened to her?" she asked breathlessly.

"I told you. She became rich and famous. And she forgot all about the man who put her in the movies."

"Is that what you think is going to happen, Eli?"

"I don't know." He shrugged. "It's what usually happens. But it's not important. What is important is that you get what you want. That's all that counts."

She wailed, wrenched her hand free. She stood suddenly, went limping off down the terrace, disappeared. He picked up her shoe, went after her. He finally found her, lying under a tall, slender bamboo palm. She was curled into a ball, weeping. He sat alongside her, stroked her back lovingly.

"Glad," he said, "what *is* it?"

"You," she sobbed. "It's *you*."

"You can kill the tail," Timmy Ryan said.

"Ahh, shit," Bernie Kaplan said. "Just when it was getting interesting."

Both men laughed and reached for their glasses on the desk. They were in Kaplan's sleazy office. The private investigator had put out a bottle of Golden Wedding.

Ryan sipped appreciatively. He held his glass up to the light coming through a dusty window.

"Now that's rare, that is," he said. "Who'd be legging stuff like this?"

"One of our boys in blue," Kaplan said. "Probably an old pal of yours."

"I never had a pal in the Feds," Ryan said indignantly. "It's a nice thing they have going. Raid a still or warehouse. Confiscate a hundred cases. Report ten, and peddle the ninety. Am I right now?"

"Something like that," Kaplan admitted. "I got a bottle for you—just to show you my heart's in the right place."

"Ah, Bernie, I know where your heart is," Ryan said. "Right in that wallet hugging your Jewish ass. How much do I owe on the shadow?"

"Two yards."

"And that includes my bottle," Ryan nodded. He unbuttoned his uniform jacket, took an envelope and a sheaf of

121

papers from an inside pocket. He counted out two hundred from the envelope, slid the bills across the desk to Kaplan.

"Want a receipt?" the PI asked.

"To be sure."

"For three hundred?"

"Ah, you're an understanding scut, Bernie."

"And you're a crook, Timmy."

"A small one, Bernie, a wee, small one. I've never been a greedy man. It's a well-known fact."

Kaplan wrote out the receipt for three hundred. Ryan tucked it carefully away. Then he opened his sheaf of papers and spread them on the desk.

"Now this is Magna business," he said. "Three employment clearances."

"That I like," Kaplan said. "Mostly paperwork, and the money's good."

"It is that. Take a look. . . ."

Kaplan read over the short biographies. They had been prepared in Henry Cushing's press department at Magna. They were the vital statistics on three new players about to be hired by Magna. The information had been provided by the actors or their agents.

Following the scandals of Wallace Reid, Fatty Arbuckle, and William Desmond Taylor—to say nothing of the divorce of America's Sweetheart and her quick remarriage to Douglas Fairbanks—most of the nation became convinced that Hollywood might give lessons to Sodom and excite the envy of Gomorrah. Executives of the movie industry, anxious to sanitize Hollywood's reputation and to encourage family moviegoing, set out to prove their hometown no more wicked than Hyrum, Utah, or Harmony, Maine.

Will Hays was appointed custodian of Hollywood virtue (president of the Motion Picture Producers and Distributors

Association) at an annual salary of one hundred thousand dollars. His instructions were to root out immorality in the movie industry. Mr. Hays had gained his knowledge of immorality, no doubt, by serving as postmaster general in the Cabinet of President Warren Gamaliel Harding, a splendid fellow.

In addition, the major studios inserted morality clauses in their employment contracts. Recognizing that easy money in the movie capital attracted prostitutes, con men, carnival barkers, drunks, dope addicts, lounge lizards, and painted women—as well, of course, as the innocent young and yearning—executives hiring new players insisted they agree to contracts stipulating, hopefully, that the signer would abstain from public sin and private vice. At least for the duration of the contract.

As a further safeguard against scandal, most of the major studios, including Magna, hired private detective agencies to make investigations of the backgrounds of those to be employed. The studios hoped thereby to avoid signing convicted sodomites or parlor house towel girls.

Bernie Kaplan did this preemployment investigative work for Magna Pictures, Inc. It was, as Kaplan told Timmy Ryan, mostly a matter of correspondence. It was clean work and paid better than shadowing an errant wife or photographing a cheating husband in a hotel room just as he was dropping his suspenders and telling the dolly his wife didn't understand him.

"They look okeydokey," Kaplan said, finishing his reading of the biographies. "I should be able to check them out in, oh, say, two weeks or so."

"Fine," Ryan said. "Now here's another one."

"I thought you said there were three?"

"This one is special. This one requires no work at all, at

all. You just okay the information as stated, Bernie, and send in your bill. Don't go poking.''

The two men stared at each other, Kaplan shaken, Ryan smiling genially. He carefully cracked the head of a cigar and lighted up, blowing blue smoke at the peeling tin ceiling.

''Jesus Christ, Timmy,'' Bernie Kaplan said hoarsely, ''you know what you're asking?''

''I know, m'boy.''

''It's my ass if it goes sour.''

''It won't go sour, Bernie. Take my word for it.''

Kaplan took the fourth biography, read it swiftly.

''Gladys Potts?'' he said. ''What's so special about her?''

''Just okay the facts as stated, Bernie.''

The PI stared at the cop a long moment.

''Is she the twist I saw with Hebron?'' he asked finally.

''Ask me no questions, and I'll tell you no lies,'' Ryan said smoking placidly. ''I can go two hundred on this, Bernie.''

''Five,'' Kaplan said. ''It could be my *ass*, Timmy. Five.''

''Three.''

''Four.''

''Three fifty and done,'' Ryan said. ''Agreed?''

''Agreed,'' Kaplan said grumpily.

''Give me your hand on that, Bernie boy,'' Ryan said heartily, holding out his big paw. ''I know you're a man of honor. I know you wouldn't cross old Timmy Ryan.''

Kaplan shook the hand resentfully. ''What would happen to me if I did?'' he asked.

''Ah, well,'' Ryan said. ''No tellin'. . . .''

Timothy Francis Edward Ryan had been head of the

Vice Squad of the Los Angeles Police Department. He had risen to this coveted and extremely profitable position by, as he said, "Loyalty up and loyalty down." His superiors believed he passed along a reasonable share of his booty. The whores, gamblers, bootleggers, drug dealers, pimps, and thieves he plundered all felt they got a fair shake. As one parlor house madam remarked, "Timmy Ryan is a man you can trust; he stays bribed."

But a politically ambitious district attorney had launched an investigation, and the powers had decided that Timmy Ryan had to take a fall. An understanding was reached with the DA that the investigation would end with Timmy. He wasn't bitter; he understood how such things worked. So he was allowed to resign in disgrace, with a discreet cash gift of five thousand dollars from those to whom he gave "loyalty up" and a final levy of almost three thousand dollars on those to whom he granted "loyalty down." Six months after his name disappeared from the front pages, he was appointed chief of studio police at Magna Pictures, Inc. At the same time a record was expunged from police files detailing how Margaret Gay was arrested in a Wilshire Boulevard hotel with five exhausted marines of the First Division.

"Ahh, Timmy," Kaplan protested, "you know I wouldn't cross you."

"I know, I know." Ryan nodded. "You're a good lad, Bernie."

"But are you sure you can trust whoever it is you're working for?"

"Have no fear," the cop said, puffing away with great satisfaction. "I'm in the driver's seat, m'boy. You see, I know where the bodies are buried. As a matter of fact,"

Timmy Ryan added, with a laugh that shriveled the soul of Bernie Kaplan, "I may have buried a few of them m'self."

Dr. Irving Blick was not a psychoanalyst. In fact, at this time there were no psychoanalysts in Los Angeles, and only seven in New York. But it was generally agreed that Blick was Hollywood's leading authority on the theories of Dr. Sigmund Freud of Vienna. He had recently added "psychic counseling" to his medical practice. And he frequently spoke at luncheons of women's groups. He urged them, after dessert had been served, to "coite freely without shame or guilt." He was much in demand.

He was a portly man who wore dark, four-button, double-breasted suits. Gold-framed pince-nez set on his fleshy nose. The glasses were attached to his buttonhole with a black ribbon. Eli Hebron thought Blick resembled the comedian Oliver Hardy, although the doctor had no mustache. But he did have Hardy's fluttery mannerisms and rubbery expressions.

Hebron finished dressing and then, as instructed, went back into the office. Dr. Blick was seated behind his desk, making notes in Hebron's file. He motioned the supervisor to a chair. Then he closed the file with a snap and leaned back. He removed his pince-nez and began to wind the black ribbon slowly about his forefinger.

"Well," he said, "our blood pressure is up slightly, but nothing to be concerned about. Our tremors persist, particularly in the right hand."

"It's getting better," Hebron said.

"Is it? Good. Results of our urinalysis will be back in a day or so. Our pulse and respiration show no significant change. Have we been taking our medication?"

"Yes. In fact, I'll need another prescription, Doctor."

"Of course. We find they help, do we?"

"Sometimes. Most of the time. They're not addictive, are they, Doctor?"

"Not necessarily."

"What does that mean?"

"They are not physically addictive. They may, however, become psychologically addictive. We would prefer they be dispensed with. But under the circumstances. . . . Is there anything about our emotional state we should know?"

"Well. . . ."

"For instance, have we been sexually active?"

"Well, ah, not, I guess, normal sex, no."

"Mr. Hebron!" Dr. Blick cried sternly. "The word 'normal' has no place in the medical lexicon. Especially in the field of psychic phenomena. And *most* especially in sexual behavior. What have we done?"

Hebron told him.

"Hmm," Blick said, unwinding the black ribbon slowly from his forefinger. "Interesting." He replaced the pince-nez, opened Hebron's file again, wrote busily. "Both these incidents were with the same partner?"

"Yes."

"A female?"

"Of course," Hebron said angrily.

"Mr. Hebron," Blick soothed, "we are trying to uncover the cause of our unhappiness. To do this, we must be absolutely open and frank and, above all, honest. We see the necessity for that, don't we?"

"I suppose so. Yes."

"Good. A young woman?"

"Yes."

"Do we feel an emotional attachment to this young woman?"

Hebron was silent a moment, then said faintly, "I'd like to."

"Like to?" the doctor repeated. "That implies we want to but cannot. Why not?"

"She's very young."

"How young?"

"Eighteen."

"And we are—how old?" Blick glanced at the file. "Forty? Hardly sufficient reason not to feel affection for this young lady."

"I do. I do feel affection."

"But we cannot love her, is that it? We cannot allow ourself to love her?"

"Something like that."

Dr. Blick set the pince-nez firmly in place. Then sat back, fat fingers spread and touching across his thick chest.

"Something blocks our ability to love this young woman. Who, incidentally, must be very loving herself. She has tried to give us pleasure in any way she can, sensing instinctively our inability to achieve satisfaction in the usual fashion. Are we correct?"

"Yes. I'd say yes."

"But in spite of her tender, loving attention to our joy, we still find ourself unable to make the breakthrough from affection to love?"

"Yes."

"What could it be that blocks our love?"

"I don't know. I've thought about it a great deal. I just don't know."

"Are we afraid?"

"Of loving? Oh, no. I loved my wife very much."

"Ah!" Dr. Blick said, eyes glittering behind heavy glass. "Our wife! Our dead wife! We loved her very much, more than we ever loved anyone before or since her death. Is that correct?"

"Yes."

"And in our mind, that great love can never be repeated? Never?"

Hebron was silent.

"Guilt!" Dr. Irving Blick said harshly, slapping one hand atop his desk. "Guilt is what prevents us from loving again. Because if we loved, we would be unfaithful to our wife."

"I—"

"Our dead wife!" Blick thundered. "Is that not true? We swore undying love. We have convinced ourself that to love again would be betraying a woman who has been dead for more than a year. Is *that* not true, Mr. Hebron?"

"Yes," he said in a low voice. "I think you're right."

"We know we're right!" Blick said definitely and happily. "Now let us discuss how we can rid our mind of this foolish, romantic, antediluvian notion. Once our guilt is conquered, our psyche is free to love again. Guilt goes out the window as love comes in the door. Pardon us a moment while we make a note of that. 'Guilt goes out the. . . .' "

Barney O'Hara was waiting in the Hispano-Suiza outside Dr. Blick's Beverly Hills office. He scrambled out to hold the door.

"Good checkup, Mr. Hebron?"

"Fine, thanks. Everything's fine. I feel great."

"Glad to hear it, Mr. Hebron. I noticed you been more cheerful lately."

"Have you?" the supervisor said, pleased. "Well, I feel more cheerful. Let's go to the studio now, Barney."

The previous evening Magna Pictures had screened a sneak preview of a new movie in a company-owned theater in Pasadena. The film was called *Jealousy*. It was a turgid love story, supervised by Eli Hebron. He had only modest hopes for the script, cast, and production crew. The movie turned out to be the mediocrity he expected. But the demand for new films remained insatiable; Hebron hoped *Jealousy* might earn back its cost and perhaps a small profit.

The story of *Jealousy* was crude. It was set in New York City at the turn of the century. A young couple, recently married, in love, live in a tenement. Both work, the husband in a railroad yard, the wife at a sewing machine in a sweatshop loft.

One day the husband is injured on the job. Not seriously, but he requires a lengthy convalescence at home. Of course, he is off the payroll. To afford food, rent, and medical care for her husband, the young wife works long hours, sometimes not coming home until midnight. She is exhausted but happy to be able to keep their little home going.

Next door lives a darkly handsome woman whose husband has died of alcoholism, leaving her a small pension. She is attracted by the injured young husband. Since they are neighbors and together all day while the wife works, the neighbor, a femme fatale, begins to flirt with the husband.

The neighbor poisons the husband's mind, hinting that his wife isn't really working late but has been having an affair with her young, handsome boss.

There is a scene in which the boss actually does try to

seduce the young wife. But she spurns him, telling him that her love for her husband will keep her unsullied and content forever.

Finally, driven mad by jealousy, the husband takes his revolver and, on his single crutch, hobbles late at night to his wife's factory, thinking to surprise her in her infamy. He assaults the young, handsome boss and then breaks into an inner room, believing he will find his wife in a compromising position. Instead, he finds her in a large loft, one of fifty women busy at their sewing machines.

Two endings were filmed for this primitive work. In one, the husband falls sobbing to his knees before his angelic wife and begs forgiveness for his jealousy. She gently reproaches him for his lack of faith in her, pardons him, and strokes his hair tenderly. Fade-out.

The second ending, used in the version of the film shown at the preview, is sterner stuff. The hardworking wife is outraged by her husband's vile suspicions. She tells him (in a ringing speech that requires three subtitles) that his contemptible jealousy has destroyed her love and wrecked their marriage. She leaves home, stalking off with head held high. In the last scene, the woebegone husband is being comforted by the femme fatale neighbor. To assuage his sorrow, she offers him a bottle of whiskey. He drinks deeply. Fade-out.

The principals connected with the production of *Jealousy* were waiting for Eli Hebron when he arrived at the studio following his visit to Dr. Irving Blick. In the outer office were the director, three leading players, and the cameraman. Henry Cushing was also present with a compilation of the cards distributed to the audience after the preview, requesting their frank opinion of the new movie they had just viewed. This rough and frequently inaccurate method of gauging audience response was employed before multiple prints of a film negative were made for national distribution.

Hebron saw from the expressions that the sneak preview had not gone well. He understood their gloom. The success or failure of *Jealousy* was the supervisor's responsibility. But ultimately the careers of everyone involved in its production would be affected.

"All right," Hebron said, "let's hear the bad news."

He ushered them all into his inner office, and got them seated. Henry Cushing started off. . . .

A total of two hundred and eighty-eight preview cards had been filled out and collected. There were the usual crank notes: "Too long." "Too short." "Too much lovey-dovey stuff." "Not enough s-x!" "The husband is lousy." "Too dark. Should be brighter." And so forth.

But more important, a hundred and forty-nine of those who filled out preview cards had objected to the ending. A few of them wrote: "Wife should have taken husband back." "It is Christian to forgive and forget." "Ending unsatisfactory. Wife should understand, kiss, and make up!"

"Well, anyway, we shot that ending," the director said nervously. "I guess we'll switch to that—right, Mr. Hebron?"

"You think we should go with the happy ending?"

"Well . . . sure. That's what everyone wants."

"Hank?"

"I guess so," Cushing said, wiping his sweated face. "More than half of them hate the ending we got."

Hebron asked the others. They all felt the ending should be changed so the movie finished on a happy note, the young couple back together again.

The supervisor thrust his hands into his trouser pockets. He wandered to the windows, stood with his back to the others. He looked down into the yard. He saw Gladys Divine come out of Makeup & Costume. She was wearing a blond wig done up in a bun and the clothes of a Western schoolmarm of fifty years ago. She stopped to talk to Bea Winks. As they chatted, Winks adjusted the wig slightly, smoothed the long skirt, fluffed the leg-o'-mutton sleeves. Then they separated. Hebron watched Gladys move to Indoor Stage Two. She walked lithely, head high, spine straight, long thighs snapping the skirt taut. Men turned to see that stride. Hebron smiled.

"No," he said loudly. "We'll go with the ending we have now. The happy ending would be such a cliché that I'd be ashamed to have Magna's name on the film. People would forget the picture before they got out of the lobby. They'll remember the ending we're using. They'll talk about it, argue about whether or not the wife did right to leave her husband."

"Mr. Hebron . . ." someone faltered.

"More important," he went on, "there's a new breed of women in this country. Women whose future and happiness don't depend on a man's whim, on subservience to husband or lover. Independent women with the courage to go their own way. With a sense of their own dignity. Brave enough to try their dreams. New women. More every day. They'll like this picture and understand the ending we have. I think it'll cause talk and make money. I don't want to hear any arguments. That's all."

They filed out silently. He sensed their anger and frustration. He stared at the closed door of Indoor Stage Two.

After a while he took one of the orange pills. He washed

it down with a swallow of warm gin. He wandered about his office, head down. Finally, he went out. . . .

"I'll be back in half an hour," he told Mildred Eljer. He took the LaSalle. He parked in front of the Mexican curio shop on La Brea.

Last time, he promised himself.

Madame Ortiz came pushing through the bead curtain.

"Meester?" she said.

"The last time I was here," he said, "you told me I would meet a young woman. You said she would bring me happiness, but to beware of her. I want to know more about her."

They sat at the rickety table. The greasy cards were slapped down.

"No," Madame Ortiz said, peering. "No beware. Only 'appiness."

"The young girl will bring me happiness?"

"Much 'appiness. Much love. What you want. Everything."

He sat a moment in silence.

"Thank you," he said finally, paid her, and left.

Back at the studio, he left the car in front of the administration building for Barney O'Hara to garage. He went directly to Indoor Stage Two and slipped inside. They were setting up for a scene in a one-room schoolhouse. The director was explaining the action to Gladys Divine.

"The heavy is drunk—see? He comes stumbling in. He goes for you, tries to kiss you. The kids are scared. But you stand up to the bully. He crowds you back toward the wall. You grab up a broom and start whacking him. He covers his head and shoulders with his arms, but you keep smacking away at him. Finally, you drive him out the door. The kids cheer and come clustering around. They hug you. Got it? Let's try a walk-through while they're setting up. Watch the chalk marks so you don't go off camera."

Charlie Royce was standing near the big white sheet. It cut the glare of the noonday sun flooding through the huge windows. Hebron sauntered casually over to him.

"How's she doing, Charlie?" he asked in a low voice.

"I don't know where she gets it, Eli, but she can act like nobody's business."

They watched Glad and the heavy walk through their scene. The director demonstrated how he wanted them to stand, move, turn. The girl listened intently, biting at her lower lip.

"She never makes the same mistake twice," Royce said.

"How's the food in your hotel dining room these days?" Hebron asked.

"What?" Royce said, startled. "Why?"

"I thought I'd ask her to dinner. Some nice place. . . ."

"Oh," Royce said, without expression. "The food's fine. Try the roast beef."

Then, as if realizing what Hebron had said, he turned to look at him, smiling faintly. "She getting under your skin?" he said.

"Yes," Eli Hebron said.

Three

HE was wearing a Norfolk suit of white duck. Pale blue silk shirt with white knotted tie. His olive complexion seemed to keep a year-round tan. He still wore his gold wedding band. Tina Rambaugh thought he had never looked so handsome. And—and elegant. She was conscious of her own chunky body. Fingernails bitten down to the quick. Heavy thighs.

He perched on the edge of Jenkins' desk, sipping the writer's gin. One foot swung lazily. The white suede shoe was spotless.

"That ending," Eli Hebron said. "The final scene where they walk off into the sunset together. We'll shoot that straight. Without the diffusion lens."

"But we'll lose the bite," Tina objected. "You said yourself it was a nice, ironic ending."

"The movie will be ironic enough without it."

"Annenberg didn't like it," Jenkins guessed. "Right, boss?"

"Right," Hebron said, not smiling. "And I didn't argue because I think he's correct. Most of our customers have made exactly the compromise with life we're showing them. Should we tell them they're fools?"

"Snow again," Jenkins said, "I don't get your drift."

"The hero has put away his fantasies," Hebron explained patiently. "As a child puts away his toys when he becomes a man. He accepts a smaller measure of real happiness in place of the ecstatic dreams that only brought pain and frustration."

"The happy ending." Tina sighed. "Again."

"Yes," Hebron agreed. "A happy ending. Only because it holds out a *chance* of happiness. No guarantee. The dreams were doomed. We show that."

"You turned down the happy ending for *Jealousy*," Jenkins said.

"Oh-ho," Hebron said. "Word gets around."

"It's a small world, boss."

"As a matter of fact, the ending we're going with *is* a happy ending, and a lot of women are going to see it that way. The wife in *Jealousy* leaves her husband, granted. Because his suspicion has killed her love. She knows what she's facing as a single woman. Loneliness. Maybe despair. But she has the courage, the strength to dare the unknown, realizing it's her only chance for happiness. Exactly the same reason why the hero of *The Dream Lover* decides to settle down with his plain wife."

Jenkins took the pint bottle of gin from under his desk. He took a deep swallow.

"I still say Annenberg changed your mind," he said. "Boss," he added.

The supervisor stared at him. Inspected the sandy hair, pitted cheeks, eyes of water-blue.

"You have talent, Ed," he said coldly. "Not as much as you think, but some. That's why I keep you around. But you also have a big mouth. Let me tell you something about *Mr*. Annenberg. He doesn't have your formal education and learning. But he's got something you don't have, and you don't, Tina, and I don't either. And that's an almost unerring sense or instinct for what the American people want in their movies. Because his taste is exactly theirs. When you and I make a decision, we usually have to reject our own taste and inclination and ask ourselves, 'Would the public go for this?' Mr. Annenberg doesn't have to make that intellectual leap. What he likes, they like. And what they reject, he rejects. Instantly, automatically, instinctively. It's elemental. Without agonizing over it, intellectualizing, figuring out reasons and motives. So don't feel so fucking superior to Mr. Annenberg. He's way ahead of you."

"I didn't . . ." Jenkins started.

"Get moving on the scenario," Eli Hebron said shortly. "I'll give you a week for a first draft."

"Plenty of time, Mr. Hebron," Tina Rambaugh said hastily.

"Good." He nodded. He put down the empty glass. "Jenkins"—he grinned—"you drink too much."

The screen door slammed behind him.

The girl looked at Jenkins. "Satisfied?" she asked.

"The son of a bitch," he said bitterly. He filled his glass, adding ice chips. "I hate his guts."

"No, you don't. You like him and admire him and wish you had half his talent."

"He's so goddamned *neat!*" Jenkins exploded. "He makes me feel like a bum. Jesus, doesn't he *ever* sweat?"

"Ed, he was right about the happy ending."

"Was he, fatso? Are you sure? You give up your dreams, and you have a chance for the brass ring. Is that it?"

"It's better than no ring at all," she said.

"Ah, the hell with it," he grumbled. "He treats every movie he makes like it's going to be another *Intolerance*."

"Maybe that's why his films make money."

"You're prejudiced," he said. "You got a crush on him?"

"No," she said. "That's one dream I've given up. But he's a beautiful man. So sad and haunted."

"Bullshit," Jenkins said. "He's getting his. Gladys Divine."

"Where did you hear that?"

"I read it. In Louella's column yesterday. E.H. and G.D. were seen smiling into each other's eyes over a fried flounder somewhere or other."

"Oh," she said faintly. "I didn't know."

"The dream dies hard, huh?" he jeered. "Now you can't comfort that sad, haunted man. Cheer up, babe; I know just the thing to take your mind off your disappointment."

"What?"

"The bum's rush."

They both laughed. She came around behind him, stroking his bristly hair. She leaned suddenly to kiss his lips. His free hand fell to her silk-stockinged calf, stroked upward. He pulled her garter, then let it snap back.

"Ouch," she said.

"Let's get to work," he said. "I'll talk, and you type."

"Yes, boss," she said.

Barney O'Hara had a pal, an ex-stunt man named Jack Newton. About a year previously, Newton was working a movie being shot in the High Sierras. The script called for a train of locomotive, tender, and six flatcars to race out of control down a steep mountainside. It would then plunge into a deep ravine after the bridge had been blown by the bad guys.

Jack Newton, dressed like the hero, would start at the rear flatbed and then leap from car to car as the train careened down the mountainside. He would jump from the locomotive just before it sailed into the gorge.

Newton studied the train, the track, the surrounding forest, the ravine, and he told the director the stunt couldn't be done. The director said Newton was yellow, and if he didn't do the stunt, the director would make certain he never worked in Hollywood again.

So Jack Newton did the stunt perfectly in one take. He escaped with a broken arm and minor bruises. He then returned to base camp, collected his pay, and kicked the shit out of the director. He went back to Los Angeles and opened a speak in the rear of a garage on Cahuenga. For six months he had been calling Barney O'Hara, urging him to stop by, inspect the premises, and bend an elbow for old times' sake.

Late one afternoon O'Hara drove Eli Hebron and Gladys Divine back to Beverly Hills in the limousine. The supervisor said O'Hara could take the rest of the day off. The chauffeur decided it was a good time to visit Jack Newton. He drove his Hupmobile to the speak and noted the number of cars parked outside the garage. Everything from a Daimler Double-Six to a Maxwell Club Sedan. Barney figured Newton was on easy street.

You entered the speakeasy by walking through one of the repair bays, past a grease pit, and knocked on a door marked PRIVATE. Then a judas opened, and a heavy looked you over.

"Friend of Fig's," O'Hara rasped, and the door was immediately opened.

It wasn't much of a room, not luxurious, but it had a bar for stand-up drinkers, tables and chairs, and a line of high-walled booths along one of the stuccoed walls. There was a big photograph of President Coolidge at one end of the room, draped with American flags. Someone had drawn a mustache on Silent Cal. There were also framed movie stills here and there. O'Hara guessed the speak got a good film crowd at night. Right now most of the customers looked like working stiffs and door-to-door salesmen resting their bunions.

Jack Newton was behind the stick. He grinned when O'Hara bellied up.

"You mick bastard," he said, holding out a wet hand. "What took you so long?"

"Fig," Barney O'Hara said, "sorry I couldn't make it sooner. Nice place you got here."

"Getting by," Newton said, winking. "Just getting by."

"I bet," O'Hara scoffed. "You selling anything that won't blind me?"

"For you, something special. Right off the boat. Brew for a wash?"

"Sounds good," O'Hara nodded.

"Eddie," Newton called to one of the waiters, "take over for me, will you?"

He took an unlabeled quart bottle from under the bar. Then he filled a pitcher with beer. Carrying both, he led the way to a back booth. They slid in opposite each other. Another waiter brought four empty glasses that were almost clean. Newton poured the whiskey and beer chasers.

He was a slender, dapper man. Or had been. The beer

was beginning to get to him; his apron bulged. But his scarred, cheerful face was still bony, and he had a laugh that boomed the walls. He had fought in the Meuse-Argonne offensive, but no one knew it. He had hocked his medals.

"Here's to Prohibition," he toasted, lifting his glass. "Long may it wave."

They drank their whiskeys. Fig looked at his guest anxiously.

"All right?"

"Smooth as a baby's ass," O'Hara assured him. "Canadian?"

"That's right. They run it down the coast in fishing boats. How's the back, Barney?"

The chauffeur turned his head slowly back and forth in the neck brace.

"Not too bad," he said. "Hell when it rains. But generally, I forget all about it. I'm lucky to be alive."

"Ain't we all?" Newton said. "Pour your own; I'm not going to wait on you."

They drank slowly, steadily, gossiping lazily about mutual friends. Who was working where, who had been killed, who had left the business to buy an orange grove.

"I guess you're doing all right," Newton said. "Right, Barney?"

"Oh, sure," O'Hara nodded. "No complaints. Hebron treats me square. The man's a saint."

"I hear the saint's got a little something going for him," Newton said. "A young little something."

"Ain't we all?" O'Hara repeated, smiling.

Newton's laugh boomed out. "That's a fact. Anyone who's not getting it in this town just ain't trying."

"Get a good movie crowd, Fig?"

"Plenty." Newton nodded. "Later, when the studios close. Then I got three guys behind the bar to handle the crowd."

"The cops leave you alone?"

"Oh, sure. They're on my side. They should be, the bastards; I pay enough. The Feds are another matter. So far I've been lucky. But I got some important people drinking here. From MGM, RKO, United Artists, Fox— you name it. Executives, stars, supervisors, directors—A-Number One people. I figure the Feds ain't too anxious to roust the big shots. Anyways, they've left me alone—so far."

"Get any Magna people?" Barney O'Hara asked idly, just to keep the talk going.

"Oh, sure. For instance, the top buttons. The chief of the studio police. What's his name? He used to be with the LA cops, then got the boot when they found out he was on the take."

"Timmy Ryan?" O'Hara said, amused. "He drinks here?"

"Sure he does. At least once a week. Usually more. He started coming in with his uniform on. I spoke to him about it. Nicely, you know. So now he wears a regular suit, or if he's in uniform, he keeps a raincoat on. I told him those brass buttons would scare the customers."

"I can see where it would." O'Hara laughed. "I never figured Timmy was on the sauce."

"He does all right." Newton nodded. "Usually sits in that back booth. In the corner. Drinks with another Magna guy. I don't know his name."

"Oh? What's he look like?"

"Big guy. Dresses like he's important. Wears a vest— you know? Big, heavy guy."

O'Hara thought a moment. "A big, heavy guy? Wears a vest? Is he reddish in the face?"

"That's the gink. You know him?"

"Maybe," Barney O'Hara said slowly. "Sounds like Charles Royce. He's a supervisor. Big shot. Lots of spondulicks. He and Timmy Ryan meet here often?"

"Once or twice a week, at least. Usually Ryan comes in first, then the other guy comes in and joins him in the booth. They put their heads together. Thick as thieves, those two."

"What time is this, Fig? When do they usually meet?"

"Oh, it's late. Like one or two in the morning. After the crowd thins out. Why the third degree, Barney?"

"Just wondering," O'Hara said casually. "Timmy Ryan and Charlie Royce. Well, well, well. . . ."

"We shouldn't drink so much," he said.

"Why not?" she said.

"I don't know." He giggled.

Robert and Mrs. Birkin lived in apartments over the garage. But their lights were out. The lights of the adjoining mansions were out. There was a weak beacon atop the hill where Douglas Fairbanks had once owned a hunting lodge and shot coyotes. But other than that twinkling light, the only illumination came from the cold stare of stars, the moon's pale glow.

A crazy breeze blew from west, south, east, swirling merrily. It brought alternating puffs of warm and chill. The whole sky tipped, and they were alone on earth. In the close darkness. They sat on the pool edge. Their shoes and stockings were off. Hebron had rolled his trouser cuffs. Bare feet paddled the black water.

"Toes are funny," Glad said.

"So are ears," he said. "You ever look at ears? Really *look* at them? They're funny, too."

"Lips are nice," she said.

"Eyes are nice," he said.

"Fingers are nice."

"So are breasts," he said, touching her lightly. "Nice."
Things soughed, creaked, waved.

They kissed seriously. Mouths meeting, pressing, drawing slowly away.

"Oh," she said. Then: "Is the flask empty?"

"Never," he said. "It will go on forever. Glad. . . ."

"Yes?"

"Just Glad."

"Now I think what I will do," she said thoughtfully, "what I think what I will do is take off all my clothes and have a swim. Okay?"

"Okay," he said.

"You too?"

"No," he said. "I will sit here and guard your clothes. So no one sneaks in and ties knots in them."

"Eli," she said, "that's smart."

"Right. I'm a smarty-pants."

She began to undress. He lay back on the tiled pool border. He gazed upward. It seemed to him that a perforated bowl had been lowered over the earth. Behind the bowl was blazing light. White. It came piercing through the tiny perforations. He wondered, if you went beyond the black bowl, outside, if you could endure that perfect light.

"Look at me," she said.

He sat up, looked, and laughed. She was standing in a "September Morn" pose: one knee bent, hands covering nipples and bush, with a look of unutterable coyness.

"Peekaboo," he said. "I see you."

She flung her arms wide.

"Introducing," she said loudly, "the one and only . . . the greatest . . . the sexiest . . . the newest . . . Gertrude Ederle!" she shouted, and flung herself into the pool, limbs flailing.

He pulled his feet from the water. He sat clasping his knees. He watched her splashing, yelling, swimming frantically to warm up. Then she quieted. She floated on her back in the middle of the pool. Her arms and legs were spread. She stared wide-eyed at the lowery night.

He saw only a specter, a slick, white ghost. He saw her face, half her body: wet breasts gleaming, long star of stretched limbs. The sea anemone rose and fell gently on the ripples. She drifted away from him, moon-touched, body pinwheeling slowly. She lifted a hand languidly. Drops of water fell sparkling from limp fingers. Silence pressed in. He sat motionless, staring. Then closed his eyes. Still he saw the bobbing white star.

She paddled slowly back to him. He stretched down a hand, hauled her up dripping. He put a hand lightly on her long back. He touched cool flesh, all of her as tender as wet lips. Her hardened nipples looked like cherry gumdrops.

"Cold?" he asked.

She nodded, clenching her teeth. He started to take off his flannel blazer, to drape it about her shoulders. But she shook her head.

"I want your undershirt," she said.

"Why? Why do you want that, Glad?"

"I want to wear what was close to you. Closest to you."

He removed jacket and shirt. He pulled his balbriggan undershirt over his head. He put it about her shoulders,

short sleeves hanging down before her breasts. She rubbed
the material along her cheek, smelled it, kissed it.

They wandered to the far end of the pool, arms about
each other. He spread his jacket under a low magnolia. He
sat down, then lay back, hands clasped behind his head.
She knelt alongside him, leaning forward, propped on her
hands. The undershirt floated about her shoulders. He
looked at her, trying to identify the image. The White
Rock girl!

"Why are you laughing?" she asked him.

He told her, and she smiled. She sat back on her heels.
She put one hand flat against the left side of his chest.

"My heart," he said.

"I can feel it," she said. "Pounding. Thump, thump,
thump."

She leaned forward to kiss his heart.

"Come live with me, Glad," he said. "Here, in my
home. Live with me."

"All right," she said. "I will. As long as you want.
When you want me to go, tell me and I will. All right,
Eli?"

"All right," he said. "But if *you* want to go, then you
just leave. No explanations."

"I won't want to go. All my life I've dreamed of a
home like this. I'll never leave."

"Not right away," he said. "But maybe. . . ."

"I won't," she said. She touched him. "I want you
inside me, Eli. Will you?"

"Are you a virgin, Glad?"

"Yes. Will you show me how?"

"If I can. Do you want to go up to the bedroom?"

"No," she said. "That's still her room. Here. Now."

She stretched out, lay down slowly atop him. He felt her

cool leather skin. He held her sinuous back. She moved her face close until they swam in each other's eyes.

"I love you," she said.

"I love you," he said.

"I don't see where it changes one damned thing," Charlie Royce said. "If anything, it makes the cheese more binding."

"You sure?" Bea Winks said doubtfully. "If she goes to live with him of her own free will? That proves she volunteered. There was no force or coercion. He didn't kidnap her, rape her, or anything like that."

"Timmy?" Royce asked.

"The law's the law," Ryan said firmly. "Whether the girl submitted willingly or under force and duress. Statutory rape. Contributing to the delinquency of a minor. Even kidnapping, if the DA is hunting for headlines. I'd say you've got him, Mr. Royce, as of this minute. Whether the girl moves in with him or not."

"The man's a fool," Royce said, almost angrily.

"Oh, there's no doubt about that at all, at all. Pussy-mad, he is. Not the first to lose his senses, and not the last."

They were in Bea Winks' chintzy second-floor bedroom. Royce had brought a bottle of prewar White Horse. They were mixing it with Vernor's ginger ale.

"Maybe we should wait," Bea Winks said. "Maybe the girl will get pregnant. Bigger headlines."

"Did he use a rubber?" Royce asked. "Did the girl say?"

"She didn't say, and I don't think she knows."

"Disgusting," Royce said.

"Ah, well," Timmy Ryan said genially, "it's the nature of the beast. Don't count on a babe, Mr. Royce. Hebron could have it knocked easy enough. By his rich Beverly Hills doctor or a quick trip to Mexico. As I see the situation, you've got enough right now. You could blow the whistle tomorrow.''

"Sure, sure," Royce muttered.

He rose suddenly, began to pace jerkily about the room. The others continued a desultory conversation in low voices. Royce listened with half an ear. Timmy Ryan wanted to spread the word of Eli Hebron's wicked behavior by tipping a reporter who had treated Ryan kindly during his recent unpleasantness with the law. Timmy felt he owed the reporter a favor.

Bea Winks thought an anonymous phone call to Louella or one of the other gossip reporters would be wiser. It would have the same result while minimizing the risk of revealing the conspirators' identity.

Listening to them, watching their movements as they talked, drank, smoked, Royce wondered again at their motives. Ryan's weren't too hard to figure: greed and a taste for mischief. Bea Winks' eagerness to join in the plot was more difficult to analyze. Affronts suffered, Royce supposed; insults from Hebron; real and fancied slights by that cool, withdrawn man, who probably never comprehended the hate and fear he inspired, not only by the position of authority he occupied, but by his sureness, careless elegance of dress, and a superiority expressed in a manner no less obnoxious for being natural and justified.

In addition, Royce guessed, Bea Winks' motive might have some link to her sexuality. She seemed to have made Eli Hebron a target for her virulent hatred of men. As if his downfall would be her personal triumph against a sex that had rewarded her talent and ambitions by relegating her to a low-paying job and reducing her—she wasn't quite certain how it had been done—to the status of a parlor house madam, treated with cynical and cheerful contempt.

Charlie Royce was suddenly conscious the other two had broken off their conversation. They were looking at him curiously, waiting. . . .

"I never thought he'd pull a bonehead stunt like that," Royce said. "Asking her to move in. Annenberg will hit the ceiling. If he doesn't tie a can to Hebron, the bank will. Magna couldn't weather the scandal. I just can't believe he could be so stupid."

"I do believe the man's in love," Ryan said mildly. "He's thinking with his balls—begging your pardon, Miss Winks."

"I think I've heard the word before, Timmy," she said.

Charlie Royce went back to his armchair and slumped down again.

"You know," he said, with pleased wonder, "we don't have to blow the whistle at all. Don't tell your reporter, Timmy. We don't have to do anything. The word will get around; you know Hollywood. If nothing breaks in a week or two, an anonymous telephone call to Louella about the girl's real age should get the ball rolling, like Bea says. Or we'll have the mother show up at the studio and make a ruckus. But we'll keep out of it, as far away from it as we can."

"Ah, you're a sly one, Mr. Royce," Ryan beamed. "Made for politics, you are. Yes, I'd say your way is best. Just let the man hang himself."

"What shall I tell the girl?" Bea Winks asked.

"Tell her to move in," Charlie Royce said. He picked

up his glass, held it to the light, peered into it intently. "Got him," he said happily.

The home of Marcus Annenberg in Sherman Oaks was a Tudor mansion. The walls were mullioned stucco; windows were small, diamond-shaped panes of leaded glass; the roof gave the impression of thatch with cleverly designed ceramic tile.

The interior was rich, solid, gloomy. Exposed ceiling beams were everywhere. Walnut doors were two inches thick. There were wall niches, window bays, stained glass transoms. Murky oil paintings adorned the walls, mostly pastoral scenes and still lifes of fresh fruit and dead chickens. All in baroque gilt frames. The furniture was massive, mahogany, overstuffed. It was covered in brown velvet and flowered velours. With lace antimacassars crocheted by Mrs. Florence Annenberg.

Almost every evening, after they had dined alone, Mr. and Mrs. Annenberg spent an hour in their projection room. They owned an extensive collection of early movies that included rare prints of *The Great Train Robbery*, *Rescued from an Eagle's Nest*, and the Corbett-Courtenay fight of 1894. Most of the early reels of Edison, Pathé, Vitagraph, Biograph, Essanay, Imp, Bison, and Selig were in the film vault of Marcus Annenberg. He collected them because he liked to view them. They brought back memories. Of stars, directors, executives, of defeats and victories, of friends and enemies.

Marcus and Florence shared a particular taste for slapstick comedy. The early Keystone one- and two-reelers were their favorites. They watched *Cohen at Coney Island* a hundred times and still laughed. Ford Sterling, Mabel Normand, Hank Mann, Fatty Arbuckle, and Mack Swain were like family. And, of course, Charlie Chaplin. Annenberg thought Charlie's dance with Marie Dressler in *Tillie's Punctured Romance* was the funniest scene ever filmed. He could see it dozens of times and still laugh until his breath caught, his chest pained, his face became congested, and Florence turned to him in alarm.

On this particular night Annenberg had asked Jules, their black butler, to fill the screening hour with old Chaplin shorts: *The Tramp, The Adventurer, The Cure, The Immigrant,* and others. Marcus and Florence settled back with a plate of macaroons between them. When the ceiling light in the projection room went out, it was just as if they were together again in the Kinetoscope Parlor on Fourteenth Street in Manhattan.

Charlie staggered up the steps of the sanatorium and got caught in the revolving door, whirling around and around. Marcus Annenberg began to laugh.

"It's Eli," he said to Florence. "I don't like it."

"The girl?" she asked, watching Charlie falling up the wide staircase.

"First of all," he said, "she works for us. That I don't like. If he wants to go somewhere else, that I wouldn't care. But on the lot it isn't right. People talk, people gossip. Behind their hands. It upsets things."

Attendants tried to give Charlie a massage; he slipped from their grasp in an exquisitely timed ballet. Both the Annenbergs shook with laughter.

"You've seen the girl?" she asked.

"Pretty," he said. "Not like Grace Darling, but pretty. A skinny little thing. What he sees. . . ."

Charlie's steamer trunk held an enormous collection of full bottles. Whiskey was poured into the fountain from which patients dipped medicinal water. The sanatorium began to come apart. The Annenbergs rocked with delight.

"Should I say anything, Flo?" Marcus asked. "To Eli?"

"Maybe it'll pass," she counseled. "A few days, a few weeks. . . ."

"It's going on," he said. "It's bad. Bad for Eli. He's an executive. Like my son. Someday he'll run the company. He shouldn't fool around. It's not right. And also, it hurts the studio. Still no word from Boston. I don't want them to find out our top supervisor is making nice-nice with a girlie who works for us."

"How would they find out?" she asked.

"Flo, Flo, it's in all the junk columns. Everyone knows. Everyone's talking about it. I get calls. And he takes her here, there, everywhere. In public. He doesn't care! It's like he's lost his mind."

Charlie was slipping, sliding, twirling, falling down. The sanatorium was in a drunken uproar. The Annenbergs shouted with glee.

"Maybe you should talk to him, Marcus," she said. "Explain about the loan. What he's doing to the studio. And to his own job, too."

"His future," Marcus Annenberg said. "I treated him like a son we never had. Am I right, Flo?"

"You're right, Marcus."

"And he does this to me. Over some floozy. Like I didn't have enough problems. My brain—it's churning. You'll give me a pill tonight. I can't keep up anymore. Money is tight. Should we convert to sound? The Boston loan. Grosses are down. People sit home listening to the radio. What's happening? I don't know."

"Marcus," she pleaded, "retire. We got enough. Please retire."

"Retire?" he said heavily. "What would I do—wait to die?"

"Sha, sha," she said, putting a finger on his lips. "Don't talk so. Watch Charlie have a hangover."

"I'll talk to Eli," he said.

Charlie Royce came in from the back lot to find a message on his desk. A Mr. Benjamin Sturdevant, of the law firm of Sturdevant & Lee, had called. He asked that Mr. Royce return his call as soon as possible.

"What the hell?" Royce said aloud. He buzzed his secretary and asked if that Sturdevant guy had said what he wanted. She said he hadn't, only that he would appreciate Mr. Royce calling him back.

So Royce called Nate Bigelow, an attorney on retainer to Magna Pictures, Inc.

"Nate? Charlie Royce. Ever hear of a lawyer named Benjamin Sturdevant? The firm is Sturdevant & Lee."

Nate Bigelow laughed. He said Ben Sturdevant was one of the wealthiest attorneys in the Los Angeles area, if not *the* wealthiest. His firm represented big land owners, developers, a few banks, oil companies, citrus growers' associations.

"And politicians," Bigelow added. "Sturdevant is up to his asshole in politics."

"Local or state?" Royce wanted to know.

"Local, state, *and* national," Bigelow told him. "Don't you read the papers? He served as chairman of the State Republican Committee. His wife's father was involved in the Teapot Dome thing. He didn't go to jail, but he should have. Why do you want to know about Ben Sturdevant?"

"Thanks, Nate," Royce said, and hung up. He thought a moment, wondering. . . . Then he called Benjamin Sturdevant. A secretary held him for a moment, but only a moment.

"Mr. Royce?" a heavy courtroom voice said. "This is Benjamin Sturdevant. Thank you for returning my call. I believe we have a mutual friend."

"Oh?" Charlie Royce said cautiously. "Who might that be?"

"A mutual friend in Boston," the resonant voice went on smoothly. "I was hoping we might get together."

"Why not?" Royce said.

"You know the Valhalla Club?"

"I've heard of it."

"Suppose we meet there for lunch. Noon tomorrow. Would that suit you?"

"Suits me fine," Royce said.

"Good. Just ask for me at the desk. See you tomorrow, Mr. Royce."

The supervisor hung up slowly.

The Valhalla Club, on Wilshire Boulevard near Beverly Drive, was the most prestigious private club south of San Francisco. Other exclusive clubs might boast of their tennis courts, golf courses, swimming pools, gymnasiums, bridle paths, dining rooms, and trustworthy bootlegger. The Valhalla had all these things, plus a gentiles-only membership that included, at last count, fifty-nine millionaires. Bankers, politicians, newspaper publishers, ranchers, oilmen, and a few movie executives sweated together in the Valhalla's steam room. The initiation fee was five thousand dollars; annual dues had recently been raised to fifteen hundred dollars.

The club was housed in a mansion that originally belonged to a land baron. He had fled the country, to Greece, after discovering his wife *flagrante delicto* with a Mexican houseboy. The seigneur had shot both to death with a matched pair of silver-mounted Model 1776 British Tower flintlock pistols. The guns were presently displayed in a glass case in the Valhalla's billiard room.

The club had added two wings to the original mansion, enlarged the kitchen, and installed steam room, locker room, gymnasium, and showers in the basement. The chambers upstairs had been made into private dining rooms and the club's offices. The bedroom in which the murders had occurred was now the ladies' retiring room. The main dining room, ballroom, billiard room, card room, library, and reading room were on the ground floor. The original garden had been paved over for tennis courts, and a grove of olive trees chopped down to install a swimming pool. The land baron's stables now served as a garage. Even wealthy Valhalla members marveled at the profligacy of a man who paneled his stables with mahogany and paved them with Italian tiles.

Charlie Royce turned his Chrysler Imperial over to a uniformed valet for parking. He took a quick look around, then strode up the marble steps to the entrance. Another valet held the door open to him. He walked directly to the desk, not staring at the busy lobby scene, but aware of it. He asked for Mr. Benjamin Sturdevant. Another valet, this one a young boy, was dispatched immediately. Charlie Royce waited, inspecting a painted ceiling depicting clouds, cherubs, nymphs, satyrs, and a fulgent sun blessing a California chockablock with orange groves, pecan trees, missions, and oil wells.

For a moment he thought the man walking toward him, smiling, hand outstretched, was Adolphe Menjou. He wasn't, of course. But Benjamin Sturdevant was like enough to stand in for Menjou. He had the same gleaming, wavy hair parted in the middle. The same patrician nose. The same waxed mustache. Perhaps the attorney was aware of the resemblance; he was dressed like Menjou in *A Woman of Paris* (directed by Chaplin). He wore a starched wing collar with polka-dot bow tie, a double-breasted black gabardine jacket filled trigly at the waist, dove gray trousers, white spats. The handkerchief in his breast pocket was folded into three precise points.

"Mr. Royce!" he exclaimed, taking the supervisor's hand in both of his. "This *is* a pleasure! Mr. Archer told me so many good things about you. I've been anxious to make your acquaintance."

Charlie Royce knew it was flattery, but he couldn't resist it.

"Thanks," he said gruffly. "How is Archer?"

"Jim-dandy," Sturdevant said. "He sends his best. 'Lo, Harry. 'Lo, Ed." He waved at two passing men. "Harry Folsom and Ed Heinz," he said to Royce. "Down from Sacramento. Interested in politics?"

"No. Not very much."

"You should be," Sturdevant smiled. "Wonderful bunch of fellows. Our kind. Well, let's see now. . . . They don't serve hard stuff in the dining room, of course. But we fellows keep a little something in our lockers. What would you say to a small libation to keep the juices flowing?"

"Sounds good to me."

"Glad to hear you're not a 'totaler."

The attorney led the way down a corridor, through swinging doors, down a wide staircase. He paused frequently to wave at passersby, shake hands briefly, or exchange a few words.

"You seem to know everyone," Royce said, impressed.

"Well, maybe not *everyone,*" Sturdevant laughed. "But I get around. A lot of friends. A lot of *good* friends. That last fellow was Fred Warnicke. He's opening up Sherman Oaks. A mint!"

The locker room was steamy, with half-naked men rushing to showers, gymnasium, massage room. One completely naked man, very well endowed, strutted by them.

"One of our more prominent members," Benjamin Sturdevant said dryly. But the witticism was lost on Royce.

They sat on a wooden bench. The lawyer took a bottle of gin from his locker.

"You'll like this," he said. "Prewar. I usually take it on ice with a squeeze of fresh lime. How does that strike you?"

"Just right," Royce said.

"Good. Benny!" Sturdevant roared. "Where are you, Benny?"

In a moment, a man came shambling out of the massage room. He was big, soft-muscled, wearing a sweated white undershirt, white canvas pants. His flat feet were bare. One of his ears was a lumpy mass of gristle. There were deep scars over both eyes.

"You call-ed me, Mr. Sturdevant?" he rasped, in a voice as harsh as Barney O'Hara's.

"Benny, I'd like you to meet a good friend of mine, Charlie Royce. Mr. Royce, this is the famous Benny Filippo."

"Aw, Mr. Sturdevant," the big man said, crushing Royce's hand. "I ain't fam-ous."

"Sure you are. Benny fought Jack Sharkey," the lawyer explained to Royce.

"Would have tak-en him, too," the giant said. "But he

cut me, and the blood got all in my eyes. But if it wasn't for—''

"Two setups, Benny," Sturdevant said. "Ice and fresh lime slices."

"Right a-way, Mr. Sturdevant." Benny nodded and shuffled off.

"He gets started on that fight, and there's no stopping him," Sturdevant said.

"Is it usually this crowded here?" Royce asked, looking about.

"Fills up at noontime, yes. Fellows stop by for a swim or workout. Or to have a few from their locker before lunch. Ah, here we are. . . . Thanks, Benny. Don't forget to duck."

"You, too, Mr. Sturdevant."

"That's a little joke Benny and I have," the lawyer said, pouring gin. " 'Don't forget to duck.' Always makes him laugh."

"Yeah," Royce said. He held up his filled glass. "Here's to you."

"Well, let's say here's to us." Sturdevant smiled, lifting his glass. "Here's to a new and profitable friendship."

"I'll drink to that," Royce said. Then: "You weren't kidding; this is the real stuff."

"Glad you like it. If you want a case, just let me know, Mr. Royce. Say, what the hell, we're just two of the boys—right? How about 'Charlie'?"

"Suits me."

"And call me Ben. Everyone calls me Ben—when they're not calling me something worse!"

Royce smiled dutifully, sipped his drink slowly. He wondered where all this affability was leading.

They pulled back their feet to allow two plump men, towels knotted about their hips, pad by to the steam room.

"Too hot in here for you, Charlie?"

"I can take it, Ben."

"Good place to talk business," the lawyer said. "In the dining room, the tables are so close together you don't know who might be listening."

He paused to add gin to their drinks.

"Let me tell you a little something about myself," he said. "So you'll know what this is all about. Mr. Archer's bank has asked me—asked my firm, actually—to represent their interests in the Los Angeles area. I've just come back from Boston—there's a cold, damp, miserable city for you—and got in touch with you right away."

Royce didn't answer. Just listening. . . .

"Archer asked me to tell you how much he appreciates those confidential reports you've been filing. Very valuable, he said. He let me read them, and I agree. Very useful information there, Charlie. Especially about converting to sound."

"You think we will?" Royce asked eagerly. "Will Magna convert?"

"Well, there are problems, Charlie," Sturdevant said slowly. "It's an enormous investment, as you well know, and Archer and his people aren't sure the outlay would be justified. . . ."

"Oh," Royce said, defeated.

"In view of Magna's present management and policies," Sturdevant added.

"Ah," Royce said, alive again.

"We do have a problem here, Charlie. Or several problems. Now I'm going to be absolutely frank and honest and aboveboard with you. Archer told me you're a man who can be trusted to keep his mouth shut.''

"I don't blab," Royce said shortly.

"Good. One problem is the loan Magna is seeking from Archer's bank. They want a lot of money to increase production and buy more movie houses here and in foreign markets. Another problem is converting to sound. Is it worth the investment needed, or will it just be a passing fad?"

"Sound will . . ." the supervisor started.

"No, wait a minute, Charlie; let me finish. Another problem is the situation in the entire movie trade. Up to now it's been run by a bunch of hebe cloak-and-suiters who got in the business by accident and have been running it from the seat of their pants ever since. Maybe it's time for real Americans to take over moving pictures as an industry, just like any other, and to bring in modern business methods and up-to-date management procedures.''

"Exactly what I've been thinking," Charlie Royce said.

"Finally, we have a problem with the present management of Magna. From what you've been writing to Archer and from information I've been able to gather from good friends—some of them right here in this club—all I can conclude is that Marcus Annenberg is on his last legs, practically senile, and losing control of what's going on. Be honest, Charlie—am I right?''

"You're absolutely right, Mr. Sturde—Ben."

"So naturally, we thought—that is, Mr. Archer, his associates, and I thought—that Eli Hebron would take over the top job at Magna. He seemed like a capable, ambitious, talented man. But then you wrote that Hebron is involved with a young woman who, I understand, is presently working for Magna. I've heard gossip about it here in this very locker room, and I've read it in newspaper columns. So I believe it's true."

"Of course it's true," Royce said. "Ask anyone."

"There's only one thing that puzzles us, Charlie," Sturdevant said softly. "In your report you said this woman of Hebron's was under age. I haven't seen *that* in any column or heard any gossip about it. Is it true?"

Once again they pulled back. This time to let a foursome dressed in tennis flannels, carrying oval rackets, push their way through. Charlie Royce welcomed the interruption. It gave him a chance to consider where his best interests lay.

"It's the truth," he told the attorney. "I've seen the evidence. The girl is fifteen. No doubt about it. And she's living in his house right now."

"Living with him?" Sturdevant said, shocked. "Oh my God, that does it! The scandal will hurt, really hurt."

They watched two naked men come trotting out of the shower room, bellies jiggling in front of them. They were roaring with laughter, snapping at each other's puckered haunches with wet towels.

"Charlie," Ben Sturdevant said, "this evidence you've seen of the girl's age. . . . What is it—birth certificate?"

"Yes."

"No possibility of an error? A forgery?"

"No. It's legit."

"And where is the certificate now?"

Royce looked at him. "In a safe place," he said.

Sturdevant returned his stare, then slowly added more gin to their glasses. He held his high in a toast.

"To flaming youth," he said, smiling coldly. He took a sip. Then: "I'm going to make a guess, Charlie. You can tell me if I'm right or wrong. I'm guessing you don't like Eli Hebron.''

"Right," Charlie Royce said. "I hate the son of a bitch."

The words, spoken aloud, intoxicated him.

"Mind telling me why?" the lawyer asked.

"First of all, he's a Jew. Maybe that makes me narrow-minded. I don't give a goddamn. That's the way I am. I'd rather do business with hundred percent Americans."

"No need to apologize for that, Charlie. A lot of us feel the same way, including Mr. Ford."

"And Hebron's got some fancy ideas about movies that I think are a load of crap. Excuse the language, Ben. Listen to him, and you'd think every movie has to be a work of art. Me, I think movies are a commercial product, just like shredded wheat or ketchup. An entertainment product. Find out what the customers want and give it to them. As far as I'm concerned, if a movie doesn't make money, it's a bad film. Even if he's a Yid, Hebron doesn't think that way. He's a lousy businessman."

"Mmm," the attorney said thoughtfully, staring into his glass. "Interesting. Charlie, I said I was going to talk to you like a Dutch uncle, and I am. Is there anyone else who knows the real age of Hebron's girl?"

"A few. But they'll keep their traps shut if I tell them to."

"I suggest you do exactly that," Sturdevant said sharply, looking up at Royce. "I don't care what it costs. Don't worry about the money. Just keep it quiet. Now isn't the time to spread Hebron's name all over the scandal sheets. The Hays Office would come down on Magna like a ton of bricks. The churches would get into the act, and before you know it, theaters would be canceling bookings. Maybe even a public boycott. We don't want that, do we?''

"Guess not," Royce said in a low voice.

"Just hold your horses, Charlie," the lawyer urged, patting the supervisor's arm. "For a little while longer. There's a lot going on here you don't know about. But I can tell you that it's very possible Annenberg will be eased out in the near future. When he goes, Hebron goes. But quietly, without headlines. And when that happens, I can assure you the new management won't forget their friends. Think it over, Charlie."

"All right," Royce nodded. "I'll think about it, Ben."

"Yessireebob!" Sturdevant cried, slapping his shoulder. "That's my boy! Now let's go upstairs and see what the cook's got for us. Some fellows I want you to meet, Charlie. Fellows with gumption and get-up-and-go. You'll like them. Our kind."

And Charlie Royce did meet them—before, during, and after lunch. Hearty, well-dressed men with outdoor tans and the bluff assurance of big money. Mostly they talked politics. The rumor was going around that Calvin Coolidge had decided not to run in 1928. They agreed that if that was true, the Republicans couldn't do better than nominate Herbert Hoover.

"A businessman," someone said. "Good for the country."

"And a Californian," someone else said. "Good for us!"

There were winks, laughter, back slaps. A box of Coronas was passed around. Sunk in a leather club chair in the paneled library, puffing on his good cigar, listening to these rich, genial fellows, Charlie Royce decided he had come home.

*   *   *

Mildred Eljer came to the open doorway of the Makeup Costume building. She stood there, looking at Eli Hebron anxiously. He wouldn't glance in her direction. What he was doing was more important.

"I don't know, Mr. Hebron," Davey Winsor said dubiously. He sighed. "It's the biggest challenge of my career."

Davey was chief makeup man at Magna. He had a crew of three, but Davey did the stars and most of the featured players. It was Winsor who had converted Nino Cavello from an Apache chief to a Latin lover. He was also adept at covering up Margaret Gay's hickeys.

Winsor could have posed for an Arrow collar ad. He had heavy, chiseled features, flaxen hair, blue eyes, and a cleft in his chin deep enough to hold a dime. Everyone knew he was a pansy. His lover was a grip at United Artists. It was said they smoked Mary Warners and carried combs.

Bea Winks was also there. And the agent Abe Vogel and a girl he had brought over in answer to Hebron's call for a "Clara Bow type."

"She doesn't look much like Clara to me," Bea Winks said.

The girl's name was Naomi Wollheim. She stood placidly, chewing two sticks of Juicy Fruit, while they circled about her. She was short, stocky, with heavy thighs and a pneumatic bosom. There was something bovine in her plump features, but that may have been the way she was ruminating. Her hair was beautiful; everyone agreed on that. It fell in glistening chestnut waves to her waist.

"Maybe . . ." Eli Hebron mused. "Maybe we could do something with her."

166

"That hair will have to go," Davey Winsor said. "So outré."

"Is that all right with you, girlie?" Hebron asked. "If we cut off your hair?"

"Sure," she said.

"Sure, *Mr. Hebron*," Abe Vogel barked at her.

"Sure, Mr. Hebron."

"Let's do it, Davey," the supervisor said. "Just to see how it looks."

Winsor put her in a barber's chair, whipped a big cloth about her. He took a pair of heavy shears and began to cut. Long, shiny tresses fell to the floor.

"Want to save that?" Hebron asked the girl. "For a wig?"

"Nah," she said. "Mr. Hebron."

Winsor took her hair down to about four inches all around. The girl's face looked plumper than ever. It hung out.

The makeup man sprayed her hair and began working with clippers and comb.

"We'll give her deep bangs," he said. "Spit curls on the sides, coming down on her cheeks. The back will be shingled."

They watched him coif the girl's hair. The low bangs and spit curls helped reduce the size of her face.

"I'll be damned," Bea Winks said. "I think it's going to work."

"Sure it's going to work," Abe Vogel said proudly. "I told you—a natural for a flapper."

"She'll have to lose at least fifteen pounds," Eli Hebron said. "Maybe twenty."

"I guarantee, Mr. Hebron," Vogel said.

"But not too much," Hebron warned. *"Saftig."*

"Those eyebrows," Bea Winks said. "Too much, Davey?"

"Much too much," he said. "We'll shave them, and pencil in thin lines, lower down."

"And lipstick," Hebron said. "Heavy on the lower lip. Use a gloss. Like a wet pout. Maybe we'll have those front teeth pulled and a bridge put in. The teeth stick out."

They watched as Naomi Wollheim's face was transformed. Dark mascara accented her eyes and lashes. Winsor worked on her cheeks with two shades of powder and rouge to diminish the plumpness, give her cheekbones.

"How's that, Mr. Hebron?" the makeup man asked.

"Fine, Davey. Just what I wanted. She really does look like Clara. Bea, what can we do about those tits?"

"Strap them down," Winks said. "With a tight corselet to give her a waist. Heels about an inch higher than she's wearing."

Winsor whisked the cloth from the girl's neck and shoulders. He spun the barber's chair so she could see her reflection in the big mirror.

"There you are!" he said triumphantly. "How do you like the new Clara Bow?"

Naomi Wollheim burst out weeping. She sounded like a Crane-Simplex horn: Ah-oogah. Ah-oogah.

"Tell her about the money, Abe," Eli Hebron called, hurrying toward the door. Mildred Eljer was still waiting for him.

"It's Mr. Annenberg, Mr. Hebron," she whispered. "He's been calling and calling."

"About what—did he say?"

"He didn't say. Mr. Felder is with him."

Julius K. Felder, treasurer of Magna Pictures, Inc., looked like a five-foot six-inch man who had been racked an additional six inches. Ankles protruded from his trouser cuffs, wrists from his sleeves, neck from his collar. A sharp-edged Adam's apple bobbed. All of him seemed drawn, face and frame. He moved as if ready to snap, pulled apart by trouble and aggravation. No one had ever heard him laugh, although a sad, knowing smile moved his lips when he saw John Barrymore being tortured in *Don Juan*.

When Hebron entered Marcus Annenberg's mud-colored office, Felder was slumped broodingly on the overstuffed couch. Hands were deep in his trouser pockets, head bowed. The back of his neck was bared, meekly awaiting the expected ax.

"So?" Annenberg said sternly to his nephew. "You couldn't come when I called? What was so important?"

"We found the flapper for *Jazz Babies*, Uncle Marc," Hebron said happily. "A real Clara Bow—but fatter."

"She can act?"

"It's not important. She gets killed in a car crash in the first reel. What's going on?"

"Julius," the studio chief said helplessly, "you tell him. I talk about it, my chest hurts."

Felder looked up. He took his hands from his pockets. He scrubbed his face with his palms. It didn't improve a gray complexion, sunken cheeks.

"A lot of things, Eli," he said. "The loan hasn't come through. Boston keeps stalling."

"The hell with them," Hebron said angrily. "We'll go to another bank."

"Hah!" Annenberg said.

"Don't think I haven't tried, Eli. New York, San Francisco—you name it. Everyone is very polite, but everyone says no."

"You think Boston is giving us the knife?"

"I wouldn't go that far," Felder said cautiously. "But you know how banks are. They all know we've done business with Boston all these years for our big-money loans. Now we come to them, and they wonder what Boston knows that they don't know."

Eli Hebron pulled up a chair near Annenberg's desk. He look out a pack of Luckies.

"Mind if I smoke, Uncle Marc?"

"So smoke. Commit suicide. Coffin nails."

The supervisor lighted up. He stared at the treasurer. "It sounds serious, Julius."

"That's only part of it, Eli," Felder said mournfully. "Attendance is down; you know that. So grosses we were counting on haven't come through. Right now we're strapped. Our short-term notes are out at local banks. All in LA. The money we use for day-to-day expenses, salaries, and so forth, until the receipts come in. We can't meet some of those notes. Not today. All right, I thought, no problem. We've been late before, and they've given us extensions. Gladly. They know Magna is good for the money. All these years. Suddenly, no extensions. They're talking snotty. Pony up. That's all I hear: Pony up."

"Jesus Christ!" Hebron said.

"Eli, watch your language," the old man rumbled.

"Julius, it sounds to me like some kind of conspiracy."

"I wouldn't say that exactly," Felder said nervously, biting at a thumbnail. "They know what's going on in the industry. Collections are down, and they want their money."

"But collections have been slow before. This isn't the first time attendance has been off. They never pushed us to the wall before, did they?"

"No. They always extended."

"Then something's going on," Hebron said definitely. He sat back, crossed his legs. "None of the local banks have sold our paper, have they, Julius?"

"No. Not yet they haven't. Or if they have, I haven't heard of it."

"Uncle Marc, what do you think?"

"Think? Think? Who can think?" The old man held his head. "I don't like it, Eli. I don't know what's happening. Everything's falling apart. What's going on? What's going on?"

The other men averted their eyes. They didn't want to watch their chief executive scrabbling with trembling fingers at the afghan across his lap, tears welling from one frog eye.

"Take it easy, Uncle Marc," Hebron said gently. "Just relax. Breathe deeply. Everything is going to be all right."

"You promise me, Eli?" the old man quavered. "Promise? Everything is going to be all right?"

"I promise," Hebron nodded. "Now just relax. Maybe take a little nap. Julius and I will discuss the situation and see what can be done."

He motioned to the treasurer. They moved into the gloom at a far corner of the room. They talked in whispers, their eyes on Marcus Annenberg. His big head came slowly down, jerked up, then sank again. His jowls rested on his chest. One hand fluttered. They heard occasional moans.

"Just how bad is it, Julius?" Hebron asked. "What's the worst that could happen?"

"The worst? Let's assume that no receipts come in the next two months, and we can't float a loan. Then we close. That's the worst."

"Two months? Julius, *two* months?"

"That's all. And that would be stretching our cash reserve. Unless you want to cancel production and start firing people."

"No. Never. That would be the stupidest thing we could do. Then word would get around that we're bleeding, and the banks would close in. We'll keep on just like we're doing."

"Two months, Eli. That's all we have."

"No, Julius, we have three. I have enough to keep us going another month. More, if I sell Paradiso."

"You'd do that, Eli?"

"If I have to. But first, here's what you do. . . . Call in Levine and Al Klinger. Read them the riot act. Tell them to put pressure on their foreign distributors and U.S. exhibitors. Get them scared. Tell them we need the cash. Tell them to call, cable, go see those guys—whatever it takes. Really lean on the exhibitors. If they don't come through, we'll cut them off. Let them try to run a house without movies. They'll pony up, you'll see."

"We may have to take a part, Eli. They're strapped, too."

"Take anything you can get. Take pennies! But tell Meyer and Al to talk hard. Now is when we'll find out who our friends are—when the chips are down. Meyer and Al should tell the exhibitors that. They come through, or they'll get shit from us. We'll fire the managers or take over the independents. Listen, banks aren't the only ones who can throw their weight around. The name Magna still means something; let's use it. Got that, Julius?"

"Sure, Eli. I'll tell them just what you said."

"Good. Lay it on. One other thing. . . . Do you know anyone in the local banks—not a president or anyone like that, but a lower-down—a guy you're close to and could talk to? To find out if anything is going on. You know? I don't like the sound of it. It's like they're all of a sudden ganging up on us. Someone who might be willing to talk to you? His name would never be mentioned, of course. He'd be safe. And maybe a contribution to his favorite charity, if that's what it takes to make him talk. You understand?''

"Sure, Eli," Felder said slowly. "Maybe . . . I can't promise anything definite, but I know a couple of guys like that. I play pinochle with them on Friday night. One works at a bank that doesn't hold any of our paper. Maybe he knows something or could find out.''

"Good," Hebron said. He put his hand on the treasurer's shoulder, pressed him to the door. "Do what you can, Julius. Get that cash coming in, and see if you can find out why suddenly we're being treated this way.''

After Felder left, Eli Hebron came back to stand close to his uncle. Marcus Annenberg was dozing fitfully, with little groans, sudden twitches, muttered words. His heavy hulk was slanted in his wing chair, head hanging, limbs slack. The supervisor shook his shoulder gently.

"Uncle Marc," he whispered. "Time to get up, Uncle Marc. . . .''

Annenberg roused slowly. He looked up with bleary eyes.

"Florence?" he said. "Time to get up?''

"No, Uncle Marc. It's Eli. You're in your office. It's time to go home.''

"Time? What time is it?''

"Late," Hebron said. "It's late. I'll call your car.''

"I have to go to the toilet first," Annenberg said fretfully.

"Sure, Uncle Marc. Do you want me to help you?''

"I can do it," the old man protested. "I don't need any help."

Hebron went into the outer office. He told Annenberg's secretary to have his car brought around. When the chief executive came out of the lavatory, his fly was open, his shirttail hanging out. Hebron buttoned him up, tucked him in, straightened his tie, smoothed his jacket.

"All right, all right!" Annenberg said grumpily, batting his hands away. "Enough already."

The supervisor took his arm. They walked slowly down the outside stairway. They rested a moment on each landing. Annenberg's face was blotchy. He looked about vaguely at the bustling yard.

"You got a flapper for *Jazz Babies,* Eli? You said?"

"Perfect for the part, Uncle Marc. Just like Clara Bow."

"Clara Bow!" Annenberg snorted. "Clara Kimball Young. *There* was something. And Norma Talmadge. Mae Marsh. Marguerite Clark. May Allison. You never heard of them."

"I've heard of them, Uncle Marc."

"Shirley Mason," the old man muttered. "Mary Miles Minter."

The big, black Pierce-Arrow was waiting in front of the administration building. The uniformed chauffeur was standing at an opened door.

"Get in," Annenberg said to Eli Hebron.

"Uncle Marc, I have work to do."

"A minute. To talk. You," he said to the chauffeur, "go away. Come back in five minutes. Like that."

They climbed into the back seat. Hebron slammed the door. He tucked the lap robe about his uncle's knees.

"Eli, Eli," Annenberg wailed, "why are you doing this to me?"

174

The supervisor, shocked, turned to stare at him.

"Doing what?" he demanded. "What am I doing, Uncle Marc?"

"A *shiksa* makes no difference," the old man shouted. "No difference at all. You understand?"

"Oh," Hebron said. "That."

"But what you're doing to me. The studio. A girl who works on the lot? In your house? Eli, it's all over town. Everyone's talking."

"Let them talk."

"The scandal," Annenberg groaned. "We've got to be so careful. You know what people think. The rest of the country about Hollywood. They hear about this, and we're bums. You understand? Bums! Boston won't give us our money. Maybe they heard. They wouldn't lend money to bums!"

"Uncle Marc, that isn't—"

"And if not for me and your Aunt Flo—how you're hurting us!—and not for the business, then for yourself. A nice, clean boy like you. A son! Yes, a son to me and your Aunt Flo! It's shameful. All right, a little fooling around I could understand. A weekend even. But living in the same house? In your dead wife's bedroom. God should rest her soul. Have you lost your senses, Eli? Is that it? You're out of your head? To do what you're doing it must be. Why? Tell me why? I'm listening."

"I love her, Uncle Marc."

"You love her?" the old man gasped, jerking back as if struck across the face. "You love her? *Gott zol uphieten!*"

They sat in silence. The activity of the yard surged around them. A man herded a gaggle of geese toward Outdoor Stage Two. A Chinese princess was carried by in a palanquin. A red Stutz Bearcat was driven to the back

175

lot. A troop of French Zouaves trotted along, carrying their muskets at port arms. General Grant held a match for Mark Antony. A crowd of girls in one-piece bathing costumes ran giggling to Indoor Stage One. The radio in the gate hut was blaring "Ain't We Got Fun."

"You going to marry her, Eli?" Marcus Annenberg asked timorously.

"I don't know."

"Maybe you should, Eli," he said in a low voice. "It don't look right. I'm tired. I'll go home now."

"Do that, Uncle Marc. Get a good night's sleep."

"Sleep!" the old man said bitterly.

Charlie Royce sat behind the wheel of his Chrysler Imperial, parked in front of Bea Winks' home. For the third time, he hauled his dollar Ingersoll from his watch pocket and peered at it in the darkness. The girl's lateness angered him. It made him the supplicant.

Finally, the porch light came on. The door opened. Gladys Divine came out slowly, pulling a white polo coat about her shoulders, sleeves swinging free. A silk scarf was tied, bandeau fashion, about her dark hair. She sauntered toward Royce's car, then paused briefly to light a cigarette. It could have been a take, she moved so artfully.

He leaned across to open the door for her. She got in without saying a word. She slammed the door, pressed back against it. She was as far away from Charlie Royce as she could get. He saw her dimly in the gloom, but he caught her young, fresh scent. She smelled like a baby, he thought. For a moment, just a moment, he envied Eli Hebron, hated him, wanted to be him. The last realization shocked him.

"What's the problem?" he asked harshly. "Bea says you're making trouble."

"No trouble," she said, looking straight ahead, staring through the windshield. "I'm living with him. I'm in his house. That's what you wanted, isn't it?"

"That part of it's true," he acknowledged. "No problem there. Now I want to move in your mother and brother. Under fake names, of course. As cook and butler."

"What for?"

"Just to keep an eye on you." He grinned.

Then she turned to look at him.

"You're full of shit," she said. "You want to take him over. You want to own him. Because he's so much better than—"

He leaned forward casually and slapped her across the face. A cruel, hard blow. It snapped her head around.

"Don't horse me, girlie," he said in a rough voice. "Don't ask me why I do what I do. Don't even wonder about it."

She didn't weep or even rub her cheek.

"I'll kill you," she said.

"No, you won't," he said. "You think I'm the only one in on this? Kill me, and another man takes my place. And another. There's no way out for you, kiddo."

She was silent.

"Listen," he said, "why are we squabbling? We can be friends. I treat you square on the lot, don't I? Good parts, plenty of footage. All the right angles. You see that item in Louella's column? The interview in *Motion Picture Story?* You're on your way, Glad. Everything you ever wanted. You're going to be a star. Everyone says so. You'll have the lead in my next. We start shooting Monday. A great scenario. You'll love it. A costume thing.

You're Mary, Queen of Scots. How's that? Just what you wanted—right? Maybe a big premiere at Grauman's. You want to give all that away?''

"I don't like what you're doing to him," she muttered. "It's dirty."

"Don't play innocent with me, toots," he said coldly. "I know better. You'd sell your soul to get away from that shithouse with the chickens and goats. And that's smart. Just think about yourself. Your own career. You don't need Hebron. You'll be a star without him. That's what you want, isn't it? You want to be a star. Loved by millions." He took a cigar from his breast pocket, bit off the tip. He spit the loose tobacco out the open window. Then he lighted the cigar with a wooden kitchen match. He twirled the cigar in his lips. He blew smoke up into the air with great enjoyment. The dark car filled with smoke. A coffin of smoke.

"Look at it this way," he said. "Suppose you go to Hebron and tell him your real age. That's the end of you as far as he's concerned. You're out of his life and out of the business. But that still wouldn't stop your mother from screaming to the cops. You're a minor, Glad. Your mother has got to protect you. So she destroys Hebron. And you end up in the family pigpen with the smelly Chick Sale out back. Is that what you want?''

"No," she said dully.

"So you really can't do anything, can you?"

"I can kill myself," she said in a low voice.

"Not you," he laughed. "Never. You're not a star—yet. And if you welsh, we find someone else. It's that simple. So play along with me. It's a mean, hard business, baby.''

"That's what he said."

"Did he? Well, for once he was right. Take it while you can, Glad. Look out for Number One. That's all you've got to do. Give him some excuse for firing the cook and butler. They got fresh with you, you don't like them, any excuse. He'll do whatever you ask; you know that. Then we'll move in Bertha and Leo. Your own flesh and blood. Won't that be swell?"

She didn't answer. She seemed to shrink down within her coat. Her head was pulled in, shoulders bowed, all of her in shriveled despair.

He leaned forward. He put a hand lightly on her thigh. He gripped the springiness. Young warmth.

"Listen, girlie," he said hoarsely, "there's nothing he's giving you that I can't give you better. What say you and me, we go—"

But she was out of the car with a high-pitched wail and running. Down the darking street. Heels clacking. He let her go. He finished his cigar before he went up to Bea's place.

In 1927 a few men still rode horses to work at Magna Studios. They tethered them in the back lot. Occasionally they rented them out for the day, if Charlie Royce was shooting a Western scene or if horses were needed for a medieval joust or a farm sequence.

But most Magna employees drove to work in their own cars. Early arrivals found space in the dusty parking lot. Latecomers parked at curbs around the fenced compound and walked through the gate. There was a roofed garage behind the administration building, but that was reserved for executives' cars. Most of them were chauffeur-driven.

The executive garage was Magna's forum. With eight hours or more each day with nothing to do, idle chauffeurs engaged in a nonstop debate on such subjects as Dempsey vs. Tunney, the possibility of Babe Ruth setting a new home run record, the value of Judge Lindsay's suggestion of "companionate marriage," the activities of Al Capone in Chicago, auction vs. contract bridge, the titillating case of Daddy Browning, the Scopes trial, Red Grange, Mah-Jongg vs. checkers, Floyd Collins, the tribulations of Andy Gump, Loeb and Leopold, and Roxy and His Gang vs. The Happiness Boys.

On this day the subject under heated discussion was the trial and conviction of Nicola Sacco and Bartolomeo Vanzetti. The two Italian-born anarchists were scheduled for execution in September. Their guilt or innocence was furiously debated by the chauffeurs, with fists brandished, feet stamped, and sputtering confrontations, nose to nose.

Barney O'Hara took no part in this argument. He leaned against the fender of Hebron's limousine, much amused, sucking on a matchstick. Timmy Ryan, in uniform, came into the garage. He listened to the uproar a few moments, then sauntered over to O'Hara.

"You care what happens to a couple of dagoes, Barney?" he grinned.

"Not so much," O'Hara said in his raspy voice. "But it helps pass the time. Listen to them go!"

"Dandy lawyers they are," Ryan scoffed. "Wouldn't have a pint on you, would you now?"

" 'Fraid not, Timmy."

"Anything in Hebron's car?"

"Nary a drop," O'Hara said. "Isn't Sammy around?"

"If he is, I can't find him," Ryan said. "And me with fur on my tongue."

"You'll have to make a run to Jack Newton's speak." Barney O'Hara laughed. "I hear you're a regular customer."

Timmy Ryan stared at him. He showed his store choppers.

"Oh?" he said casually. "Now who'd be telling you that?"

"Fig mentioned it," O'Hara said just as casually. "Said you stop by two or three times a week."

"Ah, well," Ryan smiled. "It's a nice place. Quiet like. And Fig doesn't water his booze."

"With Charlie Royce?" Barney O'Hara said. "The two of you drink there?"

"With Charlie Royce?" Ryan cried. "Now what would I be doing drinking with the likes of him? Too rich for my blood. A man with his mazuma wouldn't be drinking in Newton's blind pig."

"That's what I figured," O'Hara nodded. He eased his neck brace. "But Jack described him to a T."

"Nah," Timmy Ryan said. "He must have meant a buddy of mine. A dick on the city Bunco Squad. Big, lumbering lad he is. Red in the face, like Royce. I've had a few with him at Newton's. That must be the boyo Jack saw."

"Like as not," O'Hara said indifferently. "This buddy of yours on the Bunco Squad—wears vests, does he?"

"Oh, sure," Ryan said. "All the time."

"Well, that's who it was then," Barney O'Hara said. "See you around, Timmy."

He lounged away. Ryan watched him go. Then he walked slowly to the gate hut. He chased Mac out and used the hut Dictograph to call Charlie Royce's office. The secretary told him the supervisor was out on the back lot shooting a wagon spill for one of his Westerns.

Timmy Ryan hitched a ride on the commissary truck taking sandwiches, coffee, and soda pop to back-lot crews. It took him awhile to find Royce.

He saw the supervisor and his production crew clustered around a Conestoga that had thrown a wheel. A hostler had unhitched the six horses and led them away. Several men were straining at the tilted rear corner of the wagon that rested on a bare axle. They couldn't lift the bed high enough for the big wheel to be slipped back on.

Ryan watched Charlie Royce shuck his heavy tweed jacket. He rolled it up and put the pad across his shoulders.

"All right," he commanded the men, "try it again."

His crew strained at the wagon. They got it almost level. Then Royce, bent over, hands on knees, got his shoulders and back underneath. He grimaced as he pressed upward. His bent legs trembled. Veins stood out in his neck and forehead. The tilted corner rose slowly. Two men rammed the wheel back onto the spindle.

"Got it!" one of them shouted exultantly.

The lifting men eased their burden down, letting the wheel take the weight gradually. Charlie Royce crawled out from underneath. He straightened up, arched his back, stretched his spine and neck. Then he shook out his tweed jacket. He put it on again, straightened his tie, dusted his trouser cuffs.

"Take a break," he called to his crew. "Ten minutes."

He saw Timmy Ryan standing there. He motioned with his head. Ryan followed him to the shade of a magnificent monkeypod.

"That was something, that was, Mr. Royce," Ryan said admiringly. "Wouldn't care to be in your boots if your lads had let the wagon slip."

Royce shrugged. "What brings you out in the wilds, Timmy? Want to see me?"

Ryan told him about his conversation with Barney O'Hara. Charlie Royce listened intently. His expression didn't change. When the chief finished, the supervisor wandered up and down, hands in pockets, staring at the packed earth.

"That's it?" he asked finally.

"That's it."

"You think he bought your story?"

"No," Ryan said. "He had you dead to rights, Mr. Royce—vest and all."

"Shit." Charlie Royce sighed. "Bad luck. But who could have figured the saloonkeeper would remember us? You think O'Hara will tell Hebron?"

"He might," Timmy Ryan said. "And he might start prying."

"Yes," Royce nodded, "he might. I can't chance it, Timmy. Not right now. Too much riding on this. Can you buy him off?"

"I can try."

"Then try."

"And if he won't take?"

"Use your own judgment. I don't want to know about it."

"It'll cost."

"No problem," Charlie Royce said.

"Gimme a little kiss," Eli Hebron sang, "will ya, huh?"

"Okeydoke," Gladys Divine said promptly, and kissed him.

"You call that a kiss?" he scoffed. "The cutting-room floor for that kiss. Bosco used to give me better kisses."

"Like this?" she asked, and began to lap his mouth, nose, eyes, cheeks, ears. . . .

"Glad," he laughed, pushing her away. "All right, all right. I'm sorry, I apologize. You're a great kisser."

"And that's not all?" she said intently, staring at him in one of her lightning changes of mood.

"That's not all," he agreed.

"Really?" she whispered eagerly. "Really and truly? Am I a good lover, Eli? Do I do everything you want me to do?"

"Everything," he nodded, frightened by her fervor. "You're much woman."

"Yes, I am," she said fiercely. "A woman. I *am* a woman." She gripped his hand tightly. "Much woman," she repeated.

They stood on the porch, impatiently waiting for Leo to bring the car around. He was a miserable butler, as Bertha was a disastrous housekeeper-cook. Both of them slovenly and impudent.

Hebron had fired Robert and Mrs. Birkin at Glad's urging. Robert, she had said, was sanctimonious. Mrs. Birkin was dictatorial. To take their place she found Leo and Bertha. Hebron was disgusted by the butler's ineptitude, revolted by the housekeeper's cooking. But if it made Glad happy. . . .

Leo finally brought the Packard roadster from the garage. He pulled up abruptly with a spray of gravel. He got out grinning, tossing lank blond hair from his forehead.

"Here's your jalopy, Eli," he said.

"It's *Mr. Hebron*," Gladys said angrily. "You remember that."

"Sure," Leo smiled insolently. "I'll remember. You folks have a nice time."

Glad had learned to drive. She slid behind the wheel. Hebron walked around to the passenger side. He hardly had the door closed when she took off with a jerk that snapped his head back.

"Take it easy," he said mildly.

"I can't stand him," she cried furiously.

He said nothing to that.

"Well," she sighed finally, "he needs the job."

"I suppose."

"You're so sweet," she said. "Letting him and Bertha stay on. They're awful, aren't they?"

"Yes," he said.

"Let's not talk about them," she said firmly. "Let's talk about us. Are you hungry, Eli?"

"Not much. Why?"

"Let's drive up the coast. Can we, Eli? Please?"

"Sure, Glad. Whatever you say. I know a nice place in Ventura. We could drive up there for dinner."

"Is it fancy?" she asked anxiously. "Am I dressed all right for it?"

"You look beautiful," he assured her.

"Thank you," she said faintly.

He was content to let her drive. He sat back in the corner, turned so he could watch her. She handled the car expertly, moving easily through the business of clutching and shifting gears that he found so difficult.

"Didn't get your license yet, did you?" he asked.

"I've been so busy. You know that. But I'll get around to it, Eli. Maybe next week."

"You'd better," he warned. "If we get stopped, we'll both go to jail."

"As long as we're together," she giggled. "Come closer to me, Eli."

He slid across the seat.

"Closer," she commanded. "Right up tight."

So he did. Then he said, "Keep both hands on the wheel, Miss Divine."

The inn was south of Ventura. It was an Italian restaurant, set between highway and ocean. There was no sign; just a brightly lighted doorway. But the parking area was almost filled. They both took a drink from Hebron's silver flask before they got out of the car.

The headwaiter knew Hebron; they were ushered to a table on the glassed terrace overlooking the sea. After a whispered confab, a mustachioed waiter brought them tea cups and saucers. Everyone in the crowded restaurant seemed to be drinking tea.

They held up their cups to each other. The straight rye was powerful. Gladys gasped and coughed. Hebron added a little water to her cup.

"Sip, don't gulp," he advised. "Now . . . what shall we start with?"

"You order, Eli. I always love what you order."

"You love all food," he smiled. "I've never known a woman with your appetite. It's a pleasure to watch you."

"I don't eat too much, do I, Eli? I'm not getting fat, am I?"

"Of course not."

"Good," she said happily. "And tonight I'm going to use all the right forks and spoons. You'll see. I start at the outside and work in—right?"

"Right," he laughed. "Didn't you use salad forks back in New Jersey?"

"Oh," she said casually, turning her head to inspect the other diners, "sometimes, I guess."

This evening she was wearing a gown borrowed from the studio. It had been designed for Margaret Gay and worn in *Broken Hearts*. It was a short chemise of silver bugle beads, sleeveless, suspended from narrow straps. She wore a headband of the same material, with a white aigrette, and strapped silver pumps tied with silver ribbon bows. There were snake bracelets around the biceps of both arms.

Hebron thought her the most exciting woman in the room. And the admiring stares she attracted seemed as much a compliment to him as to her. She was conscious of the attention, he knew. She had already learned the demeanor of a movie actress on public display—gestures a little broader, laugh a little louder, expressions more artful: wide smiles, delicious pouts, a sinuous twisting of bosom and hips. He had seen Grace Darling do the same thing. He did not resent it. They were players; adulation was their mirror.

"Why are you looking at me that way?" she said. "You seem so sad."

The waiter began serving their baked clams, and Hebron did not answer. But she continued staring at him. He was wearing a black tight-waisted tuxedo with a wing collar and studs and cuff links of black onyx. She saw him as a slender black bird with white breast and glittering eyes, and she thought him the most exciting man in the room. She lowered her glance to his long, graceful hands, and closed her eyes a moment, remembering. . . .

They spoke infrequently during dinner; Hebron had learned she preferred to devote her entire attention to her food. He watched, fascinated, as she worked her way industriously through the baked clams, salad, pasta, steaks in a garlicky tomato sauce, French fried zucchini. He couldn't finish his steak; she finished it for him. But he emptied the two Coca-Cola bottles of homemade red wine that had been served them, compliments of the management.

"Ice cream," she demanded. "Chocolate ice cream with whipped cream."

"And a cherry on top?"

"All right," she said demurely. "If you insist."

He laughed and ordered the sundae. They both had coffee. He longed for a brandy and settled for another teacup of the powerful rye.

"Satisfied?" he asked her. "Finally?"

She sighed, nodded, patted her lips delicately with a napkin, just as she had seen Pauline Frederick do it in *La Tosca*.

"Oh, that was so *good*," she said. "The best food I've ever eaten."

"You always say that, Glad. Anyone would think you'd been starved as a child."

"Could I have a cigarette, Eli?"

She had started using a long ivory holder, but he could forgive her even that. He held a match. He watched as she manipulated the holder artfully, sitting upright with her sparkling headband and aigrette, looking about as grandly as a marchioness.

"Glad," he said, shaking his head, "you really are divine."

She caught his mockery at once and collapsed, giggling.

"You don't mind it, Eli—the holder?"

"Of course I don't. Everything you do is a joy. You're the best thing that ever happened to me."

Her face whitened.

"Don't . . ." she started to say, but then a young couple was standing alongside their table. Gladys and Eli looked up, startled.

"Beg your pardon, sir," the young man said. "Hate to interrupt, but my wife she wondered if—"

"Are you Gladys Divine?" the young woman burst out. "I had to ask. Please forgive me. Are you?"

"Yes." Glad smiled. "I'm Gladys Divine."

"I knew it!" the woman cried ecstatically. "I just knew it! Didn't I tell you, Harry? I saw you in *Spring Roundup*, Miss Divine, and I thought you were simply grand."

"Thank you. Thank you very much."

"Could I have your autograph? Please, Miss Divine?"

"Of course."

But there was nothing to write on and nothing to write with. Hebron signaled a waiter. Pencil and paper were brought.

"What's your name?"

"Florence Kyle, Miss Divine."

"I'll write: 'To Florence, with much love and many thanks, Gladys Divine.' How's that?"

"Oh, thank you, Miss Divine, thank you! It means so much to me."

The bustle around Hebron's table attracted attention. In a few moments a small crowd had gathered. Pencils and pens, and paper, cuffs, napkins, and calling cards were thrust at Gladys.

"Please, Miss Divine. Something personal."

"My name's Marvin, Miss Divine."

"Please sign here, Miss Divine."

"Could you make it out to Nicky, Miss Divine?"

A wild-eyed, red-haired woman, holding paper and pen, plucked at Eli Hebron's sleeve.

"Are you somebody?" she demanded.

"No," he smiled. "I'm nobody."

Gladys danced out to the car, shouting with delight.

"The first time!" she cried. "Eli, the very first time!"

"Not the last," he assured her.

"Did I do it right, Eli? Was I, you know, nice to them and not stuck-up?"

"You handled it fine. Just right."

"Oh, I'm so happy! So happy!"

She burst out laughing again, threw her arms about him, kissed him, drank avidly from the flask. Then quieted. Calmed. Took up his hand, kissed his fingertips, one by one.

"Darling," she said huskily, "thank you, thank you, thank you."

"You did it yourself, Glad. You don't owe me anything."

"I do, I *do!*"

"No." He shook his head. "I owe you. I told you, you're the best thing that ever happened to me."

She began weeping, wobbling her head slowly from side to side. He tried to comfort her, but she would not be soothed. Nor would she tell him why she wept.

Finally, she sniffed, wiped her eyes with the back of her hand. She took off her headband and aigrette, tossed them behind the seats.

"Could we put the top down, Eli?"

"You won't be too cold?"

"No."

They lowered the canvas roof, folded it back, snapped on the cover. They drained the flask before they started back.

"Want me to drive?" he asked.

"No."

The car gained speed on the unlighted highway. Telephone poles flashed by. They overtook cars, pulled out, passed with a furious honking of horns. Cars coming in the other direction whizzed by. The road spun away beneath their wheels. Winds cut at them, whipped their hair. The darkness pulled them on, faster, faster. He turned to look at her. Wide-eyed, white teeth gleaming, head thrust forward. Her body strained to the wheel, the thundering engine. She shouted once, but her words were lost. He laughed. She heard him and she laughed. They laughed, both, laughing together, roaring, careening through the night to nowhere, daring the black, on and on, neither of them wanting to stop, ever, but to go faster, faster, leaving it all behind, escape, together, into the heart of dark. . . .

Slowly up the graveled driveway to the door of Paradiso. They were silent, drained. For a moment they had flown free. But the night was there, whole, and the present weighed them down. Hand in hand, they walked up the wide staircase to their mirrored room. Quiet clung to them. The closed room was as final as a cell.

Watery moonlight washed through curtained windows. The silvered room flickered with phantoms. Glittering wraith and gleaming ghost faced each other and touched cool lips.

He moved away, to the Victrola near the bed. He wound it slowly, gears clicking. He put on a new Louis Armstrong record. He came back to take her in his arms. Gravely they began to dance, floating in a gentle fox-trot.

"Some of these days," she sang softly, "you're gonna miss me, honey."

Around and around they went, cloudy reflections whirling across the walls. Then the room revolved about them. Mirrors flickered by until the music ended, the needle scratched and clicked, the machine stopped. Still they danced in gloom, moving with small steps, burning eyes locked. They held each other with flat, pressing hands.

She turned away from him. He watched sadly as she unhooked her dress and stepped out of it. She left it on the rug, a glistening puddle. Removed her unboned corset and let it drop. She slumped into an armchair, put her head back. Raised stockinged knees, caught her heels on the chair edge. She held white arms out to him. The stone eyes of her snake bracelets winked.

He fell to his knees before her. She pulled him close. He bent to her, head bowed. The slender bird feeding.

Sometime during the night he awoke, and she was gone from the bed. He saw her standing at the windows. At first he thought she had dressed again. But then, through sleep-clogged eyes, he saw her naked flesh was spangled with moonlight. She stood motionless, and he wanted to call to her. But she turned, came back to the bed.

"Glad?" he said drowsily.

She moved close to him, took him into her young arms. He fell asleep again, a soft nipple pressed gently between his lips.

When he awoke late the next morning, a Sunday, sunlight was flaming through the room. He was alone again. He rose and went naked to the window. He stood where she had stood the night before. He parted the curtains and looked down.

He could see one end of the swimming pool, a corner of the garage. But directly below the window was the slope of lawn that Taki had tried to convert into a Japanese garden. Poor Taki. He had endured two days of Leo and Bertha. Then with hissed apologies and much bowing, he had pleaded the press of work elsewhere and disappeared from Paradiso.

Already the house and grounds showed signs of neglect: lawn unmowed, gravel unraked, shrubbery untrimmed, the terrace and swimming pool littered with twigs and fallen leaves. Hebron wondered if his home had become infected by his disorder. Could mansion and lawn suffer from disorientation, loneliness, loss of resolve?

As he gazed sadly down, he saw Gladys Divine stroll from the terrace. She wandered down the lawny slope toward the coppice that marked the rear boundary of Hebron's property. The grass was high; it covered her shoes. She had a switch, and swung it idly at golden dandelion heads that poked above the green.

She was dressed for a garden party: a gown of flowered chiffon with billowing skirt and full sleeves. And she wore a wide-brimmed straw hat that shaded her face. The hat was bound with a long scarf of white silk.

He saw her begin to run. Not, he knew, for any reason other than the sun shone, the sky was blue, it was a glorious day, and she was young. She ran across the lawn, arms outstretched. Skirt, sleeves, scarf, all sailing out behind her.

The windowpane framed her like a movie screen. He moved slightly to keep her running figure composed within the frame. He dreamed of shooting such a scene: a young, live woman floating across a lawn. And running after her, reaching, trying to capture her, a man in white. The two figures etched against a blue sky. Both vibrant in sunlight. Everything there: beauty, mystery, a hint of endless, doomed pursuit. A meaningful image.

He turned away from his dream. He went into the bathroom, shaved, bathed, dressed carefully: white flannel suit, white shirt and scarf, white shoes. Then he went downstairs, found Glad, and asked her to marry him.

Ed Jenkins was reading through the first draft of *The Dream Lover* scenario. Occasionally, mechanically, his hand rose, he took a sip from his glass of gin without lifting his eyes from the page. Tina Rambaugh, behind her desk, was watching him. Finally, Jenkins turned the last page.

"Well?" the young girl asked anxiously. "What do you think?"

He didn't answer. He refilled his glass with gin. He pulled the burlap-wrapped chunk of ice from under his desk and began to stab at it with an ice pick.

"I think it'll play," Tina said. "The vamp scene is a doozy."

Jenkins slid ice chips into his drink. He sipped, then rolled his eyes and waggled his head in an imitation of Willie Howard playing a drunk.

"Come on, Ed," the girl said. "What do you think?"

"It's philosophical," he said.

"The scenario?"

"No, fatso, not the scenario. It's good. It'll play all right. My objections are philosophical. Very deep."

She sighed, put her feet up on the desk. The soles of her shoes were turned to him.

"Oh," he said, "you're wearing bloomers today. And pink! Very hotsy-totsy."

"Let's hear your deep, philosophical objections."

"It's the whole *idea* of the movie. I'm not sure Hebron knows what he's doing. In effect, he's saying dreams and fantasies are a waste of time. We should all buckle down, face reality, and find happiness! Right?"

"Well," she said cautiously, "more or less."

"Do you believe that, Tina?" he asked sharply.

"To a point. You can daydream your life away. Mark Twain said all life is a dream."

"He was just trying to be funny."

"The hell he was; he was serious. But that's neither here nor there. Ed, the movie isn't against dreams. In fact, it makes the point that the hero's fantasies are the only way he can cope with reality. They're like booze or nose candy. They compensate for his dull-as-dishwater, bumbling existence. All his dreams are wonderfully successful. He wins a duel; he rescues a maiden; he conquers wild animals. Now get this. . . . It's only when he tries to translate one of his dreams into reality—the great lover scene—does he come to grief.''

"My point exactly. Follow that reasoning, and Columbus never should have stepped foot on board. Get it?"

"Oh, I get it," she said. "But Columbus' dream wasn't a fantasy; it was a hope based on all the scientific evidence available at the time. In *The Dream Lover* the hero's dreams are completely loony. No logic to them at all. Most people's dreams are like that."

"Are they?" he said lazily. "What do you dream about, sweetums?"

"None of your damn business," she said. "I'm just saying there's a difference between dreams as hopes and dreams as fantasies. The hopes are possible of fulfillment. The fantasies are doomed."

"Why?"

"Because," she said exasperatedly. "The world isn't built like that. It's got no time for hallucinations."

"All right, supposing you're correct—just *supposing*—is this what we should be telling the customers: that their dreams are a crock of shit?"

"I like the deep, philosophical way you have of putting things, dear."

"Take Eli Hebron, our esteemed boss," Jenkins said moodily. "What was his dream? Based on hope, not an illusion. To find a beautiful young bimbo, woo her and win her, marry her, settle down and live happily ever after. So what happens? He finds her and woos her all right. Then he pops the question, and she turns him down flat. Exit dream.''

Tina Rambaugh brought her feet down with a thud. She leaned across the desk, staring at him.

''Ed, how the hell do you know that?''

''I'll tell you exactly how I know it. Hebron had a screaming argument with old man Annenberg in Annenberg's office. It was so loud that Annenberg's secretary, Sue Marsh, overheard it. She says. She probably was on the Erie right next to the door. Anyway, she heard Hebron say he had asked Gladys Divine to marry him, and she turned him down. So Annenberg told him to kick Divine out of his house or the scandal would ruin the studio. Hebron said he wouldn't do it, that he loved the girl, needed her, and she could stay as long as she wanted.''

''But how did you find out about this?''

''Simple. Sue Marsh was in the can and told Betty Novack. Betty is Al Klinger's secretary. Betty is also keeping house with Fred Driscoll! He's one of Eddie Durant's carpenters. Fred and I share a jug of dago red occasionally. So Sue Marsh told Betty Novack, who told Fred Driscoll, who told me.''

''Why did Divine turn Hebron down?''

''According to what I heard—or what Sue Marsh heard—she said she was afraid marriage would hurt her career. She's just starting out and beginning to attract a following. Hank Cushing is already talking about starting a Gladys Divine fan club here in LA. Divine thinks getting hitched right now wouldn't help her. She wants a little of the fast life first. You know: lots of beaux, wild parties, travel to glamorous places. To give her fans something to dream about. She doesn't want to become a housewife like everyone else. Not right now she doesn't. She's probably right. But my point is, there's Hebron's dream—not a wild fantasy, but a hopeful dream—brought to dust, as the poets say. Is that what we want to show the customers in *The Dream Lover?* That their hopes are doomed? It's a downbeat movie, kiddo. I don't think the public will go for it.''

''You're saying that just because Hebron struck out with Gladys Divine.''

''Nah.'' He shook his head gloomily. ''I'm saying it because it's true. Let's face it: All our dreams are bullshit. We're just kidding ourselves. But I don't think this particular truth is commercial. I don't think we should rub the customers' noses in it. They won't thank us for it. And they won't like the movie.''

''What's so terrible about settling down with wife and kiddies?''

''Nothing—if you haven't dreamed of something better.''

''Jesus Christ, Ed!'' she burst out. ''You're a sour old cynic.''

''No, I'm not. Just realistic.''

She came over behind his desk. She sat on his lap, put a plump arm around his neck.

''What if the boss comes in?'' he said.

''We'll tell him we're doing research on a love scene. When the hell are you going to introduce me to a fate worse than death?''

He looked at her speculatively, blue eyes narrowing. ''Soon,'' he said, taking hold of her thick waist.

Her eyes widened. Then she ran her stubby fingers through his sandy hair. She smiled nervously.

''You're on,'' she said, a tremor in her voice. ''You won't back out?''

"Not me."

"I thought you told me you didn't go for young inexperienced women?"

"You ever hear about the forty-year-old man who fell in love with a ten-year-old girl? He married her, even though he was four times older than she was. But in five years, she was fifteen and he was forty-five, and he was only three times as old as she was. And fifteen years later, she was thirty and he was sixty, and he was only twice as old. Now the question is: How long do they have to be married before they're the same age?"

"You're dizzy, you know that, Ed?"

"I know."

"About us—you weren't kidding?"

"I wasn't kidding."

"I finally got to you, huh?"

"Nah," he said cruelly, "I just want to demolish your dream."

"You bastard!" she cried.

Charlie Royce hadn't been invited to the party. That was the girl's doing, he was certain, not Hebron's. He would have enjoyed seeing the inside of Hebron's mansion. It would have been a pleasure to watch the two of them, knowing. But he supposed his presence would have spoiled Glad's evening. That was understandable. Still, his exclusion rankled.

He could have walked over from his hotel bungalow, but pedestrians weren't welcome in Beverly Hills. So he drove around awhile, thinking to pass and observe Hebron's·place on his way home. For what reason he could not have said.

Driving at night gave him a chance to sort things out

and plan what had to be done. The girl had handled Hebron's proposal for marriage cleverly, he had to give her that. Her excuse for rejecting him was logical and reasonable. As a movie supervisor Hebron would appreciate how the girl felt and accept it. That wasn't worrying Charlie Royce.

What did concern him was the report he had heard of a violent argument between Hebron and Annenberg. If Royce's information was correct, the old man had ordered Hebron to get the girl out of his house, and Hebron had refused. If both remained adamant, Annenberg would have no choice but to fire the supervisor. That might please Archer, Sturdevant, and their gang. It wouldn't please Charlie Royce. He didn't want Eli Hebron merely fired; he wanted him humbled, ridiculed publicly, ruined. Royce didn't waste time pondering his motives; he was not an introspective man.

It was after midnight when he drove slowly up the hill to Paradiso. The graveled driveway leading to the house was jammed with cars. And more cars were parked along the shoulders of the paved access road. Charlie Royce drove onto the verge just ahead of a white Rolls-Royce. He killed his lights and motor. He put a match to a cigar, puffed deeply, slumped down in the seat. He could see the mansion clearly.

It blazed with light. There were guests in evening clothes on the porch, the terrace, strolling across the lawns, coming and going through the open French doors. The caterer's waiters moved about with silver trays of drinks. A buffet had been set up around one end of the swimming pool. There were even a few people in swimming, shrieking and splashing, although the night was cool.

A five-piece band was playing in the marble entrance

hall: "Valencia." "Do-Do-Do." "If I Could Be with You One Hour Tonight." "Blue Skies!" "Girl of My Dreams." "Let a Smile Be Your Umbrella. . . ." There was a singer, a gravel-voiced black woman. "Baby face," she sang, "you've got the cutest little baby face." Charlie Royce heard it all. He saw the couples dancing. Fox-trot, Charleston, Black Bottom, Turkey Trot, tango. Everyone was laughing. Everyone was having fun.

Cars pulled away; new cars arrived. Couples stood in the middle of the road drinking from flasks. Couples went dashing into the copse of trees. Couples crawled into the back seats of cars—anyone's car. Almost against his will, Charlie Royce found himself smiling at all this drunken gaiety, tapping his foot to the music, becoming a part of the pleasure and joy.

He had almost finished his cigar when the happiness in this bright, laughing home gave him the idea of how he might destroy Eli Hebron. He tossed his cigar butt into the bushes, started up, and drove slowly back to his dark, silent hotel bungalow.

Not much longer, he promised himself.

Iggy Vaccaro and Hymie "Little Lou" Elman had been collectors for Dion O'Banion in Chicago. When their chief was rubbed out—among his gardenias and American Beauty roses—Iggy and Hymie had thought it best to seek more salubrious climes. They trained west and settled in Los Angeles. It was their kind of town: understanding cops and plenty of golden-haired, long-legged trixies.

Jobs were easy to find. They worked as strikebreakers, enforcers for loan sharks, bodyguards for professional gamblers, bouncers in blind pigs—anything that required muscle and a willingness to use it. They lived together in a hotel on Figueroa and had some high old times.

At midnight Iggy and Hymie were waiting patiently in an alley not far from their hotel. Iggy wore a chalk-striped, single-button, tight-waisted suit with wide lapels. His little bow tie was black leather. Hymie's horse-blanket plaid suit was double-breasted, but just as tight. He wore no tie, but his starched collar was closed with a gold stud. Both men wore tweed caps with buttons, the peaks curled and tilted low over their right eyes, Chicago-style.

A black Nash pulled up at the entrance to the alley. The back door was opened from inside. Iggy and Hymie sauntered up, climbed in, slammed the door.

"Evening, boys," Timmy Ryan said with a beamy smile. "Now what mischief have you two lads been up to?"

"Oh . . . this and that," Iggy said.

"Getting by," Hymie said. "How's with you, Timmy?"

"No complaints," Ryan said. "Well . . . a few, but who'd be listening?" He laughed with enjoyment. "I'm happy you boys could help me out on this."

"What's on, Timmy?" Vaccaro asked.

"Well, it's in the nature of a business discussion, you might say. I'm going to meet a certain party at Jack Newton's speak. I go in alone. You wait outside in a far corner of the parking lot. It's Fig's night off—I made sure of that—and I doubt if any of the waiters will make me. But that's neither here nor there. Now I'll suggest a business proposition to this certain party, and should he accept, why, I'll nip out and drive you boys back here, and it'll be fifty simoleons for your time and trouble. Now how does that sound?"

"Fifty for the two of us?" Elman asked.

"Right you are," Ryan said. "Cash on the line."

"Sounds all right," Vaccaro said slowly. "But what if this party don't go for your proposition?"

"Ah," Timmy Ryan said. "The plot, as they say, thickens. You lads carrying your repeaters?"

"Waddya think?" Hymie said.

"Well, if this party won't listen to reason—and he's a hardheaded, stubborn scut and probably won't—why, then I'll walk him out to the car. I suspect that may be what will happen."

"And then?" Iggy asked.

"Why, then," Ryan said thoughtfully, "we'll have to take a little trip up into the mountains and leave him there. Now for this little job of work, I'm prepared to pay the princely sum of one thousand of America's best."

"Each?" Hymie said.

"No, no," Ryan said hastily. "For the two of you. Five hundred each."

"You kidding?" Vaccaro said indignantly. "You know what I paid for breakfast this morning, Timmy? Thirty-five cents!"

"And eggs twenty cents a dozen," Hymie Elman chimed in. "Little-bitty eggs, twenty cents a dozen. Can you beat it? Prices are going up, Timmy."

"You got to do better than a grand," Iggy said firmly, "or it's no deal."

They discussed the matter for several minutes. They finally came to an amicable agreement: fifteen hundred dollars for Iggy and Hymie to be split any way they desired. Timmy Ryan then drove to Jack Newton's speakeasy. He was gratified to find few cars in the parking area of the garage. He put the Nash in a far, dark corner and left Vaccaro and Elman still sitting in the back seat. He passed inspection at the barred door, went into the speak, and took the corner booth. He ordered a boilermaker and paid for it immediately. Then he waited.

It was fifteen minutes before Barney O'Hara showed up. He was wearing a suede windbreaker over a shirt open at the throat to accommodate his neck brace. He looked around the room. He spotted Ryan, came to the booth, and slid in opposite him.

"Barney, m'boy!" Timmy Ryan shouted, as if it was a chance meeting. "You're a sight for sore eyes."

"This better be good, Timmy," O'Hara grumbled. "Bringing me out at this hour."

"It's as I told you on the phone, Barney: a wonderful opportunity for you. A once-in-a-lifetime chance. But first things first; what're you drinking?"

"I'll pass. For the time being."

"Suit yourself. Barney," Timmy Ryan said with a smile of great charm. "I got a confession to make to you."

"Oh?"

"You'll be remembering that little talk we had in the garage? Well, it was Charlie Royce I been drinking with. In this very booth."

"Thought it was," the chauffeur nodded.

"Haven't mentioned it to anyone, have you now?"

O'Hara looked at the other man narrowly.

"Why, no, I haven't, Timmy," he said softly. "Not yet I haven't."

"Well now, I'm a happy man to hear that. To speak the truth, Barney, my meeting here with Mr. Royce might prove to be a wee bit embarrassing to his nibs should word get about."

"Embarrassing? How's that, Timmy?"

"Well, you see Charlie Royce is by way of being a shy

man. Oh yes he is, Barney. Very shy. Everyone thinks he's a rough, bang-about kind of fellow, but if the truth be known, he's shy as a schoolboy. Oh yes. And tongue-tied when it comes to talking to women. So what I've been doing on these one or two meetings I've had here with Mr. Royce is to pass along the names and addresses and telephone numbers of a few cuties. A few little sweethearts with the gift of making a man's shyness be of no account whatsoever. You catch my drift? Certain ladies I met during my service on the Vice Squad. I've been making life easier for Mr. Royce by—''

"Cut it out, Timmy," O'Hara interrupted disgustedly. "You think I'm right off the boat?"

"You don't believe me?"

"Of course not," O'Hara rasped. "Charlie Royce don't need the likes of you to pimp for him."

Timmy Ryan finished his drink. He set the empty glass gently down. He regarded it thoughtfully.

"You don't believe me," he said musingly. "Think of that." Suddenly he raised his eyes, locked stares with O'Hara. "How much would it take to make you believe?" he asked.

"What?"

"How much money, man? To make you swallow my story whole and forget all about my meeting here with Charlie Royce and keep your mouth shut?"

O'Hara looked at him, shaking his head in bewilderment. "Timmy, what the hell is this all about? If you hadn't said another word about it, I'd have forgotten the whole thing. You can drink with the Prince of Wales for all I care. But now you drag me out in the middle of the night and offer me money to keep my mouth shut. I've got to think something is going on, Timmy. Something maybe I should know more about."

"You're right!" Timmy Ryan cried, slapping his palm down on the table. "You're absolutely right! I'll offer him money like you want, Mr. Royce, I says, but Barney O'Hara won't touch it. I know the man, I told Royce. He'll want to know what's going on, I says. Oh, I told him straight out, Barney. Well, if that's the case, Mr. Royce says, if he won't take money to keep his mouth shut, then there's nothing for it but to tell him what's going on. You bring Barney O'Hara to me, and I'll put it to him straight, Mr. Royce says. So let's go, Barney. Mr. Royce is waiting in the car."

"Waiting?" O'Hara said confusedly. "Waiting where?"

"Why, right here," Ryan said. "Out in the parking lot. Waiting to tell you why him and me had those meetings and what it's all about. Let's go; my drink's paid for."

They rose, and Timmy Ryan led the way briskly toward the door. As they came out into the unlighted parking area, he let Barney O'Hara catch up to him. He slid an arm about O'Hara's shoulders.

"It's happy I am we're clearing up this little misunderstanding, Barney," he said in a throaty voice. "There should be no lies or bad feeling between us, being from the old sod like we are."

"Old sod?" O'Hara laughed shortly. "I was born in Brooklyn."

"Sure, and don't I know it?" Ryan said. "But we're both micks, are we not, and blood is thicker than water, and no man can say different. Ah, Barney, it's something to be Irish after all. Like brothers we are and. . . ."

Babbling along in this vein, Timmy Ryan guided O'Hara alongside the black Nash. The back door opened suddenly.

At the same time Ryan's hand fell to the back of O'Hara's back, and he pushed hard. O'Hara went stumbling forward, ducking to keep from hitting his head on the car roof. He saw the two men in the back seat. He saw their glinting revolvers. His eyes lifted, and he saw their faces.

"Jesus, Mary, and Joseph," he said hoarsely, "it's the end of Barney O'Hara."

Four

In 1913 Cecil B. DeMille brought a troupe of players out to Hollywood to make *The Squaw Man*. In their wake, like a camp follower, came Abe Vogel. He had been an agent for vaudeville artistes in New York. But he foresaw what the burgeoning movie industry would become. So he sold his business and moved west to rent an office on Sunset Boulevard, not far from DeMille's original barn, now part of the Paramount lot.

In the fourteen years since he opened his doors with four clients—a stunt man, a director, a vamp, and a tango team—Abe Vogel had seen made-in-Hollywood movies come to dominate world markets, just as they had overwhelmed the community in which they were produced. Hollywood, in the minds of most Americans, meant glamour, high living, fantasy.

Abe Vogel saw it all happen and was part of it. He saw cowboys who had once worked for bed and board become national heroes at a salary of ten thousand dollars a week.

He saw schoolgirls, waitresses, and not a few prostitutes become, literally, the "idols of millions," with sable-trimmed nightgowns, Russian wolfhounds, and Rolls-Royce New Phantoms.

And he saw men of no talent, imagination, or taste rise in film business councils to achieve incredible power over their employees and the products shown on the world's movie screens. Having a taste for melancholy, Abe Vogel often wondered how these ex-buttonhole makers, ex-circus roustabouts, ex-patent medicine peddlers had managed to scramble, claw, fight their way to the top levels of an industry that, even in its pioneer days, earned a reputation for Byzantine plots, frantic finagling, and the business practices of a Levantine camel auction.

He concluded that most of the executives who rose to eminence had what Vogel termed (to himself) a "dead center." This he defined as an implacable will to power and a cold contempt for moral principle. Such men could be charming friends, devoted husbands, doting fathers, or ardent lovers. It was only when their dreams of glory were threatened that the "dead center" loomed and the poniard was unsheathed.

Such a man, Vogel was convinced, was Charlie Royce.

There was one other factor in the success of Hollywood's top executives that bemused the agent: Most of them were incredibly lucky! Again, Royce was an example. He had come to Vogel asking him only to find an attractive underage girl ambitious for a motion-picture career. It was never detailed in so many words, but Vogel understood that this girl would be used to entrap Eli Hebron.

The plan succeeded far beyond anyone's expectations. Not only was Hebron compromised, but the girl proved to be one of the hottest young properties in Hollywood. As her agent Vogel profited, of course, but Royce was the main beneficiary. The agent was not surprised; the man was a winner. Vogel admired Eli Hebron but sadly recognized that the supervisor lacked sufficient ruthlessness to twist his way through the Hollywood maze. So Abe Vogel had thrown in with Charlie Royce. It was purely a business decision. And if it resulted in self-disgust, that was frequently the cost of doing business in Hollywood. The hundred percent happy endings were all on the screen.

Vogel's present office was a suite of four rooms in a new one-story building on Wilshire Boulevard. It was one of the first offices in Hollywood decorated in the Bauhaus style. All the furnishings were clean and functional. Eli Hebron called it "a factory with ferns." But in Vogel's mind, the rooms' lack of clutter, their gleaming spareness and open simplicity were necessary relief from the tangled and steamy Hollywood jungle.

Bea Winks, at least, had the wit to appreciate the lean and serene beauty of Vogel's private office. Sitting in a deceptively simple leather and teak chair alongside his boxy desk, she looked around at the bare white walls and nodded approval.

"At first it seems empty," she told the agent. "Then after a while you begin to like the openness. Maybe I'll do over my place like this."

"Why not?" he shrugged, forebearing to tell her what the decorating job had cost.

"So, Abe," she said, "you got what Royce wanted?"

"To a T. One father type, one mother type, one kid type. They're sitting outside. You'll coach them?"

"In a few minutes. You're sure Hebron never saw them?"

"How could he see them?" Vogel said. "The father

type is the only one who's been in front of a camera, and that was a three-second walk-on in a Warner's costume thing about two years ago. He wore a full beard and a fright wig. If Hebron ever saw the movie, which I doubt, he'd never remember this guy. The mother type is a cootch dancer—or was. The closest to LA she ever worked was San Diego."

"The sweetheart of the fleet?"

"Something like that," Abe Vogel said shortly. "I was married to her once."

"Oh. I'm sorry, Abe."

"That's okay."

"And the kid?"

"He belongs to the cootch dancer's sister. She was happy to rent him out. She's got six more just like him at home. The kid's bright and can keep his mouth shut. In fact, after this is all over, I might try to place him."

Bea Winks sighed. "After this is all over," she repeated. "You think it ever will be?"

"Sure. Royce knows what he's doing."

"Does he, Abe? I think this family idea is dumb. What's the point?"

Vogel stared at the skinny, neurasthenic woman. He reflected sorrowfully that they were much alike. But her twitches were on the outside.

"Bea, darling," he said softly, "Charlie Royce is not an educated man. Maybe not even an intelligent man. But he's got—what? An instinct. He goes for the jugular. He looks at people—people like you, me, everyone—and he says, 'What's their weakness?' He studies Eli Hebron, and he sees a high-strung, romantic, impractical boy with the gift of putting his fantasies on film. A very elegant, poetic boy! Yes, a poet. So Charlie Royce will create a dream for this poet or help the poet make his own dream come true. Then Royce will become Harry Houdini. Now you see it, now you don't. He will whisk the cloth away, and the dream will go *pouf!* Disappeared into air. What do you think Eli Hebron will do then?''

"I don't know, Abe," she said breathlessly, fascinated. "What will he do?"

"Please, sweetheart"—the agent sighed—"go talk to the father type, the mother type, the kid type. Tell me how they work out. If okay, tell Royce they go on salary."

"Where's all the money coming from?" Bea Winks wondered.

"Who cares?" Abe Vogel said wearily. "It's coming."

The shrouded home smelled of must and lentil soup. He was scarcely inside the door when Florence Annenberg attacked him.

"You!" she screamed. "You!"

Claws reached for his eyes. He had to grip her wrists.

"Don't," he pleaded. "Aunt Flo, please don't!"

She shrieked, wailed, hooted with anguish. She said it was his fault, he had driven Marcus to it, they had trusted him like a son, from worry and aggravation Marcus had suffered, how could he do this, on a bed of pain, what had they done to deserve it, because of his treachery, a dear, sweet man brought down, he had done it, at death's door, he had struck him down, a curse on his head, suffering, humiliation, destruction, death.

He climbed the stairs, feeling wrung, twisted tight and dry. The orange pills hadn't helped. He paused at the door of the bedroom. Escape tempted him. Go. Somewhere, anywhere. Away. For the first time in his life he could comprehend suicide. That was a way. He pushed the door open, went into the bedroom.

The butler, Jules, sat at the bedside. Black hands folded limply in his lap. White eyes glittered in a basalt face. He looked at Hebron, rose, came to him on tiptoe. Perhaps he saw something in Hebron's eyes. He put a hand lightly beneath the supervisor's elbow, supporting, guiding him to the bedside.

Marcus Annenberg lay massively still. He was covered to the waist with sheet and worn patchwork quilt. He had been cut in half with giant shears down the length of his body. Then the left half had been slyly shifted an eighth-inch lower. The right eye was closed. The left glared furiously at the world. Saliva dribbled from the left corner of his mouth.

Hebron bent over the bed.

"Uncle Marc," he breathed. "Uncle Marc, it's Eli. Eli, Uncle Marc. I'm here. Eli."

Nothing.

Jules leaned by him to swipe the slobber tenderly away with a dampened cloth.

"Oh, now isn't that just fine there," Jules crooned. "Get him all cleaned up and neat there. Be downstairs and watching the moving pictures any minute now, I swear. Doin' fine. Doin' fine. Alive and breathing, that's the spirit. Come along there, Mr. Annenberg, sir. Just come along and keep doin' fine. Nice and easy. Plenty rest. Yes, *sir*."

The right eyelid rose slowly like a curtain going up. The glazed eye moved up, down, right, left. Hebron bent over the bed again.

"Uncle Marc. It's Eli. I'm here. Eli. How are you feeling, Uncle Marc?"

Nothing. Then the snarled lips moved. Hebron bent lower.

"What?" he said. "I didn't hear. What did you say, Uncle Marc? Say it again."

He straightened up. He looked at Jules. Tears were on his cheeks now. One plopped from his chin.

"He said something," he told Jules. "Like 'Tub oba.' I thought he said, 'Tub oba.' See if you can make it out."

Jules leaned down. He tilted his head, put his ear close to Annenberg's trembling lips. He listened a moment, face solemnly intent. Then he straightened up.

"Take over," he said. "He says, 'Take over,' Mr. Hebron."

Hebron nodded dumbly. He bent close to Marcus Annenberg again.

"It's going to be all right, Uncle Marc," he whispered. "Don't worry about the studio. The loan will come through, you'll see. Everything will be all right. And the girl's parents are coming to visit. They'll stay in my house. For as long as they want. The girl's mother and father and a young cousin, a little boy. All living in my house. That makes it all right, doesn't it, Uncle Marc? Her mother and father right there? Uncle Marc?"

No answer. No sign the hulk had understood or even heard. Hebron reached down, stroked his uncle's shoulder. He turned away. He wanted to kiss the stricken man, but could not, could not. He dragged to the door, stopped with his hand on the knob. If I leave now, I will be dead for the rest of my life.

He turned, came back to the bedside. He bent over again, pressed his mouth against those raw, tortured lips.

"Live," he breathed. "Live."

The right eyelid lowered slowly.

Then Eli Hebron left the room, hearing again Jules'
croon: "Doin' fine. Doin' fine. Nice and easy. Be up and
about any minute now. Yes, *sir*. That's the spirit. . . ."

He came out into the bright sunlight, grinding the heels
of his hands into his eyes. Leo was slumped behind the
wheel of the Hispano-Suiza, peaked cap pulled low over
his eyes. Gladys had bought him maroon livery, to match
the limousine's color. He heard the rear door open, heard
Hebron crawl in. He straightened up, pushed back his cap.

"How's the old man doing?" he asked breezily.

Hebron didn't answer.

"Guess you'll be running things now," Leo said.

"Shut your filthy mouth," Hebron shouted at him.

Leo, shaken, started the motor, drove slowly down the
driveway to the street. Hebron gave him the address.

"And how are we feeling today?" Dr. Irving Blick
asked. "Tiptop?"

Hebron poured it all out! He was losing control. Events
could no longer be managed. The girl had spurned his
proposal of marriage. His chauffeur and bodyguard, a
good friend, had mysteriously disappeared; the police were
investigating. Business problems grew increasingly serious. And now his uncle, Marcus Annenberg, had suffered
a second near-fatal stroke for which he was blamed. He
was being taken over. He had no influence. His desires
were ignored. He was alone, alienated. His mind was a
stew of anxieties. What was happening? The orange pills
no longer had the power to soothe.

"Well now," Dr. Blick said slowly. "Well, well, well."

Winding the black ribbon of his pince-nez about his
plump forefinger, he began to dispose of Eli Hebron's
fears.

The girl's rejection, for the reasons she stated, was

reasonable; we had to admit that. She had not withdrawn herself, her body from our embrace, her psyche from our love. We were not being personally rejected. It was merely business. Surely we could see that.

The chauffeur's disappearance could have been due to a hundred causes, none of them related to us. He had cruelly deserted wife and children. Were we responsible for that? Were we responsible for the vagaries of all friends and acquaintances? For the mad behavior of the human race?

Business problems were a constant. Some could be solved; some could not. Some simply disappeared with the passage of time. But no matter how serious, they were rarely critical to psychic health. They were on a level with the weather, a broken shoelace, the price of pork chops.

Must we feel guilt for our uncle's stroke? Understandable, but illogical. The man was old, suffering from a deteriorative disorder. We could not guarantee his good health forever and ever. Then why should we blame ourself for his body's collapse?

In such a manner did Dr. Irving Blick exorcise the demons of Eli Hebron. Having cleansed him, the Oliver Hardy doctor began spinning more hopeful images.

The girl still loved us, did she not? Her continued presence in our bed proved it. And now her parents and a child cousin would come to visit. We would be immersed in a wholesome family atmosphere and relationship, laughing and sunny. Nothing could be more beneficial to our psychic health. The approving presence of mother and father. The patter of tiny feet on marble floors. Ah! Ah! The house become a home.

The missing chauffeur might return at any moment with a hilarious tale of a gargantuan drunk. What a laugh we'll have!

Marcus Annenberg might recover and take up again the responsibilities of his office. And if he did not, Magna Studios would still flourish. It was a magnificent opportunity to produce the kind of significant movies we've always yearned to make.

As for the loss of the effect of the orange pills, we have something new to suggest: a white powder in spills, to be dissolved in a glass of water and taken as needed.

"Thank you," Eli Hebron said humbly.

Along the street of fake buildings and false fronts leading to the back lot at Magna Studios was a structure called the Palace. It was a squarish two-story building in the Egyptian-Babylonian-Roman-Greek-Etruscan style. Rows of wooden columns, painted to resemble marble, supported a simulated tile roof decorated with plaster serpents, animal heads, long-necked birds.

Inside was an open courtyard. Surrounding it were several small council chambers, a dungeon, sleeping quarters, an orgy room, a terrace built against a painted backdrop (the Mediterranean Sea with an erupting volcano in the distance), and a throne room.

This unique structure was featured in almost all of Magna's historical romances and biblical epics. Kings were assassinated there, duels fought, queens seduced, ministers poisoned, royal babies kidnapped, plots hatched, wars planned, and the fate of civilization decided.

The throne room, a hodgepodge of plaster and papier-mâché, appeared to be the opulent residence of a luxury-loving potentate. The floor was a painted mosaic. On the walls were frescoes of scantily clad nymphs, satyrs and mythological beasts, bearded gods, and armored warriors in combat.

The throne itself was impressive: all gilt griffins, ivory tusks, beaded fringe, glass jewels, and peacock feathers. It was raised on a three-step dais, handy for the prostration of obsequious ambassadors, conquered enemies, and tearful maidens pleading for the lives of their beloved gladiators.

Before the throne, at the moment, Gladys Divine and Charlie Royce stood face to face, frozen, as if waiting for the cry of "Action!"

"Make it fast," he said curtly. "I've got a crew waiting for me."

"I want you to call it off," she said, lifting her chin. "I want you to stop what you're doing to Hebron."

He stared at her. He unbuttoned his jacket, thrust hands into his hip pockets. He began to pace back and forth. He didn't take his eyes from her.

He marveled at how she had changed. The lifted chin, the challenging look. Even her body seemed stronger, more resolute. Confidence had given her an erect carriage, pride had hardened her. The baby fat was gone, from her flesh and from her character. She had a steely self-assurance. Features seemed crisper, profile more classic. Determination had firmed her mouth. The eyes seemed resolved never to weep again. The name was altered, and so was the woman.

She was wearing a lilac cloche, belted suit of crushed purple velvet, long violet scarf about her throat and trailing over one shoulder. Now she wore clothes as costumes, the styles, lines, and colors selected for visual impact. She had, he acknowledged, become a valuable studio property.

"I don't know what you think this is," he started. "Some kind of feud, I suppose. A personal grudge between me and Hebron. That's not it at all."

"No?" she said.

"No," he said. "It's a lot more than that. Sure, I'd like to be making bigger pictures. Bigger budgets. More money for me. I want it. I admit it."

"Head of production?" she asked shrewdly. "Hebron's boss?"

"Maybe that, too," he shrugged. "But it's more important than that."

Suddenly it was necessary to him that she understand the stakes involved. That she understand *him*.

"It's the future of Magna Studios," he said in evangelical tones. "It's conversion to sound. It's producing a commercial entertainment product. Christ, it's the future of Hollywood that's involved here! Who's going to control the industry—a bunch of hebe cloak-and-suiters with their business in their hats or up-to-date American businessmen with gumption and get-up-and-go? Real executives who can bring production-line savvy to this crazy business and organize it."

She looked at him coldly. "Bullshit," she said.

He laughed shortly. "You've grown up fast."

"Goddamn right I have, Royce. Fast enough to see through your line of crap. It's Eli's balls you're after. He's everything you're not: sensitive, talented, imaginative, tender. And loving. You can't love, Royce. And you know it. Hebron's everything you want to be and can't. Look at you. You're like something whittled out of a stump. You can't move; you can't laugh; you can't live. You're a dead man. Oh, maybe you breathe and all that. But you're dead. Can you bleed? Hebron can. He can cry. Can you? He can smile, from inside. Can you? He can be hurt, get drunk, act crazy, drive too fast, and go up in a nutsy airplane. Can you? You can't, you can't! Do you want to fuck me?"

218

"What?" he said sharply. "What?"

"You heard me," she said. "Fuck me. As often as you want. Anywhere, anytime. If you call it off. What you're doing. Just drop it and forget it."

He looked at her incredulously, his head turning back and forth in disbelief.

"I'll French you," she said dully. "I'll suck you off."

He made a gesture. Pushing her away. Shutting her out.

"You love him that much?" he asked.

She nodded.

"No, you don't," he said harshly. "You love yourself more."

"That's not true," she cried desperately.

"I'm betting on it," he said, already marching out of the fake palace, leaving her staring at the empty throne.

Soon after the arrival at Paradiso of Norman, Faith, and Little Stanley, introduced by Gladys as her father, mother, and cousin, it became a habit for the entire household to breakfast together on the terrace, if the day was fair. The meal was prepared by the incompetent Bertha and served by Leo. But the latter proved such a surly footman that usually the whole family pitched in, setting the table and wheeling food from the kitchen to terrace on a serving cart.

The four adults sat around the white table, under the daisy umbrella. Stanley was allowed to have his milk and muffin at the edge of the swimming pool, dangling his bare feet in the water. The morning meal sometimes lasted an hour. Then Gladys and Eli departed for the studio. Norman and Faith simply lounged about, enjoying the California sunshine. "Such a welcome change from New Jersey!" Or they went shopping, taking Stanley along and using Hebron's charge accounts, at his insistence. They did a great deal of shopping.

Her parents, Hebron told Glad, were a pleasant, charming, even jolly couple, and he enjoyed their company. He did not tell her he thought them an oddly matched pair.

Norman was tall, fair, stooped. His complexion was mottled, and he had the yellowed features of a heavy smoker. He told funny stories exceedingly well in a variety of dialects. Hebron thought his manner somewhat effete, but there was no denying his grace, casual elegance, and unflagging courtesy only slightly tinged with mockery. A teacher of mathematics he may have been, but he proved an execrable scorekeeper at their occasional bridge games.

Faith was younger. She was a dark woman running to fat but exceedingly vain about her figure. She favored dresses stretched tight through bosom and hips. Her long hair—too black to be entirely natural, Hebron decided—was usually worn up in an intricate coiffure that required a dozen hairpins and a net. One night, at a small party Hebron gave in honor of his guests, she performed an extravagant Charleston to enthusiastic applause.

Stanley, the child, was an amusing rapscallion, impudent enough for an Our Gang comedy. He did have a distressing habit of asking for money, but his gap-toothed grin was hard to resist. He seemed to be tolerated by Norman but ignored or avoided by Faith.

Which was strange, considering the sleeping arrangements that had been made. Norman occupied a guest room by himself. Faith and little Stanley slept in another bedroom. It seemed a singular arrangement to Hebron, but since no one complained, he was content. Gladys moved into a small bedroom next to Eli's, for propriety's sake. But she continued to share his bed and kept her clothes in the mirrored room. She returned to her own chamber only to sleep. And not always then.

Following three days of intermittent showers and a glowering cloud cover, the skies had cleared. The blue seemed scrubbed and polished. The new sun blazed with summer strength. The men left off their jackets for the terrace breakfast. Faith wore a Japanese kimono, and Stanley only a cotton vest and swimming shorts. Of them all, Gladys appeared the coolest, wearing a draped dress of white cotton piqué with a fringed black sash.

They drank their orange juice and exchanged information on how well they had slept. They exclaimed over the welcome appearance of the sun and reported what the radio weathermen had predicted. They traded eggs, bacon, toast, marmalade. They discussed plans for the day. Gladys and Eli to the studio, of course. Norman to a neighbor's tennis court where he had been promised a "beginner's set." Faith had shopping to do. Stanley would be left to the supervision of Bertha and some older children, neighbors, who were coming over to use the swimming pool.

This relaxed social exchange was all very ordinary, Hebron admitted. Some might have considered it stultifying. But he found its very ordinariness a comfort. Almost a delight. Blick had been right: It was exactly what he needed.

There they were: the family lounging in sunlit content. Stanley, having finished his milk, waded in the shallow end of the pool. Norman, in white tennis costume, slumped easily in his chair, sipping his third cup of coffee and smoking his fourth cigarette. Faith in her splashy kimono mused dreamily, chin propped on her fist. Glad sat with head tilted back, face outside the umbrella's shade. Her eyes were closed.

Eli Hebron observed all this and wanted the moment never to end. It seemed to him the peace he had sought, the tranquillity he had never found. He saw a radiance over all, a healthy, rosy glow. His fears were reduced to miniature worries, nothing a bold, steady man could not handle. This was what had been missing from his life, this continuum of pleasure, peace, and family love.

There was a flow to it, a constant progression. But it was not linear progression so much as a closed current. He understood now what was meant by the "family circle." It *was* a circle, a closed ring in which shared joys were enhanced and shared pain diminished. He could see the beauty of that.

Look at Norm there, in his sparkling tennis whites. Stan with his Buster Brown haircut and the bounce of youth. Faith, swaddled in brilliant silk flowers, almost drowsy with comfort. Glad stretching out her cool body, immobile in the sun, silent with ease.

And about them all the still heat of early morning. The smell of wet grass drying. Birdcalls from somewhere. A lulled world stirring. Vault of sky and the sun's glory. A meaningful image, something to be remembered, and he wondered if he might create a movie on this theme. Somehow contrive to show the bliss of the ordinary. A film about a loving family, their ups and downs, triumphs and defeats. But always the circle complete. A little world. Not a bad title: *A Little World*.

He began to dream the scenes. . . .

Later Leo drove them to the studio. Eli Hebron held hands with Gladys, told her how he felt, told her he had never been happier. She nodded, patted his hand, then pressed it tightly against her cheek.

"What is it?" he asked her.

"I'm just glad you're happy," she said huskily.

Florence Annenberg answered the door.

"Hello, Julius," she said, ignoring Hebron. "Thank you for coming."

They trooped in, the treasurer going first.

"How is he, Mrs. Annenberg?" Felder asked.

She shrugged. "The same, Julius. The paralysis is maybe a little better. The mouth looks better. The eye. But in the head—not so good."

"What does the doctor say?"

"Wait. The doctor says wait. Maybe complete recovery. Maybe partial recovery. Maybe another stroke that could take him off. Wait. That's what the doctor says."

"Could we see him, Mrs. Annenberg?"

"*You* can see him, Julius. He's in the projection room. Not too long. He gets tired fast."

"Just a few minutes."

"You go in, Julius. He'll be happy to see *you*."

She turned her back, shuffled away.

Eli Hebron sighed. "She'll never forgive me. Never."

"It wasn't your fault, Eli."

"She thinks so. Sometimes I think so."

Marcus Annenberg was seated in a wheelchair parked in the center aisle of the small projection room. He was covered to the waist with a quilt. His lower legs were raised on a cushioned footstool. The puffy, age-spotted hands lay limply on his lap.

In the light reflected from the screen they could see the thick lips, still twisted. The lid over the left eye now drooped. The whole face sagged, as if the flesh had leaked away; the empty skin hung slackly, in folds.

The two men slid into seats alongside the wheelchair. Julius K. Felder on the left, Hebron on the right. Annenberg didn't acknowledge their presence. He stared fixedly at the flickering images on the screen. Occasionally deep noises came from him: faint grunts, small groans. Only once, a short, high-pitched cry.

"Uncle Marc," Hebron whispered.

"Sha, sha," the old man said. His heavy head bobbed toward the screen.

He was watching one of Ben Stuttgart's one-reel comedies. It was called *The Bakery.* Four inept holdup men attempt to rob a bakeshop and are repulsed by the angry owners and customers. It was a classic of the pie-throwing genre. More than three hundred custard and meringue pies had been used during filming, along with cakes, cream puffs, ice cream, butter, melted chocolate, buckets of whipped cream, and, in the grand finale, a six-tier wedding cake.

When Hebron and Felder glanced at the silent screen, the pie tossing had just begun. One of the robbers was wiping custard from his blinking eyes.

"Uncle Marc," Hebron said in a low voice, "we got a letter from Boston this morning. They turned us down."

"Look, look!" Annenberg gurgled.

On the screen, one of the customers tried to call the cops. A pie mashed into the telephone receiver.

"They say our present financial situation is too precarious," Felder said bitterly. "That's their word: 'precarious.' "

"We've tried every place we can think of, Uncle Marc. No one will touch us."

On the screen, one of the holdup men ran frantically in

place as his feet slipped continually in the guck on the floor.

"Oh, oh!" Annenberg said, his body heaving.

"They're buying up our paper," Hebron said. "All our short-term notes."

"The suppliers are cutting us off," Felder said. "Especially raw stock and processing. They want cash in advance. *In advance!*"

"Boy, oh, boy," Marcus Annenberg said. "See that? Oh, boy!"

On the screen, pies and cakes flew in all directions. A fat woman lost her balance, bent over. A meringue pie splashed onto her behind.

"They're selling us out, Uncle Marc," Hebron said despairingly. "The Boston bank is backing a local group. Julius found out."

"We don't know who they are," Felder said. "The locals. But they're squeezing. We're going down, Mr. Annenberg. We need cash. We won't be able to meet the payroll."

"What can we do, Uncle Marc? Do you have any suggestions? Is there anyone we can turn to?"

On the screen a customer hefted a thick pie before throwing. One of the robbers hit his hand, smacking the pie into the customer's face. Crust and filling sprayed.

"Hoo!" the old man said. "Hey!"

Eli Hebron leaned forward, looked to his left. He caught Felder's eye, motioned with his head. The two men rose quietly, slipped from their seats. They tiptoed out.

"Oh-ho!" Marcus Annenberg was saying, shoulders shaking. "Look! Ha! Oh boy!"

225

Hebron had driven them over in the LaSalle. He had brought along a flask of gin. Both men had a drink, then lighted cigarettes.

"My cash position isn't so good," Hebron said. "I thought it was better than it is. I've had a lot of personal expenses. I didn't realize. But I still have Paradiso. I'll put that up."

"What for?" Felder said sadly. "You're just postponing the inevitable."

"The bastards!" Hebron cried. "Why are they doing this to us? Because we're Jews?"

"No," the treasurer said. "Well . . . maybe. But it could be Jews behind it. Eli, it's just business. We let ourselves get in a vulnerable position, and the pirates closed in. It's a good deal for them: a functioning studio, talented people, a chain of houses, worldwide markets. They'll pick us up for a song, pump in fresh money. In a year or two they'll be rolling. It makes me sick."

"Julius, will you stay with them?"

"Do you have to ask?" the treasurer said hotly. "Never. Even if they want me, which I doubt. Never!"

"What will you do?"

"I'll look around. I won't starve. I'll get something. If I have to start all over as a bookkeeper, so be it. What about you, Eli? If worse comes to worst?"

"I've got a contract, but I won't stay. I've never worked for anyone but Uncle Marc. Maybe I could raise enough cash to finance an independent production. Get distribution through MGM or UA. I've got a good reputation in the business. I've got some good people under personal contract. Nino Cavello. Margaret Gay. Gladys Divine.

Those names mean something. I should be able to raise money."

"Sure you could, Eli. Of course."

"One big success, and I'm on my way. With you as my general manager, Julius."

"Who else?" Felder shouted. "We'll make a mint!"

But their euphoria faded as fast as it had appeared. They hit the flask again, not looking at each other.

"Ben Stuttgart shot that slapstick in nineteen twenty-two," Hebron said in a low voice.

"I know," Felder said. "He brought it in for thirty thousand. Can you imagine? It's grossed two million so far, and it's still showing. China, India—around there."

"No one would make a thing like that today," the supervisor said. "Pies aren't enough. Audiences want something more."

"What, Eli? What do they want?"

"No one knows. Really knows. If we knew, we'd all be millionaires. Every picture would be a hit. All you can do is follow your instinct and hope. This is a business for the young, Julius. When you're young, you know everything."

"You're not so old," Felder protested.

"Today I'm old," Eli Hebron said. "Suddenly."

"My God, you're a dumpling," Edwin K. Jenkins said. "In fact, you're four dumplings: two in front and two in back."

"You certainly know how to sweet-talk an innocent girl," Tina Rambaugh said.

"Innocent? Oh, lordy. Who seduced whom?"

"Let's say it was a joint undertaking," she said. She looked around his scabrous apartment. "And this is the joint." She scrunched down under the sheet. "How'd I do, boss?"

"You show promise," he said. "Is the dream dead?"

"Not on your Aunt Fanny," she said. "Just getting cranked up."

He sighed and climbed out of bed. She watched him pad naked into the kitchen. He was a skinnymarink with long, flat feet, knobby knees, thin thighs, and no ass at all. His skin was shiny, pale, lightly freckled; he had little body hair. A small blue scar puckered his back under the right shoulder blade.

"God damn it!" he yelled in the kitchen.

"What is it?" she called.

"I forgot to empty the pan under the icebox. I got a flood in here."

She lay back in the rumpled bed, staring dreamily at the cracked ceiling. She had gone all the way; she was a fallen woman. And she was ready to fall again.

He came in carrying two quart bottles of home brew. He gave her one, then got into bed next to her.

"What did you do about the flood?" she asked.

"Threw a towel in it."

"You're a swell housekeeper, Ed. How much do you pay for these deluxe accommodations?"

"Ten a month."

"I pay eight. If we went in together, we could get a big place."

"Live together?"

"Sure," she said. "Why not?"

"Without benefit of clergy?"

"Might as well," she said cheerfully. "Who'd have me now? I've been used."

He laughed and gulped his beer.

"Try it," he told her.

She took a cautious swallow. "Not bad."

"I make it myself."

"You don't!"

"Sure I do. The crock's in the can. Be careful where you pee. I do my own bottling and capping. If I ever get a few bucks ahead, I'm going to have some fancy labels printed up: 'Jenkins Suds.' "

" 'The beer with the empty head,' " she said. "What's that scar on your back?"

"A guy shot me," he said shortly.

"I didn't know you were in the war."

"Oh, sure. I made the world safe for democracy."

"Did it hurt?" she said.

"No," he said, "it felt good. You know, you're the first woman I've had up here."

"I'll bet," she scoffed. "Since yesterday."

"No, Scout's honor. You're my first guest. What can I do to entertain you?"

"You already have."

"Would you like to hear 'My country, 'tis of thee,' played on a comb and toiletpaper?"

"No, thanks. Ed, that thing you put on—will that keep me from having a baby?"

"The benny? Sure—unless someone sneaked in here and poked a hole in it."

"I've got a lot to learn," she sighed. Then: "I liked it."

"No kidding?" he said. "All those moans and groans—I never would have known it."

"Am I supposed to keep quiet?"

"Hell no. Moan away, baby."

He set his bottle on the floor alongside the bed. He

turned, pulled the sheet down. He leaned over her, took a pink nipple between his lips. He rubbed the wet tip of his tongue back and forth.

"Jesus!" she gasped.

"A little something I picked up in Gay Paree," he said. "And now, for my second number, I will simultaneously suck both tits while my right hand is—"

"Oh, shut up," she said, setting her beer bottle aside.

She took his face between her palms, kissed his mouth lovingly.

"I really liked it," she breathed. "It was swell."

"Hurt?"

"At first. Then just good. I messed your sheets. A little. I'll wash it out."

"Don't worry about it."

He put his thin arms about her, pulled her chubby body close. She was burning, lightly sweated. Her soft skin tasted of salt.

"Got another one of those rubber things?" she whispered.

He nodded, rubbing his fingers between her heavy thighs. Then he fumbled under his pillow, found the condom, pulled it on.

"Take hold of me," he said. "Do with me what you will. I am yours."

"You're beginning to talk in subtitles," she said. She grunted, squirming around, until she got him on top of her. She guided him.

"You're hot," he said. "And tight."

"Slow, Ed."

"Like this?"

"Just like that. Oh, my God. How long has this been going on?"

"It was discovered last week."

"And you made me wait this long? Oh! Yes, there! Right there! Kiss me, you fool."

"Yes, Theda."

He rammed his tongue into her mouth. She held it gently in her lips, sucking the tip.

Her hands grasped his flat buttocks, pulled him tightly down onto her, into her. She released his tongue.

"I'm doing something," she whispered.

"I know you are."

"What is it?"

"You're coming."

"I can't stop."

"Don't try."

"I may die."

"Not today."

"What about you?"

"A few minutes. . . ."

"What shall I do?"

"Lift up and down. Not your head, dummy, your hips."

"Like this?"

"Just like that."

"I get it. It's a dance."

"You bet."

"Faster?"

"Mmm."

"I can feel you!"

"Dance, gypsy!"

Later she said, "The fade-out wasn't bad either. As long as you didn't go away from me. The first time you went right away from me. I didn't like that part. I wanted you close."

"This time I didn't have the strength to get off you."

"Can we do it again, Ed?"

"Oh, God," he groaned. "In about three years."

"Poor darling," she murmured, snuggling close to him. "All worn out. Just for me."

"I'm a basket case," he admitted. "Let me get my beer."

They sat up in bed, backs against the headboard. They pulled the sheet up to their waists. They smoked his cubebs and sipped their warm beer.

"Now I know Hebron's wrong," he said. "About *The Dream Lover,* I mean. We decided to make a dream come true, and it worked out just dandy."

"Did you dream about me?" she said eagerly.

"Don't get personal, fat one. But the fantasy turned out okay. So where does that leave our screenplay?"

"Maybe our dream was the last one in the script. Where the hero settles down with his wife. Don't get scared," she added hastily. "I'm not proposing. You know what I mean."

"Unless the whole point of the movie, the point Hebron wanted to make from the start, is that dreams and fantasies can be a waste of time, can even be dangerous, if they take the place of reality and become so pleasurable that they prevent you from taking action to get what you want. Is he saying that even action that results in compromise is better than the best dream?"

"I think so," she said thoughtfully. "At least, that's the way I see the scenario. But I'm not sure Hebron intended it that way. I think he saw the final scene, settling for second best, as a defeat."

"Well"—he grinned at her—"you and I settled for second best—each other. The scarecrow and the butterball. Some defeat!"

"Ain't we got fun?" she sang.

*   *   *

During his continuing investigation into the development of movies with sound Charlie Royce came across something that interested him mightily: an engineer at a local radio station was amassing a private collection of recorded sounds. So far it was just a hobby, but the engineer was convinced it would eventually be a money-maker.

"Say we're doing a radio play," he explained, "and the script calls for a galloping horse. We got a sound effects man right there in the studio, and he clops two coconut shells on a tabletop. Sounds just like a horse walking, trotting, or galloping, depending on how fast he handles those shells. But if we want to set a scene at the seashore, say, then the sound effects man goes to a phonograph record or wax cylinder. We call it dubbing. He dubs in the actual sounds of the waves, the wind, and so forth. Because that recording was made at the seashore."

"I get it," Royce nodded.

"Some sounds can be faked in the studio," the engineer went on. "Running water, a creaky door, a gunshot—stuff like that. But some effects need recordings, like a big explosion, a parade, jungle noises, and so forth. What I'm doing is building up a library of sounds. I got everything: musical instruments, storms, a tree crashing, a train, all kinds of whistles, thirty different birdcalls, cars crashing, wheels screaming, fifteen different dog barks, whines, and howls—you name it. I sell these to stations all over the country. I've even got crowds laughing, applauding, cheering. I can make it sound like a radio play is being given in front of an audience of thousands. And all the time it's in a little studio with maybe two or three guys there."

"It's all on phonograph records?" Royce asked.

"Most of it is. I spend all my spare time recording new sounds. If I have to go into the field to get them, I take them on wax cylinders. Then, if I figure there's enough demand for them, I'll have a master cut and put the sounds on shellac. Then I sell records like 'Fifteen Different Birdcalls' or 'Train Whistles at Night.' Stuff like that. I got more than five hundred sounds in my collection, and I'm adding about twenty a week. All kinds of great stuff."

"Could you make a phonograph record of certain sounds, no speech, and synchronize it with a short film strip?"

"Sure," the engineer said. "That's easy. What have you got in mind?"

What Royce had in mind was that barroom brawl he shot for *Drive to Abilene*. Cut and edited, it ran for almost three minutes on screen. The supervisor described it to the sound engineer, told him what he wanted, and a price was agreed on. The next day Royce had a print of the fight sequence and a rented projector delivered to the engineer's home.

A week later the engineer called to say the job was finished. Charlie Royce went over that night.

The engineer had an electric phonograph set up alongside the projector. There was a twelve-inch shellac record on the turntable. The loudspeaker was next to a stretched sheet that was serving as a screen.

"Most of the stuff I had in my collection," the engineer told Royce. "Some of it I had to improvise. Some I went out and recorded specially. Like the piano playing a ragtime tune. I know you said you didn't want any speech, but in a fight like this you'd expect some grunts and groans. So I dubbed those in, using my own voice. All set? Let's go."

He turned off the overhead light, leaving only a dim

lamp for illumination. The film and phonograph started running. The moment the first image appeared on the sheet, the engineer lowered the needle into the groove.

Charlie Royce sat transfixed. It was a totally new experience. At first he was stunned. Then he was awed. He knew exactly how it was done, but he couldn't believe it. He sat there, shaken, knowing he was in on the beginning of something greater than he had thought. Something that would turn his world upside down.

When the mirror behind the bar shattered, you heard it. You heard the thud of fist hitting flesh. You heard wood splinter as the stunt man crashed through the balcony. You heard the gasps, grunts, groans, sobs of fighting men. You heard the sounds of chair leg against skull, crunch of breaking bottles, scuffle of feet, thump of men falling.

If the silent movie of the fight convinced, the sound movie overwhelmed. Charlie Royce paid the sound engineer, gave him a bonus, and told him about another job he wanted done.

On the following Saturday, the projection room at Magna Studios filled up for the weekly showing of screen tests. One of the first to arrive was Charlie Royce. With him was a dapper man with a strong resemblance to Adolphe Menjou. Royce made no effort to introduce his companion or explain his presence. They took seats down front on the aisle.

Four tests were screened, none of them of any particular interest. Following the final comments, Eli Hebron was about to end the session when Charlie Royce stood up.

"Eli," he said, "I've got a piece of film I'd like reactions to. Take about three minutes."

"Sure, Charlie. Go ahead."

"All right," Royce called up to the projection room. "Roll that special."

The supervisors, directors, cameramen, and assistants settled back in their seats. The lights went out.

"This is from *Drive to Abilene*," Charlie Royce said loudly in the darkness. "It's footage from the final print. With additions. . . ."

Royce had instructed the engineer to place the loudspeaker behind the screen and to turn up the volume. The scene burst onto the screen with an explosion of sound. If anything, the film was more effective than when Royce first saw it. The professional screen gave a sharper image. The sound boomed off the walls and ceiling of the projection room.

The audience lurched forward eagerly when they realized what they were witnessing. They sat almost flinching under the barrage of sound. Film and recording were in perfect sync. The result was more exciting than a stage performance. For the camera showed action "in the round," which the stage could never do. Nor could a theater audience see such close-ups or hear the sounds of action in such breathtaking clarity. And film editing had condensed time, eliminating the slack moments. The viewer was swept away, brought into the screen, made part of the cast. Reason was demolished by this assault on the senses.

When the film ended and the houselights came on, Royce's companion was whispering excitedly in his ear. But the supervisor ignored him, stood up, looked about with a wide grin.

"Comments?" he said genially.

There was applause, shouts of delight, a hundred questions.

Charlie Royce told them exactly how it had been done.

He told them there was no reason why the same technique, or an improved technique, could not be used to reproduce speech on the screen. He told them the day of the subtitle was over. He told them sound movies were coming—there was no stopping them—and they would kill vaudeville and the legitimate stage and end the threat of radio as a competitive entertainment medium.

They listened to him intently, and in silence, wondering about their own jobs, careers, ambitions.

"How about you, Eli?" Royce asked suddenly. "What's your reaction?"

Hebron had been sitting quietly. He had made a steeple of his hands, pressing his forefingers against his lips as he listened to the hubbub about him. He heard Royce's challenge, sighed, stood silently. The two supervisors faced each other, the only men standing.

"It's an interesting novelty, Charlie."

"Novelty!"

"And not particularly new at that," Hebron said. "It works fine with a saloon brawl. Slam! Bang! Pow! But talking movie actors? I don't think so. I don't deny it could be done. I just question if it's desirable."

"Why not desirable?"

"Chaplin said putting sound in film would be like painting lipstick on a marble statue. This is a new art form we're developing. It's taken us thirty years, and we've come a long way. Now we've got screen actors who are artists of a very special kind of pantomime. Did you see *Flesh and the Devil?* Those kisses between Garbo and Gilbert are the most erotic love scenes I've ever seen. You think they should have been talking during those scenes? Sound wouldn't have helped; it would have hurt."

"You're talking about Garbo and Gilbert," Royce said.

"They can carry silent scenes like that because they're good. Sound would have helped anyone else."

"You're deliberately missing the point," Hebron said wrathfully. He paused a few seconds.

The assistants present who had worked with him recognized the signs of growing stress. He blinked more frequently. His fingers began drumming on the chair back in front of him. He held his head stiffly lowered, peering up at Royce.

"What are we trying to do with moving pictures?" he demanded. "Trying to capture a three-dimensional world on a two-dimensional screen. Trying to catch a succession of meaningful images. Trying to suggest more than we show. The greatest arts are those with the most limitations, the most difficult technique. It's easier to write a good popular song than a good operatic aria. It's harder to write a good poem than a greeting card. The higher the standards, the more difficult the art, and the greater result when you succeed."

He looked around the room. They all seemed to be staring at him with puzzled, concerned faces. He knew he was losing them, and it angered him.

"It's a new art form," he said loudly. "It's an original art form. It's not the stage; it's not photography with radio thrown in. It's a very special art with a very difficult technique. It rarely succeeds. When it does, there's nothing in the world that equals it. Sound is an imitative technique. It would make the art of cinema easier but not better."

"Art," Royce said, appearing to be amused. "You keep talking about art. I don't see much art around here. I see a lot of good entertainment. Come down to earth, Eli.

We're not trying to produce a Mona Lisa. If we can turn out a good Katzenjammer Kids, we ought to be satisfied.''

They all laughed, and it infuriated Hebron. He gripped the chair back with trembling hands. He looked around wildly. His lips had whitened. He began speaking, his voice cracked, he stopped. He took a deep breath, started again.

"It's exactly because of that attitude that so much shit gets on film. You don't give a fuck what it is as long as it sells. Why don't you just photograph two people screwing? It would be a sensation. Big grosses.''

"Come on, Eli,'' Royce drawled, enjoying this. "Be realistic.''

"Realistic?'' Hebron shouted. "That's your trouble, Royce: you're too fucking realistic, and so are your movies. You think we're working in a realistic art form? Have you got crap for brains? You think a real fight looks like the one you just screened? The hell it does, and you know it! There's no reality on the screen. Impossible. We're selling dreams. Can't you get that through your thick head? You think Greta Garbo is madly in love with John Gilbert? It's all fantasy. And the closer it comes to reality— like having screen actors talk—the farther you get from a good film.''

Charlie Royce shook his head.

"You're way off base, Eli,'' he said sorrowfully. "Movies should be more realistic, not less. I can see us doing war movies and films about gangsters and hot love scenes. Stuff as hard and violent as life itself. You think that won't sell? The hell it won't! Because people will recognize that it's true. We'll show them the real world, the *realistic* world, with fast action and snappy talk. Then you'll see the grosses go up. But not if you keep turning out that soft, moony, nice-nelly stuff you make. Dreams? Shit, man, you're just trying to sell your own dreams. No one's interested in someone else's dream. It's the most boring thing in the world. But if you—''

"You've got no fucking brains!" Hebron screamed at him. "You haven't understood a word I've said. You bring in sound, and it'll be the end. Movies will become just photographed vaudeville. And it'll be your fault. You and people like you who think grosses are the way to judge success or failure. Like judging a great painting by the cost of the canvas and paint. You're stupid and haven't got the sense to know it.''

"Now, now, Eli," Royce said easily. "Calm down. Cool off. This is just a friendly discussion. We're just—''

But Hebron was pushing his way furiously to the center of the room. He was muttering, jamming people aside, stumbling, flinging his arms about roughly. They scrambled out of his way, giving him access to the aisle. For a moment it appeared he meant to rush at Charlie Royce, physically assault him. But finally, he turned his back and lurched out of the projection room, mouthing obscenities, dribble on his lips and chin.

There was heavy silence after he left. Then Charlie Royce looked about without expression.

"All right," he said authoritatively, "that's all for now. Have a good weekend. I'll expect you all bright and early Monday morning. Sober."

There were a few titters of nervous laughter. The room emptied.

"After what I saw this afternoon," Benjamin Sturdevant said, straightening his polka-dot bow tie, "I intend to advise my principals to move up their timetable."

"You liked the sound film?" Charlie Royce smiled.

"The film? Oh, that was tremendous. But I wasn't referring to that. I meant Eli Hebron's conduct."

"Yeah, that was some show he put on."

"I wouldn't state for the record that he's mentally deranged," Sturdevant said, "but he certainly appears to be emotionally disturbed."

"He sure wasn't making much sense."

"Not only what he said, but his manner. He was out of control. We don't want a man like that associated with Magna Pictures. If he can't control himself, how on earth can he hope to control a studio? I had the feeling he was very close to violence."

"Hebron?" Royce said. "Nah. Not the type."

They were in Charlie Royce's hotel bungalow, chewing the fat. Both slumped down on the couch, feet up on the low cocktail table. Royce had put out a quart of White Horse scotch, a bucket of ice cubes, a seltzer bottle in wire mesh. They both sipped dark highballs.

"How will you handle it?" Royce asked curiously. "Just can him?"

"Oh, no. He has a contract. We would prefer it be done in a civilized manner. We'll just tell him the conditions of his employment and leave it to him to resign."

"What conditions?"

"A complete housecleaning of the financial staff. Felder will have to go. We'll put in our own treasurer. The other executives can stay—temporarily. We'll ease them out over a period of time. To give new men a chance to learn the jobs."

"What about sound?"

"Oh, we'll convert, no doubt about that. It'll probably

take a year or two and require a heavy investment. But I don't see where we have a choice.''

"We don't," Royce said. "Not if we want to compete. What about the production supervisors?''

"Hebron will go, of course. And probably Phil Nolan. Those travel shorts just aren't paying their way. Ben Stuttgart can stay on. And we'll bring in some new talent. To take Hebron's place and to handle the Westerns.''

Royce sat up. He turned to face Sturdevant. "The Westerns? What about me?''

The attorney stared solemnly at him for a moment. Then he smiled, put a hand on the supervisor's arm.

"Don't worry, Charlie," he said softly. "We know who our friends are. We're creating a new executive position: head of production. Another reason why Hebron will want to get out. Charlie, how would you like to be head of production of Magna Pictures, Incorporated?''

Royce drained his drink. He leaned forward, mixed himself another highball so Sturdevant wouldn't see the expression on his face.

"Sounds good," he said casually. "I'll be boss of every movie that goes out?''

"Every foot of film," the lawyer nodded. "In addition, we'll expect you to handle the conversion to sound. A big responsibility, Charlie.''

"And a big salary to go along with it?''

"That goes without saying.''

"Let's say it anyway. And how about a piece of stock?''

"Stock?" Sturdevant said cautiously. "I'm not so sure about that. I'll have to talk to my people and see if something can be worked out.''

"Sure it can," Royce said genially, settling back. "I'm

not greedy. Just a little something to give me a personal interest in the future of Magna.''

"I'll see what I can do," Benjamin Sturdevant said.

He mixed himself another drink, then held up the glass. "Here's to prosperity," he said.

"I'll drink to that."

"If we get Herbert Hoover in there, the sky's the limit," the lawyer said. "All these anarchists with beards and Russki bomb throwers won't know what hit them. These union leaders with the big mouths? They don't stand a chance. You'll see prosperity like you never believed possible. Charlie, I was much impressed with your ideas of doing war pictures and gangster films. Realistic stuff. I think you're on the right track."

"Damned right I am. That crazy Hebron with his dreams and fantasies—he doesn't know shit from Shinola."

"Fascinating business," the attorney said, shaking his head. "It's all new and strange to me, but I can tell you I find it fascinating. Honestly, I envy you."

"Envy me?"

"Oh, a lawyer's job is pretty much cut-and-dried. This Magna deal was something different. But usually it's mostly paperwork. Dull stuff. That's why I envy you—something new every day. A new movie, a new challenge."

"I guess you could say that."

"And you get to meet such interesting people. I mean talented people. Beautiful women."

Charlie Royce had been wondering how long it would take Benjamin Sturdevant to get around to that. There wasn't an executive in the movie industry who hadn't been approached in the same cautious manner by a friend or acquaintance. But he wasn't about to turn the lawyer off. Not with a stock deal in the offing.

"That's the truth, Ben," he said sincerely. "Especially about the beautiful women. One of the best parts about my job, I can tell you that!"

They traded manly chuckles.

"You wouldn't believe," Royce said earnestly, "how many there are. A hundred luscious young things for every available job. They'll do anything to get a few hours' work. A walk-on. Just a chance in front of the camera. Why, Hollywood's full of them. I could pick up my phone right now and have a dozen over here before you had time to drop your pants."

"Well now," Sturdevant said breathlessly. "Well now. Professionals, you mean?"

"Whores?" Royce said indignantly. "I should say not! I'm talking about hopeful movie actresses. Would-be stars. Young. Ambitious. From all over the country. Virgins, most of them. I'm not saying they all have the talent to make it in films, but they're all eager. My God, are they eager! Like I said, they'll do anything. And I mean *anything*."

"Well, say now," the lawyer said slowly. "I was figuring you and I would have dinner together tonight. Maybe a little female companionship might not be bad. Some out-of-the-way place. Make a party of it. Dinner, and then just let nature take its course. Right, Charlie?"

"Dinner?" Royce laughed shortly. "It's just not necessary, Ben. These girls know the score. If you give them a drink and cab fare home, they're grateful. Should I rustle up a couple for us?"

"Well . . . ah . . . it's up to you, Charlie. Whatever you want."

"Why not? We'll have a celebration. It's not every day

I get to be head of production of Magna Studios. What would you like?''

"I beg your pardon?"

"What kind of judy? Young? Mature? Blond? Dark? A redhead? Thin or plump? Shy or talkative?"

"You mean I have a choice?"

"I told you there are hundreds of them. What's your pleasure?"

"Well . . . uh . . . maybe a cuddly little blonde. You know. Heavy in the right places. Very young. Like one of these kid flappers. The kind that don't give a damn. Real wild. Smokes, takes a drink or two or three or four. I heard some of these jazz babies get up on a table and dance without a stitch on. Just a string of beads. Can you beat that? Well, you know, someone like that. . . ."

"I know just the tootsie," Royce said. "A natural flapper. Wild? You wouldn't believe!"

"Well," Sturdevant said nervously, "not *too* wild. How about you, Charlie?"

"Me? I think tonight I'll get me a small girl. Dark. Short, shingled hair. Long legs with a good wiggle to her. Slender. Limber as a whip. Cold, you know, to look at, but hell on wheels when you get her stripped down. A babe who knows how to use her tongue."

"Bring 'em on!" Benjamin Sturdevant cried. "I'm rarin' to go!"

So Charles Royce went into the bedroom and called Bea Winks. He told her what he wanted and said he'd pick up the tab.

Gladys Divine issued explicit instructions for the afternoon. She would leave the studio early, at noon. Leo would drive her to Beverly Hills in the limousine. Hebron would leave his office at two P.M., no later. He would drive home in the LaSalle.

"What's this all about?" he asked her.

She winked at him. She touched his cheek with cool fingertips.

"A secret," she said.

"A nice secret?"

"You'll like it," she promised.

He pulled up before the porch to see a deserted Paradiso. No sign of anyone anywhere. He found the front door locked. Muttering, he dug out his key, opened the door, stepped inside. And they leaped at him, shouting, "Surprise!"

He saw the serving cart set with bottles, glasses, ice. And an enormous birthday cake with lighted candles. Eyes stinging, he realized he was forty-one years old that day, and someone had remembered. He turned to say his thanks. Then he saw they were in costume for his party. In movie costume. . . .

There was spindly Leo, dressed like Rudolph Valentino in *The Four Horsemen of the Apocalypse*. Strands of dank blond hair dangled from beneath his gaucho hat.

Plump Bertha in the regal gown, tiara, and flashing necklaces of Marie Dressler in *Breakfast at Sunrise*.

Norman costumed as Francis X. Bushman's Messala in *Ben Hur*, cracking his whip delightedly.

Faith vamping in leis and grass skirt (Gilda Gray in *Aloma of the South Seas)*, doing a hula that would have inflamed Warner Baxter.

Little Stanley as Jackie Coogan in *The Kid*, with floppy cap turned sideways, baggy pants held up with suspenders.

And Gladys . . . Gladys wearing a brief, glittery gown of spangles and beads, just like Joan Crawford in *Our

Dancing Daughters. There were ribbon bows on her silver pumps.

They crowded about him, shouting their "Happy Birthdays!" Glad insisted he pop the bottle of champagne and sip the first glass. He did and suspected it might be lemonade fizzed with soda water. But no matter; Glad thought it was champagne, and that was all that counted. So they each had a small glass, even Stanley. When the bottle was empty, there was gin, scotch, rye. Eli Hebron took off his jacket, removed his tie. He welcomed the opportunity to forget.

They wheeled the cart out onto the terrace where Leo had placed his wind-up Victrola. They drank, nibbled on birthday cake, and danced to "Five Foot Two, Eyes of Blue," "If You Knew Susie . . . ," "How Come You Do Me Like You Do?" Faith did a wicked Charleston to "Don't Bring Lulu," and Gladys and Eli joined in singing "Yes, Sir, That's My Baby."

Then, at Stanley's insistence, they played games. A wild chase of tag around the swimming pool. A giggling session of hide-and-seek among the trees and shrubs. Finally, on the weedy, overgrown lawn, a circle was formed for blindman's buff.

Eli Hebron was chosen as first blindman. Dazzled, willing, he looked around at the capering actors, grinning foolishly. Shebas and sheiks, he knew them all. Above, a strong sun still burned as they tied a filmy scarf about his eyes and whirled him. They turned him free to stagger about, arms outstretched.

"Here!" they cried. "Here! Here!" And he went stumbling with reaching hands to grasp, to hold, to know.

"Here!"

He fell to his knees, heard the taunting laughter, lurched to his feet.

"Here!"

He pushed to feel, to clasp. He took empty air to his breast.

"Here!"

He heard their mockery. He felt the hot sun searing. He went reeling about. But they ducked out of his reach, bending and swooping. They were not there.

"Here! Over here!"

Until exhausted, faint and gasping, he sat down suddenly. He fell back, warm earth pressing. Arms and legs stretched quivering. Their snickers faded as he lay fuddled. The world rocked beneath him. Then cool lips thrust on his.

"Glad?" he said.

"Yes," she said.

She stretched out beside him. Still masked, he touched flesh through spangles and beads, through fringe and bows.

"What I want to know . . ." he said weakly. "What I don't understand. . . ."

"What, Eli?"

"When you touch me, in public, I am so grateful, and in private, what you do, so nice, sometimes so curious and eager to learn, an innocent, or are you so experienced, and, you know, hook me to you, because I need that, but I don't understand, can't see you complete, or know, but it's best that way. Glad? Is it best?"

She made a sound, took his blindfold away. She helped him to his feet, supported him back to the house. The gargoyles had disappeared. Just gone. He could not hear their sounds. She assisted him up the wide staircase. She undressed him in the mirrored room while he swayed about. She brought a wet cloth and wiped his face and body. Then brought a scarf dampened with a sharp cologne that tingled his skin and made him shiver.

"I was drunk," he said.

"Not so much," she soothed. "The sun. You should have eaten."

"Now I'd like a tall, cold drink," he said. "Of anything."

She went away. He lay spread-eagled on the bed, dull peace flowing through him. He wondered if death was like this, strength and will just leaking away, dissolving.

She brought a chilled glass. She set it on his forehead, then pressed it against his burning face. She set it on his throat, held it to his arms and ribs. He trembled with delight, and wanted the blindfold on again.

He opened his eyes to watch her undress slowly in the early evening. At this time, on a clear day, the light was burnished, healthy. It flushed the air, put a bronze patina on living flesh. Her skin seemed dyed with russet. Nipples a warm brown. Hair in softly shifting shadow. He longed for color in films, when he might catch pastel moods and vibrant stress.

It seemed to him she came rippling to him. No wrinkles or folds, but all a gleaming smoothness. He could never know enough of her young sleekness. The helmet hair, the tight, hard haunch. She was all of a piece, nothing of her attached, no limbs. A complete one as if he might grapple a cylinder or caress a globe.

"Happy?" she kept asking. Franticness in her voice. "Does this make you happy? Does this? What?"

"I love you," he told her. "That makes me happy."

"No, no," she cried. "Let me. Let me."

He could not minister to her. Only his total surrender calmed her. She took all of him into her parched mouth.

Her sucking lips, sharp teeth meant to devour him. Skin, flesh, bone, gristle. His pounding heart.

"Thank you," she kept sobbing. "Thank you."

He could not understand her hunger, did not know her need. It was all a dream through a filmy scarf, life streaked and wavery. Wet lips dimly glimpsed. A flash of eyes. Tastes as fleeting. Perfume wisps. All smoke and floating: she, he, the imagined, intangible world, life aswirl.

He gave himself up to it. The long dissolve. . . .

Later, when they were done and silent, they bathed, dressed, and went downstairs. The others were all in the projection room, smiling and weeping through a screening of *Seventh Heaven*.

They came into Eli Hebron's office in single file, each carrying a black briefcase. All three had the smarmy solemnity of morticians. Franklin Pierce Archer led the way, wearing an earth-colored suit of hairy tweed. Following him came a man Hebron recognized as Charlie Royce's companion in the projection room on the previous Saturday. He was introduced as Benjamin Sturdevant. Hebron was certain he dressed to increase his resemblance to Adolphe Menjou. Why else would a resident of Los Angeles wear wing collar, spats, a boutonniere, and a chalk-striped suit of such constrictive cut?

The third man, Edward J. Haldwell, had the soft drawl of a Westerner, but the pallor of a banker and the long incisors of a ferret. He seemed particularly well costumed for the role of mortician, in a shiny suit of black tropical wool, white shirt, black knitted tie.

Hebron was struck by the tightness of these three men. Not only the narrowness of their jacket waists, trouser legs, the miserly fit of their starched collars, but a tightness in their manner: limbs stiff, fingers curled to fists, a wooden jerkiness to their movements. Even their speech seemed strangled: words gargled, elliptic sentences. A harsh verbal shorthand.

He offered chairs; they preferred to stand. He hoped they intended this meeting to be brief.

They told him that rather than force Magna Pictures, Inc., into bankruptcy, the creditors had met and appointed Archer, Sturdevant, and Haldwell as an ad hoc management committee to study the financial situation and devise a plan to save and revitalize Magna Studios.

"Why are you telling me this?" Hebron asked them, pleased with his composure. "I don't own Magna. I'm attempting to keep it operating during the temporary absence of Marcus Annenberg. Magna is owned and managed by Mr. Annenberg."

"No, sir," Franklin Pierce Archer said in his thin, nasal voice. "Mr. Annenberg has been declared incompetent by the courts, on the petition of Mrs. Annenberg. His wife has been granted legal power to make financial decisions in his behalf. We have reached an understanding with Mrs. Annenberg."

"Would you care to see copies of these documents, sir?" Benjamin Sturdevant asked. "We have them here."

"No," Hebron said sadly. "That won't be necessary. She sold him out, did she?"

"Sir, Mr. Annenberg is in no condition to handle his own affairs," Sturdevant said.

"And probably never will be, sir," Archer said.

"His best interests were the deciding factor in Mrs. Annenberg's decision, sir," Haldwell said. "I'm sure."

"I'm sure," Hebron nodded. "So—what now? You're in charge, is that it?"

"That's about it, sir," Haldwell agreed. "We intend to institute certain managerial changes immediately."

"What changes?"

"Charlie Royce has been appointed head of production, sir," Archer said stiffly. "With complete responsibility—and authority, I might add—for all products of Magna Studios."

"Products, eh?" Hebron said with a small laugh. "What else?"

"Sound, sir," Sturdevant said. "We intend to start converting to sound at once."

"Then you want my resignation?" Hebron asked.

The three men exchanged glances.

"That would be best all around, sir," Haldwell said. "Keeps it polite and civilized. We'll get out a story to the trade papers explaining you're leaving to explore other opportunities in the movie industry."

"And, sir," Archer said gravely, "expressing the grateful thanks of this committee for your past services to Magna Pictures."

"We want as little publicity on this changeover as possible," Sturdevant said. "Sir," he added.

"That's right." Hebron nodded. "No use getting the exhibitors nervous, is there?"

"Then you agree, sir?" Haldwell asked, apparently surprised that it had gone so easily. "I mean you agree to resign."

"We have it typed up for your signature, sir," Sturdevant said, opening his briefcase.

Eli Hebron leaned back in his swivel chair. He clasped his hands behind his head. He stared at the ceiling.

"Oh, I don't know," he said dreamily. "Perhaps I should think about it awhile. Sleep on it. I may decide to let you fire me. I may decide to issue some statements to the trade press myself. You know, the inside story of how Magna Pictures was ruined and taken over by a gang of crooked jackals headed by an Eastern bank.''

There was a taut silence for a few seconds.

"There are laws against libel," Archer said tightly.

"What will you do—sue me?" Hebron said, amused. "Give me a crowded courtroom as a theater?"

"How much do you want?" Haldwell said bluntly. "To resign and keep your goddamned mouth shut?"

"How much do I want?" the supervisor repeated thoughtfully. "At this moment I don't know what I want. But I'll consider your kind offer carefully and let you know."

"Twenty-four hours," Archer said harshly. "If we haven't heard from you by noon tomorrow, you're off the payroll. Out on your ass. We'll survive any mud you can throw at us."

"Oh, I don't think Mr. Hebron will carry out his threat." Benjamin Sturdevant smiled. "I don't think he's in any position to take his case to the newspapers."

"What does that mean?" Hebron frowned.

"Suppose we wait twenty-four hours to see?" Sturdevant said smoothly. "I'd advise you to consider your decision very, very carefully in light of your, ah, personal situation. Shall we go, gentlemen? A call to my office by noon tomorrow, Hebron."

That's how it ended. They filed out as solemnly as they had entered. Hebron stared after them, depressed and bewildered. He had expected it, although it had come more quickly than he anticipated. What he hadn't suspected was Charlie Royce's role in the takeover. That was a shock, even though he was aware of the man's enmity. But he knew the seizure of Magna would have taken place even without Royce's treachery.

He had no particular desire to hobble the prospects of Magna under the new owners. His threat to start a brouhaha in the press was merely a ploy to obtain a healthy cash settlement. That might enable him to become an independent movie producer. And the device seemed to be working until Sturdevant made his sly comments. It was that reference to his "personal situation" that puzzled and alarmed Hebron.

He went into the lavatory. He dissolved one of the powders Dr. Blick had given him and gulped it down. He came back to his desk, poured a glass of warm gin. Sipping, he wandered to the windows and looked down into the yard.

A tribe of Indians in war bonnets came laughing out of the commissary. A team of huskies dashed toward the back lot pulling a sledge on wheels. Two baggy-pants comics slouched along, carrying a ten-foot rubber ladder. Bea Winks herded a troupe of Persian harem girls toward Indoor Stage One. Two cowboys practiced their fast draw, pointing their six-shooters at Kaiser Wilhelm, riding by on an enormous white horse. The wreckage of a biplane was hauled to Outdoor Stage Three. A troop of doughboys headed for Makeup & Costume to be fitted with bloody bandages. A set designer hurried along with a papier-mâché statue of Venus on his shoulder.

Eli Hebron stared at this activity. Then he turned away to pour himself another gin, to clean out his desk. And to take the photographs of movie stars off his walls.

They were deep in leather wing chairs in the library in the Valhalla Club. Both puffing complacently on good cigars. Timmy Ryan, wearing mufti, peered about at the shelves of books, oak paneling, framed Remingtons, beamed ceiling.

"Now this is something, this is," he said. "You a regular member, Mr. Royce?"

"I will be soon," Charlie Royce said. "I'm on a guest card right now until my application goes through. Just a matter of time. I have some heavyweight sponsors."

"Very fine it is." Ryan nodded, settling back. "A real gentlemen's club."

"Damn right," Royce said. "A great bunch of fellers here. No Yids. Bankers. Politicians. I mean some big men."

"Be a great help to a man like yourself, Mr. Royce," Ryan said, tonguing out a series of perfect smoke rings. "Just starting out, in a manner of speaking. Why, there's no telling where you might go."

"Yes. Well, it was about you I wanted to talk. Timmy, I'll be moving up at Magna. Head of production, you know."

"Now I heard talk about that, Mr. Royce. They couldn't have picked a better man for the job, I'll tell the world."

"Thanks. Timmy, what have you got in mind? You've been a great help to me. I don't have to tell you that, and I'd like to see you move up along with me. But you're chief of the studio police now, and there's no place up in that department. Have you had any movie experience at all?"

"No, Mr. Royce. Nothing of any profit."

"Well, can you make any suggestions? Anything you'd like to be doing at Magna?"

"Now, that's kind of you to ask, Mr. Royce. Very kind indeed. I have been giving the matter some deep thought.

To speak the truth, I think what I'd really like to do is go back to the old country.''

"Go back to Ireland?"

''Don't take me wrong, Mr. Royce. This country has been good to me. Very good indeed. Land of opportunity it is, and that's a fact. But the missus and me are getting on. The chicks are old enough to leave the nest, and the missus and me were speaking of going back and settling in you might say.''

''Retiring, Timmy? I can't see you taking it easy, just puttering around. You're not ready for the old folks' home yet.''

"Why, no, Mr. Royce, that was far from my thinking. Now what I had in mind was opening a place over there. A drinking establishment. In Dublin maybe. Opening a place or buying a going thing. A pub is what I fancy, Mr. Royce. Always saw m'self as a pubkeeper. Himself was, you know. It's a good life. Steady like. Not that you don't have to work at it. Oh, you labor, Mr. Royce, no doubt about that. Long hours. But you build up steady customers, and you own something, if you see what I mean.''

"A pub?" Royce regarded him thoughtfully. "In Ireland? I think that's a good idea, Timmy. Make you your own man.''

"It would that, Mr. Royce." He laughed suddenly. "I can see m'self now—a respected citizen. Strollin' down Wicklow Street of a Sunday morning. White piping on the vest, and a billycock tipped over me eye just so. As the poet says, 'All's well that ends well.' ''

"Yes, a good idea, Timmy," Royce repeated. "Why don't you go over there, look around, and locate a setup to your liking. Then let me know. I'll help you out with the money. You can depend on that.''

"Oh, I have no doubts at all, Mr. Royce," Timmy Ryan said, smiling genially. "No doubts whatsoever."

He mooned in his littered office. The wreckage of his life piled up about him. Scenarios, treatments, stills, portraits, reviews, ads, interviews, programs, posters. He tried to put aside what he valued most. But everything he owned brought memories charging. He yielded to the past. He sat on the floor, glass of gin beside him, and held things in his hands. He read a few paragraphs. A few subtitles. He stared at action stills, recalling the scene, lighting, the actors.

Finally, he stopped glancing at individual items. He looked with glazed eyes at the sea around him: jagged stacks, yellowing folders, crumbling clippings, photographs with bent corners, the emulsion peeling. It seemed a shabby record of what he had done. Until he realized his history wasn't here, but on reels of film all over the world. This stuff was junk. His movies were his annals. If no one else could, he could see in his work, from first to last, a chronicle of his growth. His hand grew surer. Taste more subtle. Daring appeared, innovation. A willingness to explore. To stretch his talent, drive it to the limits, and dare.

But now, if he was removed from moviemaking, cut off and discarded, what would mark the progress of his days? What would serve as witness to his size? He would float forever, rootless, with no images caught to mark his passing. His life would be like that evening of his birthday party, in bed with Gladys, when he saw the world as smoke, drifting and impalpable.

He stood shakily, drained his gin. He put two unopened pint bottles of gin into a manila envelope. Then, at the last moment, he added three spills of Dr. Blick's magical white powder. He went stilting through the outer office. Past a tearful Mildred Eljer, who held out trembling arms to him. He staggered down to the garage, bulling his way past those who tried to stop him. He found the LaSalle, pushed Leo aside, fumbled his way behind the wheel.

Mac got the gate open just in time. Hebron roared through, crabbed forward, peering through the windshield. He made the turn, tires screaming. He drove wildly down the street. "Like a madman," people said later.

The evening was a montage. Flashing trees. Whistle screams. Scattering pedestrians. Blurred road. Glinting sun. Laughter shout. Shrieking brakes. A forest. Hill. Canyon. Cliff. A winding road. Sharp drop. City lights. Into a rainsquall and out. Billboard smear. Darkness. A streetlamp became a star. A star became headlights. Whirling. . . .

He stopped occasionally. Once to fill the gas tank. Once to buy sandwiches, and then push them into the hands of a surprised passerby. Once on a hill, high above the city. He could see twinkling necklaces and glinting gems. Flashing jewels set on black for his selection. One of his pint bottles was almost empty. With steady hands he poured a twist of white powder into the dregs. Put his thumb over the bottle mouth. Shook it energetically. Swallowed it down. He sang, "I found a rose in the devil's garden."

Then he was on the beach. He was lucid. Alert. He felt he had passed through drunkenness and was beyond. He was in a crystal world of razor perception. He might continue to drink his gin, if he chose, but nothing could cloud his vision or dim his wit. He saw plainly, he thought clearly. There was sand beneath him, a sea before him, a cloud-streaked sky above. He was aware of all that and more.

It was not just sand. Not just a tan solid. But a congress

of bright, individual grains, each different, each unique. A beach of minuscule boulders, a joined species that traded its heat and moved in concert. An association of similar sensate forms, alive to each other and sharing.

So was the ocean alive. It breathed in waves and laughed in spume. It might giggle, chuckle, guffaw, or roar as it pleased, knowing its own strength. It was an actor, a Lon Chaney, with a million disguises. No one knew the sea, the real sea. It hid itself and showed a new mask every dawn.

Just as the sky lived. Changing while you tried to catch it still. Moving clouds and moving light. Pulsing in an awful rhythm of its own. Raising and lowering, and sometimes revolving when you lay upon your back on the living sand, heard the living sea, and knew the reeling universe in all its shining splendor.

He sat up to drink again. How did you get all that on film? Those inchoate visions? Those scary dreams and fantastical imaginings? And the knotted mysteries of the human soul? The tangled stirrings of the human heart? How did you capture and reveal the wonder and the pain, love and passion, glory and death? On cold film. Show it in black and white on a poor two-dimensional screen so that a stranger might see, nod, and say, "That's so."

He drove home slowly, full and alive. He churned with ideas. New techniques to try, old techniques to burnish and make bright. He thought, with luck, his best work lay ahead. Movies of truth and revelation. Movies of bold imagination and profound understanding. This was where his life had been leading. To this night, this recognition, this resolve:

He pulled up on the graveled driveway. He killed motor and lights. He sat in darkness, listening to his heart's pump. Then the door of Paradiso opened. Gladys stood with light behind her. A radiant nimbus. She came flying down the steps, wearing something white and flowing. She yanked open the door, flung herself in, took him tightly in her arms. Teary cheeks pressed to his.

"Eli, I was so . . . I didn't know what. . . . They said you . . . God, I was so worried! I heard . . . at the studio . . . everyone was talking . . . phone calls . . . and you disappeared, just disappeared! Eli, where were you, where *were* you? I love you, I love you, I love you!"

He petted, stroked, calmed her. He smoothed her hair, held her close. Kissed wet eyes. Breathed the scent of her young flesh.

"I'll tell you everything," he promised. "Everything that happened. I've got to talk, Glad. Things to say. I feel so good. I have such plans. Wait'll you hear! I've got to get to work. So much to do!"

They left the car. They walked slowly back into the house. Arms about each other's waist. Her head lightly on his shoulder. She was uncorseted; he could feel nip of waist, soft swell of warm hip.

"Where is everyone?" he asked, looking about.

"In the kitchen, Eli. Listening to the Ipana Troubadours. For a while Leo had the Kansas City Night Hawks, but then they faded."

"Let's go in here," he said, drawing her into the living room. "I've got so much to tell you."

"I've been so worried about you, Eli. I didn't know where you'd gone. Everyone said you just rushed out."

"I got fired—did you hear that?"

"I heard," she said sorrowfully, putting the back of her hand against his cheek. "Oh, Eli. . . ."

"Best thing that ever happened to me," he said cheerily. "I've got great plans. Well, well, what have we here? What's in the shaker?"

"Just gin and bitters and ice. I had to have something while I was waiting to hear what happened to you."

He poured them drinks. He sat down heavily in a Ruhlmann armchair, pulled her onto his lap. He told her about the meeting in his office with the new owners.

"I don't blame Aunt Flo," he said. "She did what she thought was best for Uncle Marc. And maybe it *is* best. He's just not functioning."

"But, Eli, what are you going to *do?*"

"The first thing I'm going to do"—he laughed—"is hold them up for every dollar I can get. As far as I can see, everything they did was legal. Nasty, but legal. But that doesn't mean I can't threaten to give the whole story to the newspapers. It would hurt Magna, and they know it. A lot of exhibitors would hold off payments and bookings until they find out what's going on. So they'll pay me to resign quietly and keep my mouth shut. Then, with the money I get from them—they'll be putting me in business; can you imagine!—I want to make my own movies. Try to arrange distribution through MGM or United Artists."

"Your own movies? What kind of movies, Eli?"

"Great movies! I've been thinking about it all night. I know just what I want to do. Great stories! Great stars! Look, Glad, I've got personal contracts with Margaret Gay, Nino Cavello, and some others. Maybe the new owners will get to them, and they'll refuse to work. That means a lot of lawsuits, and meanwhile, I couldn't use them. But I've got a personal contract with *you.* My first movie will be *you* in a starring role! Something written specially for you. Something that'll make us rich and start

261

us on the way to our own studio. How does that sound, Glad?''

She slid off his lap. She took his empty glass over to the serving cart. She turned her back to him, fumbling with shaker and ice cubes. Something in her bowed shoulders, her lowered head, disturbed him.

"Glad?" he said. "You didn't answer me. You didn't say what you thought. About being in my first movie.''

She turned suddenly. The glass dropped from her fingers, splintered on the floor. He looked down at the shards, looked up at her face. As broken, sharp, and jagged.

"Glad,'' he said quietly, "what *is* it?''

"I can't,'' she sobbed. *"Can't!''*

"Can't?" he repeated, bewildered. "Why not? You don't have a contract with Magna. Your contract is with me.''

"No,'' she said, swinging her head wildly, hair flinging. "No, Eli. The contract's no good. Not legal. I couldn't sign it. I shouldn't have signed it. I'm underage. I'm fifteen. I'm fifteen years old, Eli.''

He stared at her.

An empty-eyed little girl standing straight. Feet together and arms down at her sides. Reciting her memorized lesson.

"My mother would have to sign to make it legal. My mother is Bertha. Not Faith. Bertha is my real mother, and Leo is my brother. Norman and Faith and Stanley are actors. Just actors. Charlie Royce hired them. To fool you. You see what they did? You can't go to the newspapers now. You can't make your own movies. Or anything. Or they'll tell. They'll destroy you. They'll make my mother, my real mother, bring charges, and they'll—''

His shriek echoed through the house. Her knuckles flew to her mouth. He lurched from the chair. She took a small step backward. He fell toward her in a stumbling rush. She paled and waited. His hands reached. She thrust her palms outward. He crushed into her. They toppled back. The cart went over with a crash of bottles, ice, glasses.

He struggled to grind her beneath him. He put a knee on her chest. He bent close, glaring at her closed eyes. His cut and bleeding hands found her throat. Slid lovingly around. He began to grip, to press, to squeeze. Lifting her neck and head from the floor. Straining to choke off blood, throttle breath, still the rise and fall. To end it. Fade-out.

She submitted meekly. No protest. No struggle. But lying limply in shy surrender. Giving herself up to him. Her fingertips floated lightly up to his clasping hands. To touch and stroke. Her mouth opened slowly. Her tongue came out slowly, a beast from a cave. The eyelids raised slowly. White bulbs bulged sightless. Her body came up in arched paroxysm, taut convulsion. Until only heels and shoulders touched the floor.

Then they were all swarming about him. Shouting, screaming, cursing, wailing. Jerking him back. Bending his fingers away. Throwing him off. Striking him. Kicking him. Dragging him by arms and legs and hair. Even Stanley, sobbing, hammering his head and face with small fists.

North of Santa Barbara the coast road curved in slightly from the sea. A narrow secondary road ran from the highway to the cliffs. Almost at the end of this graveled, tree-shaded lane, high iron gates blocked the way. The sign read HILLCREST. From the ornate gates, a tall wire fence stretched away into the forest on both sides. Just outside the gates was a small hut, occupied by a single guard.

Inside, the single-lane road curved through handsome stands of fir, pine, and oak. There was no undergrowth. The road came out to a paved courtyard before a graceful red-brick building, three stories high. Slender columns supported a peaked portico over the single door. The two wings of the building had many curtained windows. They were all covered on the outside with wire mesh painted white. This side of Hillcrest faced inland.

On the ocean side, a wide terrace ran the entire length of the building. It was set with heavy boxes of geraniums, pansies, daffodils, daisies. There were several metal umbrella tables and chairs. The tables were bolted down. The chairs were chained to the table legs. At each end of the terrace, when it was in use, a young man in white drill trousers and jacket stood silently with folded arms, or chatted amiably with the guests.

From the terrace, an expansive lawn, well tended, rose gradually to the cliff overlooking the ocean. A high chainlink fence ran along the edge of the cliff and disappeared into the trees on both sides. There were massive cement benches set out on this wide stretch of green. Guests sat or strolled about. A few went directly to the fence and, fingers clutching the wire, stood staring out to sea.

The sun blazed down onto Hillcrest, its terrace, its lawn. But usually a pleasant ocean breeze spared the guests discomfort. Outdoor entertainment was planned for every day: painting instruction, a nature lecture, a sewing circle, a Bible class. Guests were encouraged to play bridge on the terrace. Occasionally dances were held.

On this brilliant afternoon a small group of guests had gathered to watch the activity taking place at one side of the lawn. A young man in open-necked blue shirt and gray flannel bags was standing at a wooden tripod. A cigar box had been mounted on end atop the tripod. A cardboard tube from a toilet paper roll had been tacked to one side of the box in a horizontal position. On the other side, a crank from a wind-up phonograph was inserted in the box so it turned freely. The young man in charge of this equipment was wearing a buttoned tweed cap turned backward, so the peak slanted down over his neck.

Near him stood Eli Hebron. He was wearing a cap of white linen, but in the conventional manner. His candy-striped shirt had starched white cuffs and Herbert Hoover collar. He wore a narrow black knitted tie with a pearl stickpin. His knickers were tan linen, his knee hose argyle-patterned. His brown suede shoes had long, fringed tongues hanging over the laces. He was carrying a short megaphone.

Hebron was speaking to a young couple who listened intently. The girl was slender, with a great mass of dark hair that hung to her waist. She wore a full garden gown of white georgette. It had wide sleeves and billowing skirt. The handsome young man wore a Norfolk suit of white twill.

"This will be a long shot," Eli Hebron explained carefully. "Start out from that bench I showed you. Alice, you start first. You run toward the trees. You are trying to escape from Fred. But you are not frightened. It is a game, an innocent, romantic game. He wants to kiss you. You would like that, but you are pretending to be shy. Do you understand?"

They both nodded seriously.

"Fred, give Alice a head start of, oh, say, ten feet. Then you dash after her. You can run faster than she can, but you must not catch her. You can close the distance if you like, but you never catch her, never even touch her."

"Do I reach for her, Mr. Hebron?" Fred asked.

The supervisor nodded approvingly.

"Exactly. You stretch out your arms. Your fingers strain for her. And you are laughing or smiling all the time. You're lovers, and this is a pleasant pastime, a way to spend an amusing afternoon."

"Can I laugh and smile, too, Mr. Hebron?" Alice asked. "I'd like to."

"Of course you do," Hebron said. "You look back over your shoulder, smiling and laughing. Let's try to get this on one take. Now go to the bench and wait for my signal."

They walked off. Hebron turned to the young man at the tripod.

"Remember, this is the long shot," he cautioned. "We'll do the medium and close-ups later. In this take, keep them both in focus. Move your camera with them. Don't swing back and forth. I want them both in every frame. Be sure you don't cut off heads and feet."

"Yes, Mr. Hebron," the young man said.

He turned the cigar box carefully atop the tripod. He leaned forward, squinted through the cardboard tube. He put his hand lightly on the crank.

"I've got them," he said. "I'm ready, Mr. Hebron."

The supervisor glanced toward the bench where the young couple waited. He moved to stand alongside the tripod. He raised the megaphone to his lips.

"Action!" he shouted.

The young man began to turn the crank. Alice started dashing across the lawn toward the trees. Fred waited a moment, then ran after her.

She turned, smiling over her shoulder. He pursued, laughing, reaching out a hand to touch, to grasp, to hold. Her white skirt floated out behind her. Long hair whipped back.

On they flew, glowing in sunlight. Their laughter tinkled on the air. The china-blue sky curved above them. The dark green grass bent beneath their feet.

The young man yearned forward, striving. But always she was beyond, escaping. The shining figures rushed on, linked forever, burning in an image of endless want.

The young man at the tripod turned the crank steadily, his eye at the cardboard tube. As the couple ran, he moved the cigar box around to follow them. When, finally, they disappeared into the trees, he stopped cranking. He straightened up. He looked happily at the supervisor.

"I got it, Mr. Hebron," he said.

Eli Hebron smiled, put a hand on his shoulder.

"Fine," he said. "Just what I wanted. Print it."

LAWRENCE SANDERS

"America's Mr. Bestseller"